INSPECTOR HADLEY

THE AMERICAN MURDERS

by

PETER CHILD

Benbow Publications

© Copyright 2008 by Peter Child

Peter Child has asserted his right under the Copyright, Designs
and Patents Act, 1988 to be identified as the author of this work.

All rights reserved. No part of this publication may be reproduced,
stored in a retrieval system, or transmitted in any form or by any
means, electronic, mechanical photocopying, recording or
otherwise without the prior permission of the copyright owner.

Published in 2008 by Benbow Publications

British Library
Cataloguing in Publication Data.

ISBN: 978-0-9558063-1-5

Printed by Lightning Source UK Limited,
Chapter House, Pitfield, Kiln Farm,
Milton Keynes, MK11 3LW

First Edition

OTHER TITLES BY THE AUTHOR

MARSEILLE TAXI

AUGUST IN GRAMBOIS

CHRISTMAS IN MARSEILLE

CATASTROPHE IN LE TOUQUET

RETURN TO MARSEILLE

***

ERIC THE ROMANTIC

***

INSPECTOR HADLEY
THE TAVISTOCK SQUARE MURDERS

INSPECTOR HADLEY
THE GOLD BULLION MURDERS

INSPECTOR HADLEY
THE TOWER OF LONDON MURDERS

NON FICTION

VEHICLE PAINTER'S NOTES

VEHICLE FINE FINISHING

VEHICLE FABRICATIONS IN G.R.P.

NOTES FOR GOOD DRIVERS

NOTES FOR COMPANY DRIVERS

ACKNOWLEDGEMENTS

Once again, I wish to gratefully acknowledge the help and assistance given to me by Sue Gresham, who edited and formatted the book, and Wendy Tobitt for the excellent cover presentation. Without these talented and patient ladies this book would not have been possible.

Peter Child

INTRODUCTION

After Lord Andrew Mortlake inherited his estate and title he was disappointed to learn that his late father had spent most of the family fortune on gambling and women. As he had steadfastly followed his father in behaving irresponsibly, he realised that his only option to avoid bankruptcy was to marry well, that is financially well, and in the summer of 1880 he travelled to America searching for a suitable heiress. He left behind him a long trail of gambling debts, seduced women of all ages and a mansion in Northamptonshire, badly in need of repair.

In America at that time, many men with a flair for business, who were prepared to take risks presented by numerous new opportunities, soon became multi millionaires. When they had reached that high financial status they required their daughters to marry well and what could be more attractive to a first generation immigrant than his daughter becoming the wife of an English nobleman?

Characters and events portrayed in this book are fictional.

CHAPTER 1

It was early June when Inspector James Hadley took a week's well deserved leave from Scotland Yard and went on holiday with his wife Alice and children to Bognor Regis. He had booked half board at the Esplanade Hotel, a moderate establishment with commanding views, situated on the sea front. Since the dreadful Tower murders, the cases that Hadley and Sergeant Cooper had been called upon to investigate since had been fairly routine and without much excitement. Nevertheless, Hadley was glad to be away from London for a while and he intended to enjoy this holiday with his family. Due to overwork, Alice had become concerned for his health, but he insisted that he felt quite well and as he was not yet forty one years old, he had many good years left in him before retirement.

The family spent time on the beach when the weather allowed, strolled along the promenade and each day they enjoyed a light tea with pastries at the Royal Tea Rooms, at the far end of the esplanade. The meals served in the hotel were adequate rather than lavish, their rooms were spacious and the beds were comfortable; and the local stout was very much to Hadley's taste. Alice was anxious that her husband did not drink too much and kept a careful eye on him. Hadley accepted her guidance with a nod and a smile, knowing that his beloved wife was only looking after his interests and as he truly loved her, he did pay attention to her concerns. When the holiday came to an end, which was much too quickly for Hadley's liking, they caught the train back to London feeling relaxed and invigorated. Alice was pleased when they arrived at their home in Camden to find that Gladys, the maid, had cleaned throughout and had a hot meal ready for them. After a good night's sleep and a substantial breakfast the next day, Hadley left his home full of confidence, looking forward to being back in his office at the Yard after a relaxing holiday in Bognor.

Sergeant Cooper greeted Hadley with a big smile and inquired after his holiday and then remarked on how well he looked. George, their affable clerk beamed as he welcomed Hadley before he hurried off to make a pot of tea. As the Inspector sat behind his desk he glanced at several files before him and decided not to open them until he had enjoyed a refreshing cup of tea.

"Well, Sergeant, what's been happening since I've been away?"

"Nothing much, sir, just two robberies to report" replied Cooper.

"Were they serious at all?"

"Not really, sir, I've followed them up and my reports are on your desk."

"Good, I'll read them in due course."

"There was one other thing, sir."

"Yes?" Hadley asked as he looked up at Cooper.

"The Chief sent down a confidential file for you to read as soon as you returned from holiday, he said it was not particularly urgent and he would speak to you about it later."

"Right, do you know what it is about, Sergeant?"

"No, sir, it just says 'Lady Mortlake' on the cover."

Hadley looked through the files until he found the one marked 'Confidential – Lady Mortlake' and he was just about to open it when George arrived with the tea, so he put it to one side. The detectives chatted as they enjoyed their tea and Hadley emphasised the benefits of a holiday by the sea; recommending that Cooper should take his young wife, Doris, to Bognor Regis. As Hadley was about to open the confidential file, Mr Jenkins, Chief Inspector Bell's clerk, appeared and asked him to report to the Chief immediately. Hadley nodded and followed Jenkins up to the next floor and entered the Chief's spacious office overlooking the Thames.

"Morning, sir."

"Morning, Hadley, glad you're back from your holiday" replied Bell.

"Yes, sir."

"Did you enjoy it?"

"Yes, thank you, sir."

"I must say you look a lot better than when you went."

"It's kind of you to say so, sir."

"Now sit down and pay great attention" said Bell as he waved Hadley to a chair, which creaked under his weight.

"Have you read the file I sent down to you about Lady

Mortlake?"

"No, not yet, sir."

"Well, make it your top priority now, Hadley."

"Yes, sir."

"The Commissioner has been contacted by the American Embassy over the matter this morning and he wants immediate action" said Bell gravely.

"Can you tell me briefly what's in the file, sir?"

"Yes. Last summer, a Lord Mortlake travelled to New York, where he met and married an heiress called Nancy Riley, the only daughter of the steel magnate, Arthur J. Riley, then after the marriage they returned to his Northamptonshire home, where apparently things did not go well."

"Ah, marry in haste and repent at leisure, sir" smiled Hadley.

"This is not funny, Hadley, the young woman is now dead!"

"I'm sorry, sir…"

"Well you might be, now she is reported to have died as a result of a riding accident, but there are rumours that she was murdered."

"Rumours, sir?"

"Yes and the Northamptonshire police were not at their best in investigating this case, I'm sorry to say, and the post mortem report is less than satisfactory."

"That's unfortunate, sir."

"Indeed, now, after a hurried funeral, Lord Mortlake is pressing the family solicitors to release his wife's very substantial fortune to him but her father has managed to stop this with a court injunction."

"Why is the American Embassy involved, sir?"

"Because they've been advised by Mr Riley in New York that he is sending two agents over from the Pinkerton Detective Agency to investigate his daughter's death!"

"Oh, no, sir."

"Oh, yes, Hadley, apparently he doesn't trust the British Police!"

"How unfortunate, sir."

"Yes, it is, Hadley, and the Embassy, out of courtesy, has informed the Commissioner."

"When do they arrive, sir?"

"Their ship is due to dock next Monday in Liverpool, so they'll be down in London by the Tuesday, that means you've got just a week to get the investigation moving, Hadley."

"Yes, sir."

"And work all next weekend if necessary!"

"Right you are, sir."

"Now, read the file and get things under way, we don't want American private detectives trampling all over us!"

"Quite so, sir."

"And make sure you keep me up to date with everything!"

When Hadley returned to his office he told George that he did not want to be disturbed for any reason and then asked Cooper to draw up a chair and sit with him at his desk. He told the Sergeant what the Chief had said with regard to Lady Mortlake and Cooper listened carefully.

"Now, I'll read this file out aloud and you make notes about salient points, Sergeant."

"Right, sir."

Hadley opened the file and began. "Lady Nancy Beatrice Mortlake, nee, Riley, was married on the 30th June, 1880, to Lord Andrew Mortimer Richard Mortlake, in New York, America. The couple left New York on the 15th of July, with a female companion and travelled in first class accommodation aboard the S.S. Atlantic to Liverpool. Lord and Lady Mortlake took up residence at Holcot Manor, their mansion in Northamptonshire. Lord Mortlake apparently remained at Holcot Manor for just a week after their arrival before returning, alone, to his London house in Connaught Square. From then on, he spent time involved with business and at his club, The Dreyfus Club in Curzon Street, where he could be found most evening's playing cards with fellow members.

During the months up until Christmas, 1880, Lord Mortlake only returned three times to his mansion and stayed for less than a week on each occasion. According to the police report, some staff at the mansion suggested that there was considerable friction between Lady and Lord Mortlake every time they were together. Contact between the couple was rarely made until May of this year, when Lord Mortlake went home several times during that month. A day after he left to return to London, Lady Mortlake was found dead in the grounds of Holcot Manor, with her favourite horse roaming close by." Hadley stopped reading and glanced at Cooper.

"What do you make of this, Sergeant?"

"All very suspicious if you ask me, sir."

"Yes, make a note to remind me to find this woman companion who sailed with them from New York, Sergeant."

"I've already done that, sir."

"Well done, now let's see what our colleagues in Northampton make of it all."

"This will be interesting, sir."

"Yes" replied Hadley as he looked at the file and began to read once more.

"Investigations into the circumstances of Lady Mortlake's death were carried out by Inspector Peter West of the Northampton police. His report is attached herewith and the Inquest verdict is that Lady Mortlake's death was a tragic riding accident. According to the autopsy report issued by Doctor James Ogilvie of the Northampton Infirmary, death was instantaneous after she fell from her horse and broke her neck. Lady Mortlake was buried in the family vault at Holcot Church on the 20th of May."

"That's just over two weeks ago, sir."

"Quite right, now, apparently her will has been read and Lord Mortlake wants to get his hands on her money but her father in New York has managed to hold things up with a court injunction."

"And he is now sending the Pinkerton detectives over to investigate, sir."

"Yes, he's obviously a man with money and friends in high places."

"He must be if the American Embassy is involved, sir."

"Now you can understand why the Commissioner is so anxious."

"Yes, I can."

"Right, Sergeant, a list of what action we need to take now is required to move this investigation forward in double quick time."

By mid morning the detectives were on their way to interview

Lord Mortlake at his London home in Connaught Square. The Hansom cab rattled through the streets from the Yard, and up Park Lane to Marble Arch before turning into the Bayswater Road, then into Connaught Square where it stopped outside number 28. Cooper paid the cabbie whilst Hadley surveyed the elegant cream building before he climbed the steps and rang the bell. Just as Cooper joined him a butler opened the door, looked Hadley up and down and said "Yes?"

"Good morning, is Lord Mortlake at home?" asked Hadley firmly as he noted the butler's disdain.

"Who wants him?"

"I'm Inspector Hadley and this is Sergeant Cooper of Scotland Yard."

"In what connection may I ask?"

"Confidential inquiries; is his Lordship at home?" asked Hadley calmly.

"I'll see, please wait there" replied the butler as he closed the door firmly and Hadley glanced at Cooper and shrugged his shoulders.

"He's a bit pompous, sir."

"Well that's only to be expected if you're the butler to an English Lord" replied Hadley with a smile. They waited for several minutes before the door was opened and the butler cleared his throat before he announced "his Lordship is not receiving guests today."

"Tell his Lordship that we are not guests, we are detectives sent by the Commissioner of the Metropolitan Police to investigate the death of his wife!" On hearing that the butler went pale and replied "please wait a moment, sir" before he hurried off, leaving the door ajar. Hadley peered in and observed the faded decadence of a once fashionable house, it crossed his mind that Lord Mortlake and his forbears had probably seen better times. The butler re-appeared and said "please come in, gentlemen, his Lordship is now free to see you." They followed the butler across the hallway and through double doors that opened out into a spacious drawing room. Lord Mortlake stood up as they entered and Hadley was struck by the nobleman's aristocratic good looks. He was about the same age as Hadley but slightly taller, about six feet three inches, quite slim with a mop of hair, neat side whiskers and brown eyes that looked hard.

"The police, your Lordship" said the butler.

"Thank you, Wilson" replied Mortlake.

"I'm Inspector Hadley and this is Sergeant Cooper, sir."

"Now what's this all about, Inspector?" asked Mortlake testily.

"We're making inquiries into the death of your wife, sir."

"That's all over now, Inspector, apart from my remaining in mourning."

"With respect…"

"Listen to me, my wife died as a result of a tragic accident, the Northampton police investigated everything at the time and the Inquest verdict was accidental death, so that is the end of the matter!" interrupted Mortlake angrily.

"I'm afraid that the Commissioner has ordered a re-opening of the case, sir."

"I'll bet that's because her damned interfering father doesn't believe the truth and he's got more money than sense!"

"I can't comment on that, sir."

"More is the pity."

"Nevertheless, sir, I am ordered to proceed and I would be grateful if you would co-operate with my investigation" replied Hadley and Mortlake looked hard at him for a few moments.

"Alright then, you'd better sit down" said Mortlake and waved the detectives to the sofa. Cooper produced his note book and Hadley began.

"When did you last see your wife alive, sir?"

"On the 10th of May, the day before she died."

"I believe you returned to London that same day, sir, is that correct?"

"Yes, Inspector, I arrived back at about seven o'clock and went straight to my club."

"Would that be the Dreyfus Club in Curzon Street, sir?"

"Yes, Inspector, I signed in, dined there and stayed the night."

"When did you learn of your wife's death, sir?"

"At about six o'clock the next evening, Inspector."

"Then what did you do, sir?"

"I caught the first available train back to Northampton."

"I see. I understand that you and Lady Mortlake did not enjoy a particularly happy marriage, sir."

"What on earth has that got to do with her accident?"

"It may be linked."

"In what way, Inspector?"

"I'll come to that in a moment, sir, but would you answer my question?" Mortlake hesitated for a moment and replied "no, it wasn't the happiest experience of my life."

"Why do you think that was, sir?"

"I don't really know, Inspector, but I found marriage to be rather like a dull meal with the sweet served first" replied Mortlake.

"How unfortunate, sir."

"Yes it was" he replied wistfully and Hadley waited for a few moments before he said "it is only right that I inform you that as the case is now officially re-opened, I have to follow up and re-examine all the evidence that was first produced after your wife's death."

"I understand, Inspector."

"Thank you, sir."

"So I expect you'll want to go to my home in Northampton?"

"Yes, sir, I plan to travel up there tomorrow."

"Very well, Inspector."

"Now, when you came back from New York last year, a lady accompanied you on the voyage…"

"Yes, she's Miss Ann Wells, my late wife's closest friend and companion" replied Mortlake.

"Is the lady still at Holcot Manor, sir?"

"Yes, but I understand that she plans to leave next week and return to New York."

"For good, I presume?"

"Yes, Inspector." Hadley remained thoughtful for a few moments before he asked "how did you get along with Miss Wells, sir?"

"Quite well, although I did not see much of her after we returned to England, she always seemed to disappear when I arrived home."

"Do you know if Miss Wells comes from a wealthy family, sir?"

"I'm not sure, my wife never said too much about her."

"I expect that will come out during my inquiries, sir."

"I'm sure."

"Did your wife or Miss Wells come here very often, sir?"

"No, they never came to London."

"Why was that, sir?"

"I just preferred it that way and the arrangement suited me, Inspector." Hadley looked hard at Mortlake and waited for a few moments before he continued.

"Now I understand from Inspector West's report that your grounds-man, Mr Winters, found your wife after she had fallen from her horse, is that so, sir?"

"Yes, Inspector."

"How long has Mr Winters been in your employ?"

"His father worked for my father and he followed on, so all his life, Inspector."

"So he is a trusted servant?"

"Indeed he is" Mortlake replied and Hadley remained silent for a while.

"Lord Mortlake, I must advise you that I intend to have your wife's body exhumed and re-examined by the police pathologist, Doctor Evans…"

"Oh, God, no, surely not!" interrupted Mortlake.

"Oh, yes, sir, unpleasant as it may be, it must be done and I will require your permission."

"Well you damned well can't have it!"

"I urge you to co-operate with me, sir."

"Bloody hell, I said no!"

"Your refusal will be seen as trying to hide something."

"I've nothing to hide, my wife is now dead, let her rest in peace for God's sake!"

"I'm sorry, sir, I cannot let the matter rest, so either you give your consent or I'll have to get a warrant from your local magistrate in Northampton with all the attendant and unwelcome publicity" said Hadley firmly. Mortlake went pale before he replied "there is something evil about you, Inspector."

"So it has been said, but at the Yard we leave no stone unturned, sir."

"Turn everything to your advantage more like."

"Possibly, sir, but that's how we achieve results."

"Very well then; you have my permission, but I protest most

strongly and I will make my feelings known directly to the Commissioner."

"Your protest is noted, sir."

The detectives left the house in Connaught Square and Cooper hailed a Hansom cab.

"Where to, sir?"

"I think it's time for an early lunch" said Hadley as he looked at his fob watch.

"The Kings Head in Whitechapel, sir?"

"No, not yet, but perhaps later, I think instead, we'll try the White Horse in Holborn for lunch and afterwards call upon his Lordship's solicitors, whose offices are close by, to see what they have to say for themselves."

CHAPTER 2

After a fulsome lunch of pork pie and pints of stout, the detectives left the busy, smoke filled pub in Holborn and strolled along in the June sunshine to the offices of Olivier and Barrymore. The gleaming brass plate on the wall by the impressive black door gave the firm impression that the solicitors were very much City men of power and legal influence. Hadley knocked at the door which was opened by an elderly clerk with ink stained fingers.

"Can I help you, sir?"

"Yes, I'd like to see Mr Morton Barrymore, please" replied Hadley.

"Have you an appointment, sir?"

"No, I'm afraid I haven't."

"Is it an important matter, sir?"

"Yes, it is."

"Then in that case, I'll go and see if he is free" said the clerk.

"Thank you."

"Who shall I say is calling?"

"I'm Inspector Hadley and this is Sergeant Cooper of Scotland Yard."

"Well, in that case you had better come in, gentlemen" said the clerk as he stepped back and opened the door fully to allow the detectives into the hallway.

"Please wait here for a moment" said the clerk before he disappeared down the corridor. They waited for several minutes in the dark, oak panelled hall, with the aroma of ink and dusty paper assailing their senses, before he returned.

"Mr Barrymore will see you now, gentlemen, so if you would like to come this way please." Hadley nodded and they followed the clerk to Barrymore's office where they were announced to the solicitor. Morton Barrymore was an imposing man in his fifties with grey hair and side whiskers to match. His hard features and grey eyes made him look quite formidable. Half smiling with a curious twist of his lips, he welcomed the detectives and invited them to sit before his large desk that was full of papers bound up with pink ribbon.

"So, how can I help you, Inspector?" he asked as his eyes

hardened with suspicion.

"I believe that Lord Mortlake is a client of yours and you act for him in all matters, is that correct, sir?"

"Yes, that is so, Inspector."

"I have to inform you that the Commissioner has re-opened the case of the tragic death of Lady Mortlake and he has instructed me to carry out further investigations into…"

"But surely the Inquest found that Lady Mortlake died as the result of a riding accident and therefore the matter is closed as far as the police are concerned!" interrupted Barrymore firmly.

"It would seem not to be the case, sir, so I would be obliged if you would answer my questions concerning his Lordship."

"That's quite out of the question, Inspector."

"I will not ask anything that breaches client confidentiality, sir, as I only wish to gather background information to help me with the general direction of my inquiries" said Hadley as he fixed Barrymore with his determined look. The solicitor thought for several moments and then acquiesced.

"Very well, I'll assist you as much as I can, but be under no illusion, Inspector, I will not betray confidences under any circumstances!"

"That's clearly understood, sir."

"We agree then."

"We do, sir."

"Please proceed."

"How long has Lord Mortlake been a client of yours, sir?"

"Both my senior partner, Mr Tristram Olivier and I have represented the Mortlake family for over twenty five years, Inspector."

"So you know them well, sir."

"Indeed we do and when Lord Rupert Mortlake sadly died last year, Lady Elizabeth, his wife and Lord Andrew, relied upon us completely to attend to everything."

"How very re-assuring, sir."

"It is very rewarding to be held in such high esteem by members of England's old aristocracy" said Barrymore with a twisted smile.

"I'm sure, sir. Would you say that Lord Andrew Mortlake inherited a substantial estate from his late father?" Hadley asked and he watched Barrymore become uncomfortable before he replied "no, Inspector, to be honest, Lord Rupert had unfortunately kept somewhat undesirable company in his later years and these scallywags had taken advantage of his kind generosity."

"Did he gamble?"

"He was partial to the occasional game of cards at his club, Inspector."

"Was that the Dreyfus Club in Curzon Street?"

"Yes, it was."

"So, what did he leave to his son?"

"After all his debts had been honourably settled…" Barrymore paused.

"Yes?"

"He left just over a thousand pounds, Inspector."

"Not a great deal for a Lord of the Realm" said Hadley.

"No, Inspector."

"What about the present Lord?"

"What do you mean, Inspector?"

"Does he have pressing creditors?"

"I'm not prepared to comment on that!"

"Very well, sir. Tell me, why do you think his Lordship went to America after his father's death?"

"I believe for a holiday, to recover from the tragic loss of his father."

"How did his mother, Lady Elizabeth, cope with her loss?"

"Very well indeed, Inspector, the lady was an inspiration to us all" beamed the solicitor.

"Indeed, sir, now were you surprised when Lord Mortlake married Nancy Riley so quickly after meeting her in New York?"

"No, not at all, Inspector."

"Why was that?"

"His Lordship is a very attractive gentleman, Inspector, and as there were few suitable young ladies in London society last year, I'm not surprised that an American beauty should win his heart."

"Mr Barrymore, I must advise you that his Lordship has told me this morning that his marriage was unhappy, and the records show that he spent very little time with his wife, preferring to remain at his London home, where she never visited."

"I'm sorry to hear that, Inspector."

"I understand that Lady Mortlake's considerable fortune has been left entirely to her husband, is that so?"

"Yes, Inspector, other than a few small amounts to her companion, Miss Wells and her maid" replied Barrymore.

"How much did Lady Mortlake leave her husband?"

Barrymore hesitated before he answered and the solicitor knew that undercurrents of suspicion were firmly fixed in Hadley's mind regarding his client.

"I'm not sure of the final figure, but it is in excess of two million pounds, Inspector." Hadley said nothing but raised an eyebrow whilst Cooper wrote the amount down in his notebook with a shaking hand.

"I see" said Hadley.

"Now, if there's nothing more, I have my work to attend to, Inspector."

"I understand that there is a court injunction brought by Lady Mortlake's father, Mr Arthur J. Riley, preventing the money being released to your client, is that so?" asked Hadley, ignoring the solicitors remark.

"Yes, it's a mere formality whilst things are sorted out, paperwork you understand, the bane of the legal profession" smiled Barrymore.

"Quite so, sir, and I sympathise, as we at Scotland Yard also suffer from too much paperwork these days" replied Hadley.

"Well, Inspector, I had better get back to mine and not keep you from yours" said Barrymore with a smile.

"Yes, indeed."

The detectives left the solicitor's office and returned to Scotland Yard. Hadley remained deep in thought during the journey through the busy London streets and said nothing to Cooper until they arrived back in the office.

"A legacy of two million pounds is a very strong motive for murdering your wife, especially if she is estranged and disapproving of your life style, Sergeant."

"Yes, sir."

"If her Ladyship was murdered I think it's going to be very difficult proving it."

"Probably, sir, but we do know that her husband couldn't have done it as he was at his club when she died."

"True, but accomplices could be easily bought by a man who would have such untold wealth as soon as the deed was done."

"Are we allowing our suspicious minds to run away with us over a tragic accident, sir, or do you really think she was murdered?"

"I believe she was murdered, Sergeant, and we'll find out the truth in the end!"

They spent the rest of the afternoon writing up notes and Hadley sent a letter to Doctor Evans, the police pathologist at the Marylebone Hospital, informing him that he intended to exhume the body of Lady Mortlake. Hadley planned to organise the exhumation within a day or so of his arrival in Northampton he would then telegraph the Doctor to join him there to carry out a second autopsy. Hadley also sent a telegraph message to Inspector West, informing him that a fresh investigation into the accident had been ordered by the Commissioner and that he would make contact with him once he had arrived in Northampton.

It was early evening when the detectives left the Yard and took a cab to the Kings Head pub in Whitechapel. The bar was quite busy with early drinkers, men on their way home from the docks, costa mongers and fish wives, all enjoying a welcome drink after a hot and tiring day. Vera, the fulsome barmaid welcomed them with a smile.

"What can I get you, gentlemen?" she asked.

"Two pints of stout, please, Vera" replied Hadley, she nodded and began to pull at the pumps.

"Anything to eat?" she asked.

"No thank you, Vera."

"You look well, been on holiday or something?" asked Vera as she placed the foaming drinks on the wet bar.

"Yes, a week in Bognor Regis" replied Hadley.

"Oh, I say, it's alright for some" she said.

"It is if you're one of 'the some'" replied Hadley with a grin.

"That's what I'd like to be one day" said Vera.

Hadley nodded and said "pay Vera, Sergeant, while I find us somewhere to sit."

Finding an empty table near the open door Cooper joined him;

they sat quietly enjoying their drink and watching the characters in the pub. Hadley was waiting for Agnes Cartwright to arrive with her young associate Florrie Dean. Hadley had known Agnes for twenty years, ever since he was a young Bobbie walking his beat on the grim streets and alleyways in Whitechapel. She had suffered badly at the hands of a drunken husband, then after his death, a smart talking man had procured her for the oldest profession before leaving her to fend for herself. She was a well proportioned lady of uncertain years who gave personal relief to gentlemen for five shillings a time, two and sixpence on Mondays to encourage trade on her quiet night. Florrie Dean was much younger and the pretty blonde offered 'special services' to her clients, who were greatly appreciated by the older gentlemen. The Toffs would come down, late at night, from their clubs in the West End for relief and their casual talk to both women was a source of valuable information to Hadley, which he appreciated. He knew that there was always a grain of truth in gossip and rumour.

Suddenly from the warm, dusty street, Agnes and Florrie entered the pub. Hadley saw them straight away and called out to them, the two women smiled and sat at the table.

"Hello, Jim, Sergeant" said Agnes.

"Hello, ladies, how are you both?" asked Hadley.

"We're well thank you, and all the better for seeing you, Jim" replied Agnes and Florrie nodded.

"That's good to hear… Sergeant, two gins for our ladies if you please." Cooper nodded and made his way to the bar.

"We haven't seen you lately, Jim, so where have you been?" said Agnes.

"On holiday at Bognor Regis."

"On holiday, my how the rich live!" said Agnes.

"You flatter me, Agnes."

"I'd like to do more than flatter you, Jim."

"I know you would, but you also know that I'm a happily married man" he smiled.

"You're too good, Jim, but I think you should let your hair down now and again" she replied with a smile.

"Yes, and if you did, I could give you one of my 'specials' that I offer to the older gentlemen" said Florrie, her eyes bright with anticipation.

"You're both very kind... and please note, Florrie, I do not regard myself as an older gentleman" he smiled before he supped at his stout and Florrie giggled whilst Agnes shrugged her shoulders.

Cooper returned with their six penny gins and sat next to Florrie then Hadley asked "have you ladies ever heard of a Toff called Lord Mortlake?"

"Is he an old gent?" asked Florrie.

"No, the present Lord is about my age, but his father was an old gent who died last year" replied Hadley.

"They don't usually tell us who they are, Jim" said Agnes.

"No, I don't suppose they do."

"We only get to find out who they are if any of the other girls recognise them, or we get to know them if they're regulars" said Florrie.

"We do have a lot of older one's these days, but the good thing is they pay up quick and don't take too long about it, which is a blessed relief" said Agnes.

"They can be a worry though" said Florrie.

"Why is that?" asked Hadley.

"Last week, Daisy Wells had an old gent on top of her when he suddenly had a seizure, and she couldn't move him, so she had to call out until somebody heard her" said Florrie.

"What happened?" asked Cooper.

"Luckily, Nellie Drake was passing by outside her room and heard Daisy, so she went in and helped get the old boy off her and then called a Doctor" said Florrie.

"Was he alright?" asked Hadley.

"Yes, the doctor gave him something and then called a Hansom to take him home to his wife" replied Florrie.

"It gave Daisy a bit of a turn though" said Agnes.

"I'm sure. Now, ask around and see if any of the girls know this Lord Mortlake, I'm particularly interested in him" said Hadley.

"Why, Jim?" asked Agnes.

"I can't say too much at the moment, but he's been living in London without his wife for a year and he's bound to have come down here for some relief" replied Hadley.

"That's for sure" said Agnes.

"And I'm interested to know if he's been asking the girls about a handy man to help him."

"To do what, Jim?"

"Again, I can't say at the moment, but I'll tell you when it's all over."

"We'll keep you to that, Jim" said Agnes and Florrie nodded.

When the detectives eventually left the pub, the dusty, cobbled streets had cooled and they enjoyed a leisurely ride to Hadley's home. As the Inspector climbed down from the cab outside his house in Camden, he said to Cooper "as we're off to Northampton tomorrow and we'll be staying for several days, make sure you bring everything you need, Sergeant."

"Yes, sir."

"Meet me in the office first thing, as usual, and then after I've reported to the Chief we'll be on our way."

"Right, sir."

"You can tell your wife that we'll be back no later than Friday, Sergeant."

"I will, sir."

"Also tell her that you will probably be working all weekend, as we've a lot to investigate before our American friends arrive in London next Tuesday."

"Yes, sir."

"Goodnight, Sergeant."

"Goodnight, sir."

Hadley stood for a few moments watching the Hansom make its way back towards Marylebone High as he wondered what he and Cooper would uncover at Holcot Manor in the following days.

CHAPTER 3

The next morning they caught the ten o'clock train from Kings Cross station for the relatively short journey to Northampton. The old market town was busy when they arrived and after an early lunch at the Duke's Arms, which was full with farmers from the cattle market, they made their way to the Excelsior Hotel in Gold Street, where Hadley booked two single rooms until the Friday morning. Leaving their luggage to be taken to their rooms they left the hotel and hired a trap to take them the six miles out to Holcot. The chestnut mare made good progress and the trap turned into the driveway that led to the Manor only forty minutes after leaving the town. The forlorn looking house stood at the end of the badly maintained drive. Its timbered Tudor façade appeared to be in poor condition with gaps in the mortar holding the red bricks that were set between the stout oak timbers of the frame. The garden borders were relatively tidy and the last few yards of the drive were in fair condition. After the trap had come to a halt outside the impressive front door, Hadley stepped down and surveyed the building whilst Cooper paid the driver and arranged for him to return at six o'clock to collect them.

"This place has seen better days, Sergeant" said Hadley as Cooper joined him.

"Indeed it has, sir" replied Cooper before he knocked at the door. They waited for several minutes and then Cooper knocked much harder. Within moments the door swung open and an elderly butler stood before them.

"Yes, gentlemen, can I help you?" he inquired.

"Yes, I'm Inspector Hadley and this is Sergeant Cooper of Scotland Yard. We'd like to speak to Lady Elizabeth Mortlake, please."

"In what connection, may I ask, sir?"

"It is a confidential matter."

"Very well, please come in, sir" he replied and opened the door fully to allow them into the large hallway. After he had closed the door he said "please be good enough to wait here, whilst I inform her Ladyship of your arrival."

"Thank you" said Hadley as the butler gave a little nod and

wandered off to a door at the back of the hall. As he disappeared, the detectives looked about them. The hallway was once magnificent but wherever they looked there were signs of decay and neglect. Cracked and peeling wall paint was to be seen everywhere and the large tapestries that hung on every wall appeared threadbare and badly in need of restoration. The whole place looked gloomy, uncared for and smelled musty. Suddenly they heard footsteps from the upstairs landing and they both looked up as a young woman came into view and hurried down the stairs, she was very attractive with blonde hair and blue eyes. Hadley thought she was probably in her late twenties and he assumed that she was Ann Wells. She smiled when she reached the foot of the stairs and as she approached them asked in an American accent "good afternoon, gentlemen, who you are you?"

"Good afternoon, Miss, I'm Inspector Hadley and this is Sergeant Cooper of Scotland Yard" Hadley replied with a smile.

"Policemen, well I'm delighted you're here" she said.

"I'm pleased to hear it, Miss, and who are you?"

"I'm Ann Wells" she replied as she held out her hand.

"Ah, Lady Mortlake's companion from New York" said Hadley as he shook her hand.

"Yes, I am. So you're real live detectives from Scotland Yard?" she said as she then shook hands with Cooper.

"We are, Miss."

"Well, as I said, I'm pleased you're here and I guess it's in connection with Nancy's accident?"

"It is, Miss."

"Well, have I got lots to tell you, Inspector."

"I'm glad to hear it, Miss." Just then the butler re-appeared and announced "her Ladyship will see you now, gentlemen."

"Thank you" said Hadley.

"I'll catch you later then, Inspector" said Ann.

"You may be sure of that, Miss" he replied with a smile.

"Please follow me, gentlemen" said the butler.

Lady Elizabeth Mortlake, widow of the late Lord, sat impassively in a large winged chair close to the stone fireplace which was the centre piece of the spacious and overcrowded drawing room. She peered through her glasses at the detectives as the butler announced them.

"And who are you exactly?" she asked cocking her head to one side, Hadley assumed that she was slightly deaf, he repeated what the butler had already told her and she replied "you'd better sit down and tell me why you're here." The detectives made themselves comfortable on a threadbare sofa opposite her Ladyship and Cooper took out his notebook.

"I think we should have some tea first, Barton."

"Yes, Milady" replied the butler.

"Tell Mrs Chambers to prepare some tea and cucumber sandwiches" she said.

"Yes, Milady" Barton nodded.

"And bring some of her rock cake."

"Very well, Milady" nodded Barton before he left the room.

"Now then, why are you here?" she asked as she leaned forward in her chair.

"Lady Mortlake, we are here to re-open the investigation into your daughter-in-law's death" replied Hadley.

"Why?"

"The Commissioner has ordered it."

"Who?"

"The Commissioner of the Metropolitan Police, Milady."

"Well it's nothing to do with him, it was a tragic accident and that's all there is to it!"

"With respect, Milady…"

"The police have already investigated it and they were satisfied and so was the Coroner" she interrupted firmly.

"I appreciate that, Milady, but nevertheless…"

"Her death was accidental, and that was the verdict of the Inquest" she interrupted.

"I know…"

"Well if you know that, why are you here?"

"Because the Commissioner has ordered…"

"Speak up will you, I'm afraid I'm a bit deaf these days!" she said with a smile and a nod of her head.

Hadley sighed and speaking more loudly, he explained why they were there. As he finished, Barton arrived with a large silver tray with the tea. He put it down on a table close to his mistress and after a nod of his head he left the room.

"Now, how do you like your tea?" asked her Ladyship.

When they had finished the cucumber sandwiches and enjoyed a second cup of tea with one of Mrs Chamber's rock cakes, Hadley began his questioning of Lady Mortlake.

"When your daughter-in-law arrived from New York was she well received here, Milady?"

"What do you mean, Inspector?"

"I presume that you did not meet her before she married your son?"

"No, I didn't."

"When you met her, did you approve of her, Milady?" When she heard that she leaned back in her chair and gazed out of the window opposite for a few moments.

"Well, unfortunately she was an American, Inspector."

"And so, Milady?"

"I find them a bit uncouth and a trifle loud, I'm afraid" she replied.

"You find them disagreeable?"

"Yes, I do, and they're all the same you know, Inspector, I mean look at that girl she brought with her as her companion..."

"Miss Wells?" interrupted Hadley.

"Yes, I think she was the cause of a lot of trouble between my son and his wife."

"In what way, Milady?"

"When she wasn't making eyes at Andrew she was plotting behind his back with his wife to have me thrown out!"

"I'm sorry to hear that, Milady."

"I've lived here ever since I married my late husband and he would turn in his grave if he thought for one minute that I should be dismissed from this house on the say so of some upstart American girl!" she said with feeling. Hadley knew then that the arrival of Nancy and Miss Wells caused undisguised resentment from the old woman which probably permeated throughout the household.

"I'm sure that's true, Milady."

"Why Andrew couldn't have married an English girl with the right family connections, I simply do not know" she said firmly.

"Matters of the heart are always a mystery, Milady" said

Hadley.

"Matters of money more like" she countered firmly.

"Oh?"

"Andrew married her for her money, Inspector, and that's all there is to it."

"Did he say as much?"

"Inspector, my late husband spent a considerable fortune on living a London life of which I did not approve, but I'll say no more, Andrew followed in his father's footsteps, more is the pity. When one finds oneself in great financial difficulty then a hasty marriage to a wealthy woman is infinitely better than bankruptcy, even if she is an American!"

"So you were aware of your son's financial position, Milady?"

"Yes, but it wasn't Andrews fault, his father left him in this dreadful situation and when he said that his only option was to marry an heiress, I agreed, but I didn't expect him to arrive back with someone of such obvious low breeding" she replied with feeling.

"Does anybody else share your low opinion of the late Lady Mortlake, Milady?"

"Only everybody who matters in society, Inspector."

"And what about your son?"

"When he realised what a mistake he'd made, he spent much of his time in London, Inspector."

"I understand that Lady Mortlake never went to his house in Connaught Square" said Hadley.

"Good gracious me, no, I mean he couldn't possible expose that American to London society, I mean we'd have been the laughing stock at all the fashionable gatherings."

"I see."

"I'm glad you do, Inspector, because believe me, she was best kept hidden away here"

"Well, thank you for all your help, Milady."

"Have you finished with me, Inspector?"

"For the time being, Milady, and now I'd like to have a few words with the staff."

"Why? They don't know anything" she replied.

"Nevertheless, Milady."

"Very well, but make sure you question that American girl

who's staying here for the moment, Inspector."

"I will, Milady."

"Good, now I'll ring for Barton and get him to make the necessary arrangements."

"Thank you, Milady."

When Barton had received his instructions from Lady Mortlake and conducted the detectives out into the hall, Hadley asked him to assemble all the household staff in the kitchen and when that had been done to inform him. Before that, Hadley wanted to speak to Miss Wells, so Barton was asked to summon her. The butler nodded and then the detectives were shown into the study where they waited for her to arrive.

"First impressions, Sergeant?" asked Hadley as he sat behind the desk.

"No love lost between her Ladyship and her daughter-in-law, sir."

"No, and I would say she was positively hostile towards her" replied Hadley.

"Not hostile enough to murder her, surely, sir?"

"You never know, Sergeant, it will be interesting to hear what Miss Wells has to say" replied Hadley as the attractive American entered the study and the detectives stood up to greet her.

"This is what I like about England, you gentlemen are so attentive" she smiled as Hadley waved her to a seat.

"We do our best, Miss Wells."

"Oh, call me Ann, please, Inspector" she said as she fluttered her eyelids.

"I would prefer to remain formal, if I may, Miss Wells" replied Hadley and she smiled.

"Whatever you think is appropriate, Inspector" she whispered and Hadley blushed a little whilst Cooper grinned.

"Thank you, Miss. Now you said when we first met that you had things to tell me."

"Oh, that's for sure! So much has been going on here over the last year that makes me sure that Nancy was murdered!"

"Tell me what exactly."

"From the very beginning, after Nancy married this man, all he's done is try and get money off her, big amounts I might say"

24

she replied, with her blue eyes hardening.

"Did she tell you that?"

"You can bet your bottom dollar, Inspector!"

"I presume you mean 'yes', Miss?"

"Yes, and she was getting quite worried over it all."

"Did she confide in anybody else?"

"Yes, she wrote several letters to her father about it" she replied.

"Do you know what his reaction was?"

"I think he guessed that she was very unhappy and concerned so he said in his last letter that she should leave Andrew and come back to New York."

"And did she plan to do that?"

"Yes, Inspector, we were going to return next week, the tickets were paid for and everything."

"Presumably you plan to return, Miss?"

"Oh, yes, Inspector, I can't wait to leave this dreary place and I'm just so sorry that Nancy is not coming with me."

"Do you know if she had many arguments with her husband?"

"They were at each other's throats all the damned time!"

"What about, Miss?"

"Money, all the time it was money, he obviously married for the fortune that her Grandfather had settled on her and he didn't love her at all, not for one minute did he care" she replied angrily.

"So it was an unhappy marriage from the start?"

"Yes, it sure was, and the arguments got worse the more she refused to give him any money for his gambling debts and whatever else."

"I see" nodded Hadley.

"It was so awful, but I tell you, the man is such a liar, such a hypocrite!"

"Go on, Miss."

"Nancy met him in New York at some function that her father organised, and when Andrew found out that she was rich in her own right, he was all over her, telling her about his title and his wonderful ancestral estate, huh! I mean look at this dusty pile of broken down old bricks!" she said with venom.

"You obviously didn't approve, Miss."

"No, I didn't and neither did Nancy so when we arrived, saw

the place, then met his mother, she realised she been tricked by him and he only married her for her money because he had none and was up to his neck in debt."

"I see."

"So as she had made her will in his favour when they were first married, I think the only way he could get at her money was to murder her, and that's what he did!"

"Be careful what you say to us, Miss, we know that Lord Mortlake was staying at his club when his wife died" said Hadley.

"Sure he was, he had someone do it for him, that's obvious isn't it?" she asked and Hadley secretly agreed that she was probably correct.

"We'll find out in due course, Miss."

"Good, now let me tell you how she was murdered" she said.

"I'd be very interested to hear your theory, Miss" replied Hadley.

"Right, come with me to the murder scene and I'll tell you what happened" she said and the detectives were momentarily taken aback.

"How far away is it?" asked Hadley.

"About a mile or so, it's a lovely afternoon and the walk will do you both good!" she replied.

The detectives followed Miss Wells out of the house and walked with her in the warm June sunshine in the direction of Northampton. The grounds were very green and gently undulated towards a thick wooded copse that dominated the sky line. When they were within about thirty yards of it, she stopped and looked around at the ground before pointing down.

"Here, Inspector, this is where Nancy is supposed to have fallen off Topper" she said.

"I presume Topper is her horse?" asked Hadley.

"Yes, she's a lovely chestnut mare, as docile as a kitten and Nancy's favourite to ride."

"You said 'supposed to have fallen off'?"

"Yes, but look at the ground all around, Inspector, its flat, no potholes or anything that could cause Topper to stumble and let me tell you, Nancy was a damned fine rider!"

"She could have been at a gallop and fallen quite easily" said

Hadley.

"No, Inspector, I've looked in every direction leading up to this spot and there are no hoof marks that indicate that Topper was at a gallop when Nancy fell, or I should say, was dragged off."

"Tell me what you think happened next" said Hadley.

"Somebody stopped her and dragged her off Topper then broke her neck or strangled her, I guess."

"Who do you think did it, Miss?"

"I don't know, that's for you to find out, but I guess whoever murdered her was hiding in that copse over there, waiting for her" and she pointed at the small dense wood.

"You're quite a detective, Miss" said Hadley and Cooper smiled.

"I only want to see justice for my friend, Inspector, we were very close since our school days and she was like a sister to me." When she had finished speaking, she paused before suddenly bursting into tears and sinking to the ground, where she sat sobbing, much to the consternation of the detectives. They both rushed to comfort her and Cooper produced a clean white handkerchief which she gratefully took and wiped away her tears.

"I'm sorry, Inspector, it's not like me to get all weepy, but Nancy meant so much to me and I don't know how I'm going to manage without her."

"I understand, Miss."

"Yes, I think you do, Inspector" she said with a faint smile.

Helping her to her feet they slowly made their way back to the house.

By the time they arrived in the hall she had composed herself and told them that she would help all she could to bring the killer to justice.

"Thank you, Miss Wells, your assistance has been invaluable" said Hadley.

"Now I must tell you that I'm leaving this God awful place tomorrow to spend a few days in London before I'm due to sail back home" she said.

"Where are you staying, Miss?"

"At the Savoy Hotel in the Strand, Inspector, I want to see some of London before I leave England, it'll probably be my only chance" she said with a smile.

"Quite so, Miss, I expect we'll contact you there before you leave next week" said Hadley.

"Yes, I sail a week next Thursday from Liverpool, so I'll be leaving London on the Wednesday morning."

"Very good, Miss."

"I only hope that you find the person who murdered Nancy and see them hang!"

"I'll do my very best, Miss" replied Hadley.

"I'm sure you will, Inspector. I'll give you my address in New York, so will you promise me you'll write and let me know what happens?"

"I promise, Miss Wells" replied Hadley.

"Thank you, Inspector."

"Sergeant, make a note of Miss Well's address" said Hadley and Cooper nodded as he produced his notebook. After she had given Cooper the address, she smiled and shook hands with them before making her way upstairs to her room.

"Now let's see if Barton has got everybody in the kitchen" said Hadley, just as the butler appeared.

"All the members of staff have been assembled in the kitchen now, sir" said Barton.

"Thank you, please lead on."

CHAPTER 4

The kitchen in Holcot Manor was large and appeared as if it had not changed much since Tudor times. The huge fireplace had a black iron stove for modern cooking but other than that the place remained as it must have been for centuries. The centre of the room was taken up by a long oak table at which all the anxious staff were now seated. Barton introduced the detectives then pointed to each person at the table and announced their name followed by their position.

"This is Mrs Noakes, the housekeeper" said Barton and a thin middle aged, austere woman nodded her head at the detectives.

"This is Mrs Chambers, the cook" and the plump woman with a round face smiled.

"This is Mr Winters, the head grounds-man." The thick set man with a ruddy complexion dressed in scruffy tweeds nodded. Hadley remembered that he was the person who found Lady Mortlake after she had fallen from her horse.

"This is Mr Kelly, the head groom." The thin, pale faced young man gave a nervous smile.

"And finally, this is Kate, the house maid." She gave a nod of her head and then looked down at her clasped hands.

"Mr Barton, is this everybody?" asked Hadley as he was surprised that there were so few employed to run such a large house.

"Yes, sir, we're all that's left I'm afraid, the original number of household staff has been reduced since his Lordship died last year" replied Barton.

"I see."

"When extra work needs to be done on the estate, arrangements are made with some of the local people to come in from the village, sir" said Barton.

"I understand, Mr Barton, thank you" said Hadley; the butler nodded before he stood back.

"Now ladies and gentlemen, I just want you to know that there is to be a further investigation into the tragic death of Lady Mortlake, and I will be speaking to each of you privately in due course…"

"She fell off her horse, it was an accident, the Inquest said so" interrupted Winters.

"We are aware of that, but nevertheless, we will be carrying out further inquiries" said Hadley in a firm tone.

"She should be left to rest in peace" said Winters, and on hearing that they all nodded, except Kate, Hadley made a mental note of that.

"That's what we all want, Mr Winters, I assure you, now Sergeant Cooper and I will be back tomorrow afternoon to speak to you all, so please make yourselves available and try to remember what each of you were doing at the time of her ladyship's accident."

The staff looked at one another and Winters along with Kelly shrugged their shoulders.

"Can we go now?" asked Winters.

"You may, and thank you everybody" replied Hadley as they stood up to leave. The detectives left the kitchen and made their way outside the house, standing at the front door in the late afternoon sun. Hadley glanced at his fob watch, it was just before six o'clock. As he replaced it in his pocket he heard the sound of the horse and trap approaching up the long drive.

It was almost seven o'clock when they arrived back at the Excelsior Hotel and they just had time to wash and prepare themselves for dinner. After a glass of local brewed stout in the bar, they went through to the dining room where they enjoyed a fulsome dinner of lamb cutlets followed by fresh fruit served with cream. When they had finished their coffee in the lounge, they went up to Hadley's room to review the day in private and write notes.

"Having spoken to her Ladyship, and Miss Wells, I am now even more certain that Lady Mortlake was murdered, Sergeant."

"I must admit that Miss Wells certainly had it all worked out, sir."

"Yes, she did, and I think that she is probably right about most of the tragic events."

"Who is at the top of your list of suspects, sir?"

"If Lord Mortlake planned his wife's murder, then I suspect an unknown killer, probably hired in London, but if her Ladyship was behind this, then someone from the household committed the crime and Winters would be my top suspect."

"Do you really think her Ladyship would do such a thing, sir?"

"Why not, Sergeant? She obviously disliked her daughter-in-law intensely and knew that if she died, her son would inherit a huge fortune and he would have more than enough to settle his debts, marry a suitable young woman from acceptable London society, then restore the Manor to its original glory, where she could live out her days in splendid isolation."

"Good heavens, sir, you make her appear like a scheming monster."

"When your only son is in serious debt and you are about to be thrown out of your home by an upstart woman of inferior class, then I can assure you, Sergeant, many women have murdered for less!"

"But her Ladyship is an aristocrat, sir."

"So she is, but history tells us that they have been the worst schemers and murderers down through the ages" replied Hadley.

"Yes, I suppose you're right, sir."

"Of course I'm right, take Richard the Third for instance, when he was Duke of York, he murdered his brothers and then the Princes in the Tower to get the crown and keep it, I tell you, Sergeant, when it comes to power and money the blue bloods will stop at nothing, and that includes murder."

"So if her Ladyship did intend to kill Lady Mortlake, she would have turned to her faithful servant, Winters, who probably disliked the American as much as she did, to do the deed and make it look like an accident, sir."

"Precisely, now we shall know more after the Doctor has carried out a second autopsy."

"When do you plan to call him up from London, sir?"

"I'll telegraph him after we've spoken to Inspector West in the morning and arranged the exhumation of Lady Mortlake."

"I don't suppose he'll be too glad to see us, sir."

"No, he won't, Sergeant, because as far as he's concerned, the case is closed and interference from Scotland Yard will not be well received."

Hadley was proved right as usual and when the detectives

presented themselves at Northampton Police Station the next morning, Inspector West was not pleased to see them. After introductions and the invitation to a pot of tea, Inspector West fixed his stern gaze on Hadley, sitting opposite him in front of his paper strewn desk and asked "please explain to me, why the Commissioner wants a further investigation into Lady Mortlake's tragic accident?"

"I'm afraid it's politics, Inspector" replied Hadley.

"Well that doesn't tell me anything, I'm afraid" said West with a quizzical frown.

"Lady Mortlake was the only daughter of one of the richest men in America and her Grandfather had settled a vast sum of money for her independently. It has become clear that the impoverished Lord Mortlake married her for her money; and as her sole beneficiary, her death has raised suspicions. As a result, her father has hired agents from the Pinkerton Detective Agency to investigate the matter, whilst a court injunction is withholding the money…"

"Good grief!" exclaimed West.

"The Pinkerton men are due to arrive in London next week" said Hadley with a smile.

"Then they'll be up here, tramping about all over the place" said West.

"You may rest upon that certainty, Inspector."

"We don't want damned Americans poking their noses in here" said West.

"Precisely, so if, in the meantime, you will give me your undivided attention and support, I may be able to keep them at a distance" Hadley smiled reassuringly.

"Yes, yes, of course, I'll give you any assistance you need."

"That's splendid. Now the first thing that I need to do is exhume the body as I've arranged for our Doctor to carry out a second autopsy" said Hadley.

"Right, I'll get a warrant if you would let the vicar know at Holcot church, where Lady Mortlake is buried."

"Yes, I'll let him know this afternoon and I should point out that we do have Lord Mortlake's permission for his wife's exhumation" replied Hadley.

"Good, now you know that exhumations have to be carried out

at midnight?" asked West.

"Yes, do you think we can arrange everything for tonight?"

"I don't see why not" replied West.

"Right, as time is pressing we'll try for tonight."

"Good, meet me here at about eight o'clock and we'll travel out to Holcot to exhume the body and bring it back to the Infirmary for your Doctor to examine."

"Excellent. May I send a telegraph message to the Yard?"

"By all means, Inspector."

"Thank you, and please call me Jim"

"Er, thank you, Jim, I'm Peter" replied West hesitantly.

Hadley sent a message to Chief Inspector Bell informing of their progress so far and asking him to contact Doctor Evans to request his attendance tomorrow at the Northampton Infirmary to carry out the autopsy of Lady Mortlake. The detectives then left the police station and hired a trap to take them out to Holcot village. It was a glorious sunny day and they both enjoyed the trip out through the picturesque countryside. Hadley asked the driver to stop outside the village pub and whilst Cooper paid the driver and made arrangements for their return from Holcot Manor at six o'clock, he studied the exterior of the old pub. The oak beamed establishment was called the 'Bunch of Grapes', and going inside they found it refreshingly cool. Pints of stout were ordered along with an early lunch of cheese, pickles, ham and fresh bread. It was in the early afternoon, feeling suitably refreshed, that the detectives made their way along the quiet main street to the church. The vicarage was but a stone's throw from the quaint Norman church and as Cooper knocked on the imposing door, Hadley gazed around at the picturesque scene. The door was opened by a small, grey haired lady with dark inquisitive eyes, who asked who they were.

"I'm Inspector Hadley and this is Sergeant Cooper..."

"You're policemen then" she interrupted.

"Yes, Madam, may we see the vicar, please?"

"What's it about? He's a very busy man you know" she said and Hadley smiled as he found it hard to imagine that the vicar was overworked in this sleepy village.

"I'm sure, Madam, but it is very important" replied Hadley.

"Well, I'll see, but I can't promise anything" she said before she hurried away down the hall. Within moments the vicar appeared, he was a small, round, middle aged man with a pink, shiny angelic face and asked in a high pitched benign voice "may I help you gentlemen?"

"Yes, if you would, vicar."

"Well you'd better come in and tell me how I can help."

"Thank you" said Hadley as he stepped into the musty hall. After introductions, Hadley came straight to the point.

"We're here to investigate the death of Lady Mortlake…"

"A great tragedy that has touched us all" interrupted the vicar as he shook his head in sorrow.

"I'm sure it has, and as part of the investigation I must inform you that we intend to exhume the body of her Ladyship…"

"Exhume her body!" interrupted the vicar.

"Yes."

"What ever for, Inspector?"

"We require a second autopsy" replied Hadley.

"But the dear woman died as a result of a riding accident, and I understand that Doctor Ogilvie at the Infirmary said so in his report."

"We are aware of that, vicar, but nevertheless, we are going to exhume her body and carry out another autopsy" said Hadley.

"Well when do you propose to disturb the eternal peace of her Ladyship?"

"Tonight…"

"Tonight!"

"Yes, Inspector West is obtaining a warrant and we will return tonight to recover the body, I understand it is in the Mortlake family vault" said Hadley.

"Well it was buried there, Inspector, but Lord Mortlake had her body removed a day after the ceremony and reburied at the far end of the churchyard" said the vicar. The detectives were surprised to hear this and Hadley asked "what reason did his Lordship give for his wife's reburial?"

"He just said that both he and his mother would prefer it."

"Why?"

"Because it would be more fitting to the lasting memory of his wife, who enjoyed being out in the fresh air" replied the vicar.

"Rather than being buried deep within the family vault?" said Hadley.

"Precisely so, Inspector." Hadley remained silent for a few moments and then looked at Cooper, whose expression confirmed what Hadley was thinking.

"Would you please take us to her Ladyship's grave?"

"Yes, of course, Inspector."

The detectives followed the vicar to the far end of the church yard where the fresh unmarked grave of Lady Mortlake lay close to an oak tree of considerable size. Hadley looked down at the mound of brown earth and said in a sad tone "there's not even a wooden cross for her."

"His Lordship is organising a headstone for his wife, Inspector" said the vicar hastily. The detectives remained silent by the grave side of the American heiress who had married for love, only to discover that she had been duped and betrayed by the man she loved. Hadley dedicated himself to find her murderer and bring him to justice.

"Thank you, vicar, we'll return tonight and exhume her Ladyship. Will you please arrange for your grave diggers to be here at midnight?"

"Yes, Inspector, and I will be here as well to oversee things and to pray for her" replied the vicar.

"Thank you."

The detectives hired a trap in the village to take them out to Holcot Manor, where Barton admitted them to the house.

"I have gathered everyone in the kitchen, sir, and her Ladyship has given permission for you to interview them privately in the study" said the butler.

"Thank, you."

Barton then conducted them to the gloomy room and asked "who would you like to speak to first, sir?"

"You, Mr Barton."

"Me, sir?"

"Yes, and I suggest you sit down for a moment" replied Hadley. The butler sat nervously on the edge of the seat in front of the desk and looked at Hadley now sitting opposite.

"How can I help, sir?"

"Where were you at the time of the accident?" asked Hadley.

"I was organising the cleaning of the silver all that morning, her Ladyship insists upon it every week, sir" replied Barton.

"Who actually did the work?"

"Myself, Mrs Chambers and Kate, sir."

"And were you all together when you heard about the accident?"

"Yes, it was about eleven o'clock when Mr Kelly rushed in and said that Mr Winters had found her Ladyship in the grounds and that she had fallen from her horse" replied Barton.

"Then what happened?"

"I informed her Ladyship at once, who told me to summon Doctor Moore from the village."

"And did you?"

"Yes, of course, I told Mr Kelly to go immediately, as fast as he could" replied Barton.

"When the Doctor arrived had Lady Mortlake been moved or was she still where she fell?"

"Still where she fell, Inspector, so I and Mrs Noakes went out to see if we could give any assistance, but when we got there, Mr Winters said she was already dead."

"Go on, Mr Barton."

"We waited there until Mr Kelly arrived back with the Doctor, then after he pronounced that she was dead, Mr Kelly and Mr Winters carried her body back to the house where she was laid out on the table in the library."

"When did Miss Wells learn of Lady Mortlake's death?"

"Soon as we all knew, Mrs Noakes told her that there had been an accident and Miss Wells actually rushed out to meet us as her Ladyship's body was being carried back to the house, sir."

"I'm sure that she was deeply upset" said Hadley.

"Yes, indeed she was, sir."

"Then what happened, Mr Barton?"

"The Doctor examined her Ladyship once again and confirmed that her death was probably instantaneous and then said that he would arrange for an ambulance to come out from Northampton and remove her to the Infirmary."

"Then presumably, Lord Mortlake was advised of his wife's death?"

"I believe so, sir, because he arrived that night from London" replied Barton.

"Thank you, Mr Barton, you've been very helpful" said Hadley.

"Thank you, sir, now who would you like to speak to next?"

"Mrs Chambers if you please" replied Hadley and the butler nodded and left the study.

The cook added very little to what the detectives already knew, but she did tell them that Lady Mortlake was very kind towards her and Kate, taking a great interest in the traditional English recipes as well as the staff's general well being, much to the annoyance of his Lordship and his mother.

Mrs Noakes was next to be questioned and she was hostile from the moment she sat down in front of Hadley.

"I'm not one to gossip, but I can tell you, Inspector, that sadly, her Ladyship was not the right person for Master Andrew" she said firmly after Hadley had asked her about their relationship.

"What makes you say that, Mrs Noakes?"

"I've been the housekeeper at Holcot for more than thirty years and until that American woman arrived, I never heard a cross word" she replied.

"Really."

"Lord Rupert spent all his time at his London house along with Master Andrew, attending to important business you understand, and her Ladyship remained here at Holcot living an undisturbed, elegant and genteel life."

"Then Master Andrew went to America and arrived back from New York with his new wife" said Hadley.

"Yes, and everything changed!"

"Please go on, Mrs Noakes."

"Well she wanted to take charge of everything, her and her outspoken friend…"

"Miss Wells?"

"Yes, she left this morning for London, thank goodness" replied Mrs Noakes with relief.

"So, tell me what her Ladyship did that caused upset in the household?"

"Well, first of all she wanted to have workmen in to decorate every room, I mean have you ever heard of such a thing?"

"Yes, I have" replied Hadley but Mrs Noakes ignored his comment and carried on.

"Then she wanted Master Andrew to spend money on new furniture! Well, I was shocked, this house has been like this for years and to alter it would be a sin."

"Really, Mrs Noakes?"

"Yes, and what upset me and her Ladyship most of all was the American's suggestion that her Ladyship should move out and live in the old gate house at the end of the drive. That was a monstrous thing to say to her mother-in-law, a lady in the autumn of her life."

"Quite so, Mrs Noakes."

"Then she persisted, with her silly so called companion, in talking to the staff in friendly and familiar terms. Well, that gave them ideas above their station and made Master Andrew and her Ladyship very angry indeed."

"I can believe that, Mrs Noakes, now tell me, did you hear his Lordship often argue with his wife?"

"Yes, Inspector, all of the time, and I believe that Master Andrew could not put up with her constant nagging and returned to London for peace and quiet as often as he could."

"Did you know that Lord Mortlake was seriously in debt?" asked Hadley and the question seemed to un-nerve her.

"Well, I, er, er" she hesitated.

"Well, Mrs Noakes, you've been the housekeeper here for thirty years, you must know what goes on and you must have had an idea" Hadley persisted and she blushed.

"Well, there was some talk…" she hesitated again.

"Go on, I'm listening."

"Master Andrew had some debts that were left to him by his father, and I understand the creditors were pressing him and he asked his wife to help, but she refused, Inspector."

"And that's why they argued" said Hadley.

"I don't know, sir, as I said, I'm not one to gossip."

"Thank you, Mrs Noakes you've been very helpful."

Hadley next spoke to Kate, who was very nervous, blushing at every question. She confirmed what Barton had said and told Hadley that her Ladyship and Miss Wells were both very kind towards her, treating her well. She cried when she told them about her Ladyship being carried into the house; and Miss Wells leaving today for good. Then Hadley spoke to Kelly, who confirmed what Barton had said and when he had finished, the Inspector asked him about Topper, the horse.

"She's a lovely chestnut mare, sir, good as gold she is, and as gentle as they come."

"Before we leave this evening, I'd like to see her please, Mr Kelly" said Hadley.

"Right you are, sir."

When Winters arrived in the study he was not best pleased at being kept waiting in the kitchen until last.

"Will this take long? I've got things to attend to, you know" he said as Hadley waved him to a seat.

"I hope not, Mr Winters."

"That's good."

"Tell me how you found her Ladyship?"

"What do you mean?"

"Were you close by when she fell?" Hadley asked and Winters looked uncomfortable.

"Quite close."

"How close?" persisted Hadley.

"Well, close enough…"

"To see her fall or to hear her scream?" asked Hadley with his eyes hardening.

"I don't remember…"

"Don't remember?" interrupted Hadley angrily.

"Well, I think I was close by in the copse…"

"What were you doing there, Mr Winters?"

"Setting some traps, sir" he replied slightly nervously.

"So, did you see her fall?"

"Yes, I heard the horse coming and I looked up, saw her just as she fell" he replied.

"Was she at a gallop?"

"I don't think so…"

"At a trot?"

"Probably, sir."

"Why do you think she fell, Mr Winters?"

"I can't really say, sir."

"Her Ladyship was a good horsewoman, Topper is a gentle horse and the ground is flat with no potholes; so, I'll ask you again, why do you think she fell?" On hearing that, Winters went pale and looked distinctly anxious.

"I really can't say, sir, I just don't know."

"Perhaps you witnessed someone dragging her off Topper" said Hadley quietly and Winters went ashen faced and trembled slightly.

"No, sir, I didn't see anybody else when she fell, I rushed out from the copse and went to see if I could help her, but she lay awful quiet and I felt for a pulse but there was none, so I left her and ran to the house for help, then Mr Kelly came back with me, then Mr Barton and Mrs Noakes came out to see if they could help, but it was no use."

"What happened next?"

"Mr Kelly rode off to get Doctor Moore from the village and when he came and examined her he said she was dead, so we carried her back to the house and laid her out in the library."

"Thank you, Mr Winters, that'll be all for the time being" said Hadley abruptly and Winters nodded and left the study. Hadley then looked at his fob watch and said "just time enough to see Topper before we return to Northampton and have an early meal."

"Yes, sir" said Cooper.

"We've got a long night ahead of us, Sergeant."

CHAPTER 5

The detectives returned to the Excelsior Hotel and prepared themselves for the midnight exhumation by having an early dinner and refraining from any alcohol. Just before eight o'clock they left the hotel and walked the short distance up from Gold Street to meet Inspector West at the police station.

"I have the warrant and I've arranged for Sergeant Richards and two constables to accompany us tonight, Jim" said West.

"Very good, Peter" replied Hadley.

"Have you advised Reverend Thomas?"

"I have. He will have two grave diggers there and he said he would be present to pray for her Ladyship" replied Hadley.

"Everything is organised then" said West.

"I presume an ambulance will come from the Infirmary?" asked Hadley.

"No, Jim, we'll bring the coffin back ourselves in a police wagon" replied West and Hadley nodded.

It was a clear, warm moonlit night and the journey out to Holcot church, although very pleasant, was for a sad purpose. The detectives rode in a police four wheeler with West and Richards whilst the two constables followed in the police wagon. When they arrived at the church yard they could see a group of figures holding flickering lamps at the grave side of Lady Mortlake.

The policemen approached the figures and greeted the vicar who then gave the order for the grave diggers to do their work. They quickly removed the fresh soil from the grave and piled it up to one side. They dug at the earth smoothly and efficiently, on reaching the coffin Hadley looked at his fob watch in the flickering light of the lamps, it was a quarter to midnight.

"We have fifteen minutes to wait" he said to the assembled group and they stood in silence listening to the vicar's prayers until the moment arrived for the coffin to be raised. The constables helped the grave diggers lift the coffin and place it on the ground. Hadley looked down at the simple brass plate on the lid which just gave Lady Mortlake's name and her life span, 1855 – 1881.

"Just twenty six years old" he whispered more to himself than anyone in particular, but Cooper overheard him.

"It's a terrible tragedy, sir." Hadley looked at his young Sergeant, who was only a few years older than Lady Mortlake.

"Yes" he nodded.

"Let's get her away now" said West, interrupting their thoughts and the grave diggers assisted by the constables, carried the coffin to the police wagon. Once they had loaded the remains of Lady Mortlake into the wagon, the policemen set off back to Northampton whilst the detectives thanked the vicar for his help and prayers, before following on. When they reached the town, Inspector West made arrangements with them for later in the day and said goodnight to them outside the Excelsior Hotel. Hadley was sad and troubled by the exhumation of the young woman and the implications of her death, so he spent a few restless hours of what was left of the night, trying to get some sleep.

Doctor Evans arrived at eleven o'clock on the train from London and the detectives were at the station to meet him.

"I hope this trip is not a waste of my time, Jim" said the Doctor as the hired trap hurried away from the station towards the Infirmary.

"I'm sure it isn't, Doctor" Hadley replied.

"It's all very disconcerting for the pathologist whose already carried out the autopsy, you know, and I can assure you that it's not often we get asked for a second opinion on a deceased" said the Doctor and Hadley wanted to laugh at that, especially when he saw Cooper try and hide a grin. When they arrived at the Infirmary they were shown into Doctor Ogilvie's office, who welcomed them coolly. Then after a pot of tea, the atmosphere thawed and the two medical men discussed Ogilvie's findings whilst the detectives sat quietly and listened. Eventually they followed Doctor Ogilvie into the mortuary where the body of Lady Mortlake lay on a cold marble slab. She was strikingly beautiful with jet black hair and fine features. Her body had not decomposed too badly and the markings around her neck from the accident were still plain to see in her milk white skin.

"You can leave us now, Jim" said Doctor Evans and Hadley nodded.

"When you have finished, Doctor, would you make your way

to the police station and I'll meet you there" said Hadley.

"It won't be until late this afternoon, Jim" replied the Doctor.

"That's perfectly in order, Doctor."

"Good, now have you booked me in somewhere comfortable to stay tonight?"

"Yes, Doctor, you're with us in the Excelsior Hotel" replied Hadley.

"Is the food good?"

"Yes, it is."

"That's a relief then" he said and Hadley smiled.

The detectives left the Infirmary and called at the police station to have a few words with Inspector West before walking down to the Duke's Arms for an early lunch.

After they had finished eating and drinking in the pub, they returned to the hotel to discuss the events so far and prepare reports from Cooper's notes. It was late afternoon when they walked up to the police station to wait for Doctor Evans. When he eventually arrived and was shown into Inspector West's office he looked serious.

"Well, Doctor?" asked Hadley as the Doctor sat down and sighed.

"I think that the poor woman fell or was dragged from her horse and then strangled" replied the Doctor.

"I knew it" said Hadley whilst Cooper shook his head and West looked surprised.

"Does Doctor Ogilvie agree with your findings, sir?" asked West.

"Yes, he does now, Inspector."

"Why didn't he come to the conclusion before that her Ladyship was strangled, Doctor?" asked West.

"Because he was advised that she had fallen from her horse and he assumed that no foul play had been committed, and the original autopsy showed that she had indeed suffered serious injuries to her neck, the third and fourth vertebrae in particular, which was consistent with such a fall, but she was still alive after the event and then someone strangled her…"

"When, Doctor?" interrupted Hadley.

"Hard to tell, but I think fairly soon afterwards, her windpipe was badly crushed so her death would have been mercifully quick" replied the Doctor.

"Were there any other injuries?" asked Hadley.

"Did she fight with her attacker, do you mean?" asked the Doctor.

"Yes."

"No, I could not find anything that would indicate that, Jim" replied the Doctor.

"So, she was probably unconscious from the fall and then strangled" said Hadley.

"Yes, Jim."

"Well, I suppose this will officially open a murder investigation" said West.

"It was already open, Peter, the Doctor's report just confirms that it was the right course of action" said Hadley and West nodded.

"I don't suppose you'll be able to keep the Pinkerton men away from here now, Jim" said West.

"Pinkerton men?" asked the Doctor in surprise.

"Yes, Lady Mortlake's father is sending them over from New York to investigate her murder" replied Hadley.

"She was an American?" asked the Doctor.

"Yes."

"That'll put the cat among the pigeons" said the Doctor.

"It certainly will" replied Hadley with a sigh.

"You know how pushy American's can be, they'll be into everything and you won't be able to stop them" said the Doctor and Hadley nodded as a constable knocked and entered the office.

"Excuse me, sir, there's a telegraph message from London for Inspector Hadley" he said to West.

"Give it here, please" said Hadley and he took the buff envelope, opened it and read the message out loud "Hadley, Lord Mortlake violently attacked and kidnapped today, return to London immediately and see me. Prepare for an emergency meeting with the Commissioner at nine o'clock tomorrow, Bell." They all gasped and Hadley asked "when did this message arrive, constable?"

"Just now, sir."

"Right... Sergeant, it's back to the hotel to pick up our things and straight to the station, Peter, can you send a message back to London telling my Chief that we are on our way?" said Hadley.

"Yes, of course. I'll get a police wagon to take you to your hotel and then onto the station" replied West.

"What about me?" asked Doctor Evans.

"You can come with us if you like" replied Hadley.

"No thank you, Jim, I can't do with all this hurrying about and besides, I've got to write my report" said the Doctor.

"In that case, it looks like you'll be dining alone at the Excelsior tonight" replied Hadley with a grin.

"Yes, I suppose I will, and more is the pity."

"But the food's good!" said Hadley as he left the office followed by Cooper and West.

The London express arrived at Kings Cross just after seven o'clock and the detectives hired a Hansom to take them to the Yard as fast as the horse could go. They went straight up to Chief Inspector Bell's office, knocked and entered.

"Thank heavens you're back, both of you had better sit down" said a relieved Chief Inspector.

"What happened, sir?" asked Hadley as Cooper produced his notebook.

"Lord Mortlake's butler, Wilson, raised the alarm just about midday, according to him, Mortlake had told him that he was going to have lunch at his club and asked him to hail a Hansom, which he did, then after the cab pulled up outside the house and Mortlake came out to get into it, a closed coach pulled up behind the cab, two well built men got out and grabbed Mortlake. A fierce argument ensued then a fight broke out and before Wilson or the cab driver could assist, Mortlake was overpowered and bundled into the coach, which made off at speed towards the Bayswater Road" said Bell.

"Dear God" whispered Hadley.

"And no sign of his Lordship since" said Bell.

"This all gets worse and worse, sir" said Hadley.

"How could this get any worse?"

"Doctor Evans says that Lady Mortlake was strangled, sir."

"Oh, no" whispered Bell.

"Once the Pinkerton men know that, we'll never get rid of

them" said Hadley.

"No, not until they see us hang somebody for her murder" said Bell as he shook his head slowly.

"I'm afraid that's very true, sir."

"We're in for a very difficult time, Hadley, and when the Commissioner hears about this in the morning, he'll want immediate action followed by a quick arrest!"

"Yes, of course, sir."

"The evening papers are already full of the kidnapping, and as usual, all the lurid details are exaggerated to make the incident seem as dreadful as possible" said Bell with a sigh.

"It's always the same, but the public love it, sir" said Hadley and Bell nodded.

"I expect that once the American Ambassador is made aware of Mortlake's kidnap, he'll be asking the Commissioner awkward questions, especially as the Pinkerton men are due to arrive here on Tuesday" said Bell in a worried tone.

"That's without a doubt, sir."

"There's a lot of pressure coming from America, you know, Hadley."

"I'm sure that is so, sir."

"This Arthur Riley fella is a multi millionaire, apparently he inherited a fortune from his father then made even more money in steel and railways" said Bell.

"So I understand, sir."

"He takes an interest in politics and finances a lot of what they do over there by the back door, it certainly wouldn't be acceptable here mind you, but the American politicians are different in their approach."

"Indeed they are, sir."

"So the sudden death of his only daughter will be fully investigated by Riley, with scant regard to our efforts, and he will back that with considerable political might."

"Yes, sir."

"As I see it, the only way that we can satisfy the man is to bring his daughter's killer to justice before the Pinkerton men arrive next week" said Bell.

"What about Lord Mortlake, sir?"

"You'll need to find him by then as well" replied Bell and

Hadley knew that everything was about to fall upon his shoulders.

"I'll do my best, sir."

"You'll have to do better than that, Hadley."

"May I have some help, sir?"

"What kind of help?"

"Well, for a start, more officers, sir."

"Out of the question, we're stretched as never before, Hadley."

"But, sir, think of the implications if I don't manage to arrest the killer by Tuesday!" On hearing that Chief Inspector Bell sat back in his chair and thought for a moment before he said "alright, let me know what you want and I'll see what I can do, but no promises, mind."

"I understand, sir."

"Now, you'd better write me a full report before you go home tonight and make sure you have all the answers for the Commissioner in the morning, Hadley."

"Yes, sir."

"So from now on, prepare yourselves for late nights and working all hours until the killer is caught" said Bell.

"Right, sir" said Hadley and Cooper nodded.

"I bet you're glad you had a holiday in Bognor last week" said Bell with a grin.

"I am, sir."

"I wish I could have a holiday, but it wouldn't do me much good anyway, because I never sleep these days" said Bell with a sigh.

"I'm sorry to hear that, sir."

"So I might as well lay awake all night in Clapham worrying about everything, whilst I listen to Mrs Bell snore, as be at the seaside" said Bell gloomily.

"Indeed you might, sir" replied Hadley with a straight face as he imagined the scene. Cooper tried to hide his grin.

When the detectives had written a report and presented it to Bell, they left the Yard and took a Hansom to 28, Connaught Square. A very worried and perplexed butler opened the door to them and he asked anxiously "any news of his Lordship, sir?"

"I'm afraid not, Mr Wilson" replied Hadley.

"Oh, dear, oh, dear" said the downcast butler.

"We'd like to talk to you, may we come in?"

"Yes, of course, sir" and Wilson stood aside and the detectives entered the hall before they were conducted into the study.

"Tell me what happened today, Mr Wilson, and leave nothing out" said Hadley as Cooper produced his notebook.

"Well, sir, it was usual for his Lordship to have lunch two or three times a week at his club, that's the Dreyfus Club in Curzon Street…"

"Yes, we know it, Mr Wilson."

"So, about twelve o'clock today, he asked me to summon a Hansom for him, which I did, and then when it stopped outside the house, I informed his Lordship that it was waiting for him."

"Then tell me exactly what happened next, Mr Wilson."

"As his Lordship went out of the front door and down the steps another coach, a closed one with black horses, suddenly pulled up behind the Hansom and two men got out."

"How were they dressed?"

"I don't really recall, sir."

"Try, if you can" said Hadley.

"Ah, yes, I think I remember that the bigger of the two men had a dark green topcoat."

"Go on."

"He said something to his Lordship, which I didn't hear, and then he grabbed his Lordship by the arm, he struggled before the other man grabbed his other arm, it was awful to see it" said Wilson and Hadley thought the old man was about to cry.

"Please continue when you're ready, Mr Wilson."

"Thank you, sir, I'm alright, so then the man in the green coat punched his Lordship hard in the face, I ran down the steps to help my master, but they bundled him, half conscious, into the coach before I could get there and made off at speed towards the Bayswater Road."

"Have you ever seen these men before?"

"No, Inspector."

"Did they look like ruffians?"

"No, sir, they seemed to be quite presentable."

"Was there anything special or peculiar about the coach?"

"Not that I can remember, sir."

Hadley remained silent for a few moments and then said "Mr

Wilson, I'm going to ask you some questions about his Lordship that may offend you, but you must answer me truthfully as his Lordship's life may depend on what you tell me."

"Very good, sir."

"Does he have any close friends to whom he owes money?"

"One or two, I believe, sir."

"Do you know their names?"

"Yes, sir, Mr Oswald Linklater and Mr Henry Descoyne, they're members of the Dreyfus Club, where unfortunately the cards have not been in his Lordships favour recently" replied Wilson sadly.

"I see, do these gentlemen come here at all?"

"Yes, sir, they dine here quite often and then play cards for most of the night."

"Have you ever heard Lord Mortlake arguing with either of them?"

"No, sir, but they have often chided him about the amount of money that his Lordship owes them."

"But they are unlikely to harm him?"

"Oh, quite so, sir, they are gentlemen" replied Wilson with a touch of indignation.

"Yes, of course. Now, does his Lordship have any close lady friends?" asked Hadley and Wilson looked slightly uncomfortable.

"Well…" he hesitated.

"Come along, Mr Wilson, remember, his Lordship's life may depend on your answers."

"There is a young lady who frequently visits his Lordship" replied Wilson.

"And she is?"

"Miss Jarvis, sir, Miss Madeleine Jarvis."

"Tell me all about Miss Jarvis if you would."

"Well, she is a very attractive lady who comes here quite often for luncheon or afternoon tea and she plays the piano for his Lordship."

"Would you say that there was a romantic attachment?"

"I really don't know, sir."

"Is Miss Jarvis well connected in London society?"

"I would imagine so, sir."

"Any other ladies who you would regard as close friends of his

Lordship?"

"No, not really, sir."

"Do you have the address of Miss Jarvis?"

"I discovered one of her letters on the Master's desk yesterday and I believe that it has her address, sir."

"Please show me the letter" said Hadley and Wilson nodded before he went to the desk and produced the envelope from the top drawer then handed it to Hadley. The Inspector read the short 'thank you' note, which was written in a warm, friendly tone, regarding a recent night at the opera, and the address was 36, Regent Street.

"Thank you, Mr Wilson, you've been very helpful."

"Thank you, sir, and you will let me know if you have any news about his Lordship?"

"You may depend upon it" replied Hadley.

"Thank you, sir."

"Now, Sergeant, we'll call upon Miss Jarvis on our way to the Dreyfus Club!"

"Right, sir."

CHAPTER 6

Regent Street was very busy with the late evening traffic and the cab driver had difficulty in finding number 36. Eventually the Hansom struggled across the path of several other cabs, much to the annoyance of their drivers, and pulled up at the kerb. Whilst Cooper paid the driver, Hadley stood with his hands on his hips, studying the building. He was anxious to question Miss Jarvis closely about her relationship with Lord Mortlake, as she represented another motive for murder in his suspicious mind. A maid answered the door and Hadley introduced himself and Cooper then asked to speak to Miss Jarvis. The maid bobbed a curtsey and closed the door but she returned quite soon and admitted them to the spacious, well appointed hallway. She then conducted them into the elegant drawing room where a tall, attractive young woman of about twenty five, stood to greet them. Miss Jarvis held out her hand and said in a soft well educated voice, "good evening, Inspector."

"Good evening, Miss" replied Hadley as he took her extended hand and shook it gently, followed by Cooper.

"Please sit down, gentlemen."

"Thank you, Miss" Hadley nodded as he made himself comfortable on a plush, green sofa and Cooper joined him.

"Would you like a drink?" she smiled.

"No, thank you, Miss, I'm afraid we're on duty" replied Hadley much to Cooper's surprise.

"How may I help you?" she asked softly as she lowered her head slightly and fluttered her eyelids. Hadley thought again that this lovely woman could well be an additional motive for murder along with the two million pound inheritance.

"I believe that you are a friend of Lord Mortlake, Miss, is that so?"

"Yes, Inspector, Andrew is a good friend and we've known each other for several years."

"How close is your relationship, Miss?"

"That is an impertinent question, Inspector, and I prefer not to answer it!" she replied in an angry tone.

"Miss Jarvis, let me acquaint you with some facts that may

change your mind, firstly, the Police Commissioner himself has given me direct orders to open an investigation into the death of Lady Mortlake, because we now know that she was murdered; secondly, agents from the Pinkerton Detective Agency in America are arriving next week to carry out investigations in parallel with our own; thirdly, the American Ambassador is involved at the highest level, and lastly, Lord Mortlake was attacked and kidnapped outside his house at lunch time today. So please answer my question!" When she heard that she let out a cry and the colour drained from her face as she sank down onto a fireside chair.

"Oh, dear God, do you know what has become of Andrew?" she asked in a whisper as if terrified by the expected answer.

"No, not yet, Miss, but we'll find him that's for sure" replied Hadley.

"Please do everything you can to rescue him, Inspector."

"I will, Miss, now please tell me about your relationship with Lord Mortlake and any plans that you have for the future."

"I can't see how anything I say can help you find him" she replied as she started to dab at her eyes with a handkerchief.

"I assure you, Miss, that everything you tell me may hold a clue as to what has befallen him, so your answers may save his life" said Hadley firmly. She then began to cry and the detectives waited patiently for her to compose herself. When she was ready, she smiled a brave smile and said "I think I'll have a drink to steady me, are you sure you won't join me, Inspector?"

"No, thank you Miss" replied Hadley and Cooper raised his eyebrows.

She rang for the maid who poured a brandy for her mistress and presented it on a silver tray. After a few sips, she settled in her chair and said "as I told you, Andrew and I have known each other for a number of years and I had hoped that one day he would make me his wife, but unfortunately, my family is no longer wealthy and Andrew had to marry a woman with a considerable dowry."

"That's sad and unfortunate for you, Miss."

"Yes, it is. When he went to America last year and returned with a bride from New York, I was heartbroken."

"I'm sure, Miss."

"Then soon after he arrived back in England he started to call upon me again."

52

"I see, and what did you think about that, Miss?"

"I was flattered, of course, but my parents were very displeased."

"Did they make their feelings known to his Lordship?"

"No, but my brothers did" she replied.

"Tell me about them, Miss" said Hadley with interest.

"Robert, that's my older brother, went to Andrew and told him that as a married man he should not call here without his wife and his attentions towards me were most unwelcome" she replied.

"And then what happened?"

"Andrew took no notice and said no one would stop him seeing me because he loved me" she whispered.

"Go on, Miss."

"And we became very close" she half whispered and blushed.

"You were lovers?"

"Yes" she replied with a gentle nod of her head as she looked down at her hands.

"When did this happen?"

"It was just before Christmas, Inspector."

"Did any of your family know of your affair?"

"No, not until after Andrew's wife had her tragic accident" she replied.

"Please tell me everything, Miss."

"Well after the funeral, Andrew proposed to me and said we could get married as soon as he was out of mourning" she said.

"And you told your parents?"

"Yes, I did."

"How did they react?"

"They did not approve, but when you get to my age and are unmarried, Inspector, you have to accept any proposal before it's too late, so I told them that in no uncertain terms" she replied with a smile.

"Where are your family now, Miss?"

"My parents are on holiday in France at the moment, Inspector."

"What about your brothers?"

"I believe that Robert is at home with his wife in Kensington and George is with his Regiment at Aldershot."

"I'll need their addresses, Miss."

"Why?"

"I have to follow all lines of inquiry, Miss, and your brothers may know something about Lord Mortlake that you are unaware of" replied Hadley.

After Miss Jarvis had given all the information that Hadley required, the detectives left the house and hailed a cab to take them to the Dreyfus Club.

The receptionist recognised the detectives from their previous visits to the club and he eyed them up warily as they approached his desk.

"Good evening, gentlemen" said Smethurst.

"Good evening" said Hadley.

"May I be of some assistance, sir?" asked Smethurst anxiously as he remembered the altercation he had with Hadley during his last visit.

"Yes, I would like to speak to Mr Linklater and Mr Descoyne, if they are in this evening" said Hadley.

"I'll just check the members register for you, sir."

"Thank you" said Hadley as the bespectacled receptionist opened a large, leather bound book and ran his finger down the member's signatures for that day.

"Ah, yes, here we are, Mr Linklater is in, sir, but I can find no trace of Mr Descoyne" said Smethurst.

"Is he likely to be in later?"

"I couldn't say, sir, but Mr Linklater may know" replied the helpful Smethurst.

"Indeed, so would you let him know we are here and wish to speak to him?"

"Yes, of course, sir, it's Inspector Hadley and his Sergeant from the Yard if I'm not mistaken?"

"Yes, you are quite right" replied Hadley.

"Won't keep you a moment, Inspector" said the receptionist as he left his desk and hurried away across the spacious hallway and through double doors into an inner sanctum. They waited for some while and observed the august club members wandering from room to room, some puffing at cigars and others laughing a little too much for effect as Hadley's patience began to wear a little thin. He glanced at his fob watch then at Cooper with raised eyebrows just as Smethurst re-appeared with a tall, fair haired young man.

"This is Mr Linklater, Inspector" said Smethurst.

"Good evening, sir, I'm Inspector Hadley and this Sergeant Cooper, may we have a word or two in private?" asked Hadley.

"What's this about, Inspector?"

"It is concerning your friend Lord Mortlake, sir."

"What about him?"

"We need to discuss the matter in private, sir."

"Very well, Inspector…Smethurst, where shall we go?"

"Mr Bolting's office is vacant as he is out until later, sir" replied the receptionist.

"Good, so if you would like to come with me then, gentlemen" said Linklater. The detectives followed the young man down the corridor to the secretary's office and when they had made themselves comfortable in there, Hadley began.

"Mr Linklater, I have to advise you that Lord Mortlake was attacked and kidnapped outside his home today…"

"Good God!" exclaimed Linklater.

"The incident was widely reported in the evening papers so I presume by your reaction that you have not read them yet?"

"Quite so, Inspector" replied the shocked young man.

"Tell me, sir, when did you last see Lord Mortlake?"

"Several days ago, er, er, I can't quite remember, Inspector."

"Where was that, sir?"

"At his house in Connaught Square, we had dinner with our friend, Henry Descoyne and then played cards most of the night."

"Do you expect Mr Descoyne to come here this evening?"

"Yes, he should be in later, Inspector."

"Do you know of anybody who might wish to harm Lord Mortlake, sir?"

"No, not really."

"What do you mean by 'not really', sir?"

"Well, somebody like Andrew is bound to have made a few enemies…"

"Miss Jarvis's brothers perhaps?" mused Hadley and he watched the colour drain from Linklater's face.

"You know about them then?" he asked anxiously.

"Yes, we do, but perhaps you would like to add something to

help our investigation, sir."

"I don't know much, Inspector."

"Any information, no matter how little, is always helpful, sir" smiled Hadley.

"Well, Andrew has always been quite keen on Madeleine and we all thought that they would eventually marry, but when Andrew went off to America and came back with a wife, well, all his friends were taken by surprise."

"Continue, sir."

"Her parents were not happy at all and her brothers were very angry with Andrew and told him to stay away from Madeleine, but he took no notice, then after his wife's tragic accident, he told us, in confidence of course, that he had proposed to Madeleine."

"How did her brothers react to that, sir?"

"They were pretty bloody angry, I can tell you, Inspector."

"If their sister was engaged to be married to the man of her choice, surely they should be pleased for her?"

"Yes, normally, but they regard Andrew as the very worst of men."

"Why, sir?"

"He gambles heavily, and what's worse, he always seems to loose and owes us all a King's ransom, he spends time in flesh pots indulging himself with his perverted desires, and as his habits are well known by all in fashionable society, he's not regarded as a very suitable person for marriage."

"I see, sir, and what do you think of him?"

"Oh, he's great fun but he should never get married as I'm sure it would end in tragedy!"

"It already has, sir" said Hadley in a cold tone.

"Oh, yes, how stupid of me to say that" said Linklater apologetically.

"Quite so, sir" said Hadley in a calm tone.

"I'll do anything I can to help you find Andrew, Inspector, but for the moment I'm at a loss to know where he is."

"Don't worry, sir, you've been most helpful and I would ask you to inform your friend Mr Descoyne of what has happened to Lord Mortlake today" said Hadley.

"Yes, of course, Inspector."

"If he has any information that might be relevant to the

whereabouts of his Lordship, then would you please ask him to contact me at the Yard?"

"I will, most certainly, Inspector."

"Thank you, sir."

"Is that all, Inspector?"

"Yes, Mr Linklater, for the time being."

On the way back to their respective homes Hadley discussed the day's events with Cooper all the way to Camden. As the cab trotted into Marylebone High, Hadley said gloomily "finding Mortlake in London is going to be worse than trying to find a needle in several haystacks, Sergeant."

"That's true, sir."

"The kidnappers could have taken him anywhere" said Hadley.

"Perhaps the Jarvis brothers can shed some light on the mystery, sir."

"Yes, and at the moment they are the prime suspects" replied Hadley.

"Although Wilson said he did not recognise the men who attacked his Lordship and presumably he would have known if it had been the brothers, sir."

"Quite so, but they could have hired ruffians to do their dirty work, Sergeant."

"But Wilson said they weren't dressed like ruffians."

"Yes, he did say that" nodded Hadley.

"Or, perhaps Wilson did recognise them but didn't want to say, sir."

"Why should he do that, Sergeant?"

"I don't know, sir, but could the whole incident be part of an elaborate hoax?"

"Now there's food for thought."

"Indeed it is, sir."

"We'll track down the Jarvis brothers as soon as we can, Sergeant."

"Yes, sir."

"Right after I've faced the Commissioner tomorrow morning, Sergeant and I'm not looking forward to that, I can tell you!"

CHAPTER 7

Hadley arrived in Chief Inspector Bell's office at eight thirty the next morning clutching his latest report along with his notes for the Commissioner's meeting at nine.

"I hope you've got all the right answers to the questions that the Commissioner is bound to ask, Hadley."

"I hope so too, sir."

"No vague shilly-shallying this time, Hadley, not now the Americans are involved" said Bell firmly.

"No, sir."

"Any sign of his Lordship?"

"Not yet, sir."

"It's all beginning to smell very fishy, Hadley."

"I agree, sir."

"Where do you intend to search for him?"

"I'm not sure yet, sir…"

"Hadley! That's simply is not good enough!"

"It's the truth, sir."

"Never mind about the truth, the Commissioner wants this man found and someone arrested for the murder of his wife before the Americans arrive!"

"I'm sure he does, sir, but my inquiries take time and I'm working hard at it…"

"Obviously not hard enough!"

"I didn't arrive home until after eleven o'clock last night, sir."

"So?"

"Well, sir…"

"You've had a holiday haven't you?"

"Yes, but…"

"Well there you are then" interrupted Bell with a stony expression as Hadley struggled to control himself before he said "yes, sir, now after the meeting with the Commissioner, I intend to interview the Jarvis brothers…"

"Who are they?"

"They are the brothers of Madeleine Jarvis, Mortlake's fiancé, it's all here in my report, sir."

"His fiancé?" queried Bell as he fixed Hadley with a surprised

58

stare.

"Yes, sir."

"Bloody hell, he's only just buried his wife!" exclaimed Bell.

"That is so, sir, and the Jarvis brothers apparently are outraged at his behaviour…"

"I don't blame them, the man should be in mourning; he needs horse whipping!"

"Possibly, sir."

"And these brothers are your prime suspects?"

"Yes, they are, sir."

"Well arrest them immediately, Hadley."

"That may be premature, sir."

"Hadley, the Commissioner wants results and it puts him in a favourable light when news of arrests are reported in the Press."

"They may be totally innocent, sir."

"Never mind about their innocence, Hadley, you know that I stand firmly on my principle of locking them all up until we get at the truth" said Bell firmly.

"I do, sir."

"A spell in solitary works wonders when it comes to loosening tongues, especially if they're innocent."

"Yes, sir."

"Now tell me about the wife? What more do we know about her murder?"

"Only that she was strangled after she fell or was dragged from her horse, sir. I'll hopefully know more when I receive Doctor Evan's report" replied Hadley.

"Have you any suspects?"

"Yes, the prime suspect is Winters, the grounds-man who found her, sir."

"Is he in custody?"

"Not yet, sir."

"Why not, Hadley?"

"I've got to build a case against him, sir."

"Good God man, there's killers and kidnappers running around all over the place and you seem to be paralysed by the fear that arrest might upset them!"

"Not at all, sir, I just must make sure that I'm in possession of all the facts" replied Hadley.

"Oh, well, if you must make every inquiry slow and laborious it is inevitable that there will be delays in arrests" said Bell with a sigh as Hadley looked at his fob watch.

"It's almost nine o'clock, sir."

"Right, let's go and see if we can convince the Commissioner that we are making some progress" said Bell.

The Commissioner's face grew a little redder than usual and his side whiskers twitched as he listened to Bell's detailed statement regarding the investigation into the murder of Lady Mortlake and the kidnapping of her husband. When Bell had finished the Commissioner remained silent for a few moments before he said "Chief Inspector, do you realise the precarious position that I am in over this infernal affair?"

"Yes, I'm sure I do, sir" replied Bell nervously.

"And do you, Hadley?"

"Yes, sir."

"Why oh, why, then, do I have to give you both instructions to make arrests?"

"Well, sir…" began Bell.

"Are you damned well frightened or something?" interrupted the Commissioner angrily.

"No, sir…"

"You behave like silly, shy school girls in the park, now, I've heard enough!"

"Yes, sir."

"Hadley, arrest both the Jarvis brothers and the peasant up at Holcot who found her Ladyship" thundered the Commissioner.

"Very good, sir" replied Hadley.

"I demand action!"

"Of course, sir" said Bell anxiously.

"What with the damned Press and the interfering politicians, my life is a constant misery" said the Commissioner forcefully.

"I'm sure it is, sir" said Bell in a sympathetic tone.

"I hardly sleep these days, Chief Inspector."

"I know how you feel, sir."

"To make things worse, the American Ambassador has been in contact with Sir Roger Belgrave the Home Office Minister, asking him to 'move things along' in the investigation as he is coming under pressure from senior Congressmen in Washington!" said the Commissioner.

"Oh, dear" whispered Bell.

"You may well say 'oh, dear' Chief Inspector, but it seems that now we have to produce immediate results, not only for our masters but the American Congress as well, have you ever heard the like?"

"No, sir, I haven't" replied Bell with a shake of his head.

"This Arthur Riley must have a lot of friends in high places" said the Commissioner.

"I believe that is the case, sir."

"So, Hadley, it all rests on your shoulders now" said the Commissioner.

"Yes, sir" replied Hadley as he felt the wet blanket of total responsibility fall on him from a great height.

"Get all the suspects into custody, start questioning them and I'll announce it to the Press this afternoon."

"Isn't that a little premature, sir?" queried Hadley.

"Hadley! Remember where you are and never question the Commissioner's decision" said Bell sharply.

"I'm sorry, sir, but I have to actually arrest these suspects before the news of it is printed in the Press" persisted Hadley.

"I have confidence that you'll do it in plenty of time, Hadley" said the Commissioner.

"If you say so, sir" said Hadley lamely.

"I do, Hadley, now get to it, good morning, gentlemen" said the Commissioner as he returned his gaze to the paperwork in front of him.

When they returned to the Chief Inspector's office, Hadley protested that he simply did not have time to arrest Winters and the Jarvis brothers by this afternoon.

"Very well, Hadley, you arrest Robert Jarvis and send Cooper down to Aldershot to arrest his brother George and I'll telegraph Inspector West in Northampton to go out to Holcot and bring Winters in" said Bell.

"I think that is most unsatisfactory, sir."

"Hadley, for once do as you are told."

"Yes, sir."

Hadley sat at his desk and sipped at a cup of George's tea whilst he told Cooper what the Commissioner had ordered.

"This will be tight for time, sir" said Cooper anxiously.

"I realise that, Sergeant, so I suggest you get away to Aldershot as quickly as possible."

"Right, sir."

"Take a constable with you, just in case Mr Jarvis objects to being arrested on a charge of kidnapping his future brother-in-law."

"Yes, sir."

"Then return with him as soon as possible."

"I will, sir."

"Meanwhile, I'll go to Kensington and see if I can find his brother, Robert."

After Cooper had left the office, Hadley studied his report for a while before going down to Custody and requesting a duty sergeant to accompany him to Kensington. He was pleased that he was allocated Sergeant Preston, an ambitious young man who was keen to get on and prove himself. They were just about to leave the Yard when George hurried down and managed to stop Hadley at the front door.

"Oh, sir, I'm glad I've caught you" said the clerk.

"Yes, George?"

"There's a Mr Morton Barrymore in your office, sir, he's just arrived and he says he needs to see you urgently."

"Right, George…wait here if you would, Sergeant, I shouldn't be too long."

"Very good, sir" nodded Preston.

Hadley followed George back to the office where the solicitor sat looking anxious.

"Inspector, good morning" said Barrymore as he stood and shook hands.

"Mr Barrymore, good morning, how can I help you?" asked Hadley as he sat behind his desk and waved Barrymore to sit once more.

"Inspector, this letter arrived this morning for my attention and I think you had better read it" said the solicitor as he handed the envelope to Hadley.

"Posted yesterday in London at four o'clock" said Hadley as he looked at the envelope before he removed the letter.

"Yes, Inspector" whispered Barrymore as Hadley began to read it aloud.

"To Mr Morton Barrymore, Solicitor, Sir, this is to inform you that we have your client Lord Mortlake in captivity and will hold him until a ransom of one hundred thousand pounds has been deposited into a numbered account held in Banque Suisse Credite in Geneva. For the next seven days Lord Mortlake will be fed only on bread and water, after then, all sustenance will be withheld until he dies a painful and agonising death from starvation. Then his body will be placed into a weighted sack and thrown into the Thames where it will remain undisturbed forever. When the Banque Suisse Credite confirms that the sum has been deposited then Lord Mortlake will be released in London. If you fail to provide this sum within seven days then your client will surely die and his death will be your responsibility. The Bank details are as follows: Banque Suisse Credite, Boulevard Foche, Geneva, Switzerland, account number 23-462-967-1940." Hadley sat silent and contemplated the letter once again.

"Have you such a large sum at your disposal, Mr Barrymore?"

"Well, yes, er, more than that is held in the client account, Inspector."

"Then my advice is to make arrangements to pay the ransom as soon as possible, sir."

"Good heavens I can't do that, Inspector!"

"Then your client's death will be your responsibility, sir."

"Aren't you going to do anything?" asked Barrymore angrily.

"The chances of me finding Lord Mortlake in London within the next six days are practically nil, sir."

"But if I take such a large sum from the account, how will I ever replace it?"

"Presumably after Lord Mortlake is released and inherits his fortune from his late wife, sir" replied Hadley.

"I'm amazed at your attitude, Inspector!"

"I often amaze people, sir, but let me be blunt, the only chance we have of releasing his Lordship in time and bringing the kidnappers to justice, lies in your ability to pay this ransom immediately."

"Oh, dear God help us" whispered Barrymore.

"In this instance, Lord Mortlake needs your assistance as well as the Almighty's, sir."

"I'll have to tell Mr Olivier about all this."

"Yes, I'm sure you will."

"What if he says 'no' to this payment, after all he is the senior partner, Inspector?"

"Show him the letter and tell him that Lord Mortlake's death is his responsibility if he objects" replied Hadley.

"Oh, dear."

"And I suggest that it would be helpful if you remind him of the fees you could charge a grateful client who has just inherited two million pounds, sir" said Hadley with a knowing smile.

"Oh, yes, I'm sure that would encourage him, Inspector."

"Without a shadow of a doubt, sir" nodded Hadley.

"I'll go at once and make the necessary arrangements after I've told Mr Olivier."

"Very good, sir, and I'm sure it's the right course of action to save his Lordship."

Half an hour later, Hadley and Sergeant Preston arrived outside 48, Abingdon Road, just off Kensington High, and knocked at the door. A pretty young maid opened the door and Hadley announced himself and asked to see Mr Jarvis.

"I'm afraid he's not here, sir, would you like to speak to Mrs Jarvis?"

"Yes, please" nodded Hadley and the maid bobbed a curtsey and disappeared into a room to the left of the hallway. She reappeared a short while later, invited them in and they followed her into the drawing room.

"Good morning, Inspector" said Mrs Jarvis as she stood.

"Good morning, Madam" replied Hadley as he looked at the elegant young woman.

"Now tell me what this is all about" she said firmly as she sat down in a winged chair and waved them to the sofa opposite.

"I'm anxious to speak to your husband about the kidnapping of Lord Mortlake, Madam."

"A dreadful business, Inspector, it's reported in all the London papers" she said.

"Yes, indeed."

"But my husband had nothing to do with it, Inspector."

"I'm sure that is so, Madam, but nevertheless, I need to speak to him."

"Well I'm afraid that won't be possible for a week or so."

"Why is that, Madam?"

"He's gone abroad on business, Inspector."

"May I ask where to?"

"He's gone to Geneva, in Switzerland, Inspector, and he left yesterday afternoon to catch the boat train from Waterloo."

"Has he now" mused Hadley as his mind raced at the news.

"Yes, but as I say, he'll be back in about a week."

"I'll have to wait until then, Madam."

"Yes."

"Tell me, what business is your husband in, Madam?"

"He is a senior manager with a Merchant Bank in the City, Inspector" she replied proudly.

"And the name of the Bank is, Madam?"

"It's the London branch of the Banque Suisse Credite, Inspector."

"And where are they in the City, Madam?"

"In Threadneedle Street, Inspector."

"Thank you, Mrs Jarvis, you've been very helpful."

"I'm glad to have been of some assistance, and please feel free to call again, Inspector."

"Oh, I will, Madam, of that you can be sure!"

CHAPTER 8

Hadley returned to the Yard and waited patiently for a telegraph message from Inspector West regarding the arrest of Winters and the return of Cooper with George Jarvis. It was just after midday when the message arrived from West confirming that he had Winters in custody and Hadley telegraphed back saying that he would come up to Northampton to question him. Cooper arrived back with Lieutenant Jarvis of the Queen's Fusiliers at five o'clock and took him straight to custody. When Cooper reported to Hadley that he had the suspect, Hadley went immediately up to see Chief Inspector Bell.

The Chief listened to Hadley then said "well I suppose two out of three suspects in custody is not bad."

"No, sir, but I'm anxious that the Commissioner is careful to just say in his Press statement that arrests have been made and not to go into any more detail."

"Hadley, the Commissioner is not a fool you know, that's why he's the Commissioner" replied Bell testily.

"I'm sure that's the case, sir, but I am anxious that his enthusiasm about early arrests doesn't run away with him."

"You need not worry. Now, what do you plan to do next?"

"Question George Jarvis and when I've finished with him, I'll travel up to Northampton to interview Winters, sir."

"Good, and don't hesitate to bring Winters back here if necessary, Hadley."

"I won't, sir."

"Right, now I'll inform the Commissioner of the good news and he can release it to the Press."

"Yes, sir."

"You try and get confessions out of the two in custody, Winters for murder and Jarvis for kidnapping, then all you have to do is find Mortlake and we can close the case before the Americans arrive."

"I hope it is that easy, sir."

"I know you'll do it somehow, Hadley."

"I'm not so confident, sir."

"Oh, Hadley, you disappoint me when you say things like

that."

"It's the truth, sir."

"Listen, Hadley, I do not want any more sleepless nights for a while, so I'm relying on you to get results!"

"Yes, sir, I'll do my best."

After a pot of George's tea and a briefing from Cooper, the detectives went down to custody to interview Lieutenant Jarvis. The young man sat anxiously at the table opposite Hadley whilst Cooper prepared to take notes.

"Mr Jarvis, you have been arrested on suspicion of kidnapping Lord Mortlake, what do you say to that charge?" asked Hadley.

"I've already told your Sergeant many times, Inspector, I know nothing at all about it!" replied Jarvis in a forceful tone.

"Where were you yesterday?"

"What a stupid question, Inspector!"

"Nevertheless, I have to ask it for the record" replied Hadley.

"I was with my Regiment all day and up to lunch time today when your Sergeant arrived at the Mess to arrest me!"

"I see."

"In fact I rejoined my Regiment at the beginning of May after a week's leave in London, when I stayed with my brother and his wife, and I've not left the Garrison since, so the kidnapping is news to me, Inspector."

"What do you know about your brother's business career?"

"Robert is a manager with a Swiss Merchant Bank in the City, Inspector, why do you ask?"

"Do you know if he goes abroad on Bank business?"

"Yes, he often travels to Paris and Geneva, where the Bank has its headquarters."

"I see."

"What's that got to do with Andrew's kidnapping?"

"I ask the questions, sir, and you give the answers."

"So it seems, Inspector."

"Tell me, what is your relationship like with Lord Mortlake?"

"Well to tell the truth, I never cared much for him."

"Why is that?"

"I think he behaves very badly and he's a cad, Inspector."

"Continue if you would."

"There's not a lot to say, he's a heavy gambler and always seems to loose, he's always in debt and he leads a promiscuous life."

"So you and your brother were unhappy to say the least, when your sister told you that he had proposed to her?"

"We all were, Inspector, especially so soon after the death of Mortlake's wife. My father forbade Madeleine to have anything to do with him."

"Apparently she took no notice."

"That is so, but she is very headstrong, Inspector."

"Can you think of anybody who would wish to harm Lord Mortlake?"

"Yes, I can."

"Who, sir?"

"Well, for a start, all the people that he owes money too…"

"Give me a list" interrupted Hadley.

"All his fellow club members that he gambles with, all the trade's men in London and Northampton, all the husbands of his various indiscreet conquests; the list is endless, Inspector."

"Quite a list it seems, sir."

"A very long one, Inspector."

"Thank you, sir, that will be all for the time being."

"Am I free to return to my Regiment?"

"Not yet, sir, I have to make some further inquiries before I can let you go."

"How long will they take, Inspector?"

"I promise to be as quick as possible, sir" replied Hadley with a smile.

The detectives returned to the office and discussed the day's events and made plans for the next day. Hadley was conscious of time running out before the arrival of the Pinkerton agents and that made him anxious because he knew that they would prove to be a total distraction once they were on the case.

"First we'll go to the Swiss Bank in the City, make our inquiries and after we've finished over there we'll catch a train to Northampton and see what Winters has to say for himself."

"Will we be staying up there, sir?"

"I don't plan to but you'd better bring your overnight bag just in case" replied Hadley.

Alice was pleased to see her husband home at a reasonable time for once and after an evening meal with the children, they sat alone in the small secluded garden relaxing in the warm breeze.

"This case is proving very difficult, my dear, I'm going up to Northampton tomorrow and I hope to be back later that night, but I can't be sure" Hadley said to his wife.

"I understand, dear."

"And with things as they are, I'll probably be on duty all weekend."

"Well, in that case, it's jolly good that we had our holiday otherwise you'd be half dead with exhaustion" she said firmly.

"Yes, indeed."

"How's your Sergeant coping with all this?"

"Very well, dear, I'm glad I've got him with me."

"And his wife, how is she managing?"

"I think she's learning to have patience and understanding."

"That's very necessary for a policeman's wife. Now, I suggest we have an early night" Alice smiled.

"An excellent idea, I shall need all my strength for what lies ahead tomorrow" replied Hadley.

"Never mind about tomorrow, Jim, it's what lies ahead tonight that I'm concerned with!"

"Alice!"

"We women have needs as well as you men and I'm still in the holiday mood" she laughed.

"Bognor has a lot to answer for" smiled Hadley.

"Oh, yes it certainly does, now come on, Jim!" she giggled.

"Shh, the children might hear you" whispered Hadley.

Cooper was already at his desk the next morning when Hadley arrived and George brought a pot of tea in with the mail as the Inspector sat behind his desk.

"Any thoughts overnight, Sergeant?"

"Not really, sir, although the notion that the kidnap of Mortlake is not what it appears to be, still haunts me."

"Hmm, but I think it is more than a coincidence that Robert Jarvis works for the same Bank as in the ransom demand."

"True, sir, but why would Jarvis get involved in a crime that would jeopardise his whole way of life and his career along with the certainty of a long imprisonment?"

"Only if he was caught, Sergeant, and criminals always intend not to get caught and plan accordingly" replied Hadley.

"Well, going off to Geneva when he knows that we would be bound to interview him about the kidnap, is hardly throwing us off the scent, sir" replied Cooper.

"True enough, Sergeant, but as usual, when dealing with members of the human race, there's always more questions than answers."

The detectives arrived at the prestigious building of the Banque Suisse Credite in Threadneedle Street. They went into the magnificent marble pillared reception where Hadley introduced them to the aloof receptionist and asked to speak to Mr Robert Jarvis's immediate superior.

"That would be Mr Desmond Moncrieff, sir" said the aloof young man.

"Kindly inform him that we wish to see him" said Hadley as he removed his battered top hat.

"I'm not sure he'll see you without an appointment because he's a very busy and important person, sir."

"So am I!" shouted Hadley and the young man flinched.

"But I'll see if he is free, sir."

"Yes, and let him know that we are conducting a kidnap and murder investigation, I'm sure that will help concentrate his priority of business engagements into the right order" said Hadley firmly and the young man went pale.

"Yes, sir" he stammered before he left his desk and hurried away up the marble staircase. Cooper grinned and said "you really must get a new hat, sir."

"Why?"

"You frighten everybody with that old one."

"Good, I like them to be frightened when they are obstructing me" said Hadley and Cooper laughed.

"You sometimes look like a street ruffian, sir."

"Only sometimes?" said Hadley and Cooper laughed again.

"You look like you're more at home in the Kings Head than in a Merchant Bank, sir."

"Precisely, Sergeant, my skill at blending in has many advantages."

"You don't blend in here, sir" replied Cooper with a grin.

"Are you criticising my modus operandi?"

"No sir, only your battered hat and scruffy coat!"

"I beg your pardon, Sergeant" said Hadley with mock indignation as the receptionist returned.

"Mr Moncrieff will see you now, gentlemen, so if you would like to follow me" said the young man and Hadley winked at Cooper, then picked up his hat as the receptionist turned and headed once more towards the stairs.

Mr Desmond Moncrieff was the very model of a Merchant Banker, he was tall and distinguished looking with an air of total superiority about him which he directed at the detectives as they entered his palatial office. After the formal introductions they were invited to sit and Hadley began by saying "we are currently investigating the disappearance of Lord Mortlake…"

"A shocking business; the Times reports that he was attacked by ruffians outside his London home in broad daylight, I was aghast and it begs the question, what are the police doing about it?" interrupted Moncrieff.

"We are following up lines of inquiry…"

"Well, you'd better be quick about it, Inspector, I mean to say, are any of us safe in London whilst these ruffians are at large?" he interrupted again.

"I believe that there is no immediate danger to your good self, sir" replied Hadley.

"You may say that, Inspector, but I am far from convinced!" exclaimed Moncrieff but Hadley ignored the remark and said "sir, I'm here to make inquiries into the whereabouts of Mr Robert Jarvis, who I understand, is responsible to you."

"Yes, he is."

"Can you confirm that he has gone to Geneva on Bank business?"

"Yes, but how do you know that?" asked Moncrieff indignantly.

"It's our business to know, when do you expect him back in

London, sir?"

"Er, next week sometime, probably Friday, Inspector" replied Moncrieff as he was caught off guard.

"Does Mr Jarvis have the authority to open a numbered account at your head office in Geneva?" asked Hadley and the question seemed to perplex Moncrieff.

"Well, er , no, that is to say, yes, if a client wished to open an account then Mr Jarvis would arrange that with the relevant person in Geneva" replied the Banker in an uncertain tone.

"You don't seem too sure about this, sir."

"Nonsense, Inspector, I'm fully aware of all the Bank procedures, both in London and Geneva."

"What about Paris, sir?"

"What do you mean, Inspector?"

"Could Mr Jarvis open an account in Paris which was then transferred to Geneva?"

"Yes, in theory…"

"What about in practice, sir?" interrupted Hadley.

"Really, Inspector, your line of questioning is most inappropriate" said Moncrieff as he hurriedly mopped his brow with a handkerchief.

"I don't think so, sir, because I'm not only investigating a kidnapping but also a murder that may be linked…"

"A murder?" interrupted Moncrieff, his air of superiority now completely gone.

"Yes, a murder, and I have to inform you that your bank is involved…"

"Good God, no, that can't be!"

"Indeed it is, sir."

"Oh, we'll all be ruined" wailed the Banker.

"Possibly, sir" said Hadley piling on the pressure.

"I must call a board meeting at once" said Moncrieff.

"I think that's a very wise precaution sir, because once the Press get hold of this information, who knows where it will end?"

"Oh, dear God" whispered Moncrieff as he mopped his brow once again.

"I must tell you that a ransom note from the kidnappers of Lord Mortlake has been delivered and it demands payment into a numbered account held in Geneva and I want to know who holds that account, sir."

"That could prove difficult, Inspector."

"Why, sir?"

"Numbered accounts held in Geneva are protected from any disclosure by Bank protocol" replied a shaken Moncrieff.

"Well, you'd better find a way around the protocol in this case" said Hadley.

"I can't see how I can, Inspector."

"Then I suggest you have your board meeting as soon as possible to find a way, sir."

"Really, Inspector, you can't come into my office and tell me how to run the Bank!"

"As you please, but today is Friday, so I'll give you until Monday when I will call again and expect the information regarding the account in Geneva" said Hadley.

"Impossible!"

"Then you may have to be ready with an answer for the Americans when they arrive on Tuesday"

"The Americans?"

"Yes, agents from the Pinkerton Detective Agency will be in London to investigate the case in parallel with Scotland Yard" said Hadley.

"Why, for heaven's sake?"

"Lady Mortlake was murdered. She was the only daughter of Arthur Riley, one of the richest men in America and he has hired the Pinkerton agents."

"Good grief" whispered the pale faced Banker.

"I think it is important for you to know that Mr Riley financially supports Congressmen in the American Senate and they are already applying pressure for a quick resolution of the investigation. Your Bank is bound to be involved as Mr Jarvis is under suspicion regarding the kidnap of Lord Mortlake, which will mean the whole case will be widely reported in the American Press as well as our own" Hadley said with a mischievous smile.

"This is an absolute nightmare" whispered Moncrieff.

"In my experience, murder always is, sir."

"Indeed."

"I look forward to seeing you on Monday then. I wish you a good morning, sir" said Hadley brightly as he stood and smiled at the shattered Banker, who nodded lamely.

The detectives caught the train from London and arrived in Northampton for an early lunch at the Dukes Arms before they booked into the Excelsior Hotel once again, just in case they were forced to stay the night by unforeseen circumstances. They walked up Gold Street in the warm June sunshine to the Police station where they met, by chance, Inspector West in the entrance.

"I was just going out to Holcot, Jim, care to join me?" said West with a smile.

"Has something interesting developed, Peter?"

"Possibly, I can't be too sure, but after arresting Winters and questioning him, I think that Kelly, the groom may be implicated more than he's admitted to so far" replied West.

"That's interesting" said Hadley.

"So, do you want to come along or would you rather stay here and interview Winters?"

"No, he can wait, we'll come with you, Peter and you can brief us on the way" replied Hadley.

The police four wheeler made the journey to Holcot Manor in quick time as the horses pulled well and on the way Inspector West told Hadley that Winters changed his recollection of events to implicate Kelly, the groom.

"I wondered about him from the start" said Hadley.

"According to Winters, it was Kelly who found Lady Mortlake after her horse trotted back to the stables on its own" said West.

"Then Winters lied about setting traps in the copse and seeing her fall from her horse" said Hadley.

"That seems to be the case" replied West.

"Does he say where he was at the time?" asked Hadley.

"He claims that he was the other side of the copse to where she fell and didn't see anything and only when he heard Kelly shout out for help did he run round and when he arrived at the scene, she was already dead" replied West.

"It's all very suspicious" said Hadley.

"And you don't know who to believe out of those two" said West.

"In my experience the thought of the hangman's noose makes

liars of just about everybody who comes under any suspicion" said Hadley as the police four wheeler turned into the long driveway up to the Manor House.

Barton opened the door to the detectives and greeted them before asking Hadley "is there any news of his Lordship yet, Inspector?"

"Not at the moment, Mr Barton, but I'm confident that he will be free quite soon" replied Hadley.

"That is good to hear, sir, now I expect you'll be wishing to speak to her ladyship?"

"In a moment, but first I'd like to have a few words with Mr Kelly…"

"Oh, I'm afraid you can't, sir" interrupted Barton.

"Why is that?"

"He's gone home to Ireland, sir" replied Barton.

"What!"

"He had a letter from his sister saying that his invalid mother was very ill and not expected to live, so her Ladyship gave her permission for Mr Kelly to go first thing this morning, sir" replied Barton in a sad tone.

"My God" whispered Hadley as he turned to Cooper and West who looked as surprised as he was.

"Do you know from which ferry port he intends to travel?" asked Hadley.

"I'm afraid not, sir."

"Do you have his address in Ireland?"

"Yes, sir, it will be in the house book" replied Barton.

"May I have it, please?"

"Yes, of course, sir, if you would care to come in and wait in the hall, I'll get it from Mrs Noakes."

"Thank you" said Hadley as Barton gave a little bow and wandered off towards the kitchen.

"Well, gentlemen, what do think about that?" asked Hadley.

"Too suspicious for words" replied West.

"I agree, sir" nodded Cooper.

"Then I suggest we return to Northampton and try and discover which route Kelly may have taken from his Irish address and telegraph the police to stop him at the ferry port" said Hadley.

"Yes, and Winters may be able to give us some clues about

that" said West.

"I hope so" said Hadley as Barton arrived back with the house book.

"Here we are, sir." Hadley took the open book and said "Sergeant, make a note of the address."

"Sir" nodded Cooper producing his note book and writing it down.

"Will you wish to see her Ladyship now, sir?" asked Barton.

"No thank you, we'll have to postpone that for a while" replied Hadley.

"Very good, sir, but I will tell her Ladyship that you called."

"Thank you, Mr Barton."

The police driver raced the horses back to Northampton at speed whilst the detectives discussed the latest twist in the investigation. As Kelly's address was in Dundalk, they assumed that he would go via Liverpool to Belfast and then travel down the coast to the town. They arrived back at the station and West produced maps of Ireland for them to peruse. It was obvious that Kelly would go to Liverpool and a telegraph message was sent to the police there requesting the arrest of Kelly. No sooner had the message been telegraphed when one arrived for Hadley from London. He read it twice before he whispered "my God" and handed it to Cooper to read aloud.

"Hadley, Ann Wells found dead in the Savoy Hotel, return to London immediately and bring Winters with you. Bell."

CHAPTER 9

The detectives travelled in a locked compartment on the train with the disagreeable Winters who protested his innocence most of the way to London. Eventually, Hadley told him to be quiet, contemplate his position and save his comments for the formal interview that he would have at Scotland Yard.

"That's alright for you to say, but I'm under arrest on suspicion of murder!" exclaimed the ruddy faced grounds man.

"Yes, we know that, Mr Winters, but you'd be well advised to hold your tongue and then tell us the whole truth when you are interviewed" replied Hadley.

"Well when's that going to be?"

"As soon as possible, believe me!" replied Hadley and Winters then remained silent for the rest of the journey.

When they arrived at the Yard, Cooper escorted Winters to custody whilst Hadley hurried upstairs to Chief Inspector Bell's office.

"Glad you're back, Hadley, this is a bad business."

"Indeed it is, sir" replied Hadley as he sat down in a creaking chair.

"A chamber maid found Miss Wells about midday and called the floor manager, who contacted us. Initial examination showed that she had been strangled, but we'll have to wait for the full report from Doctor Evans."

"Yes, sir."

"Now, Inspector Walters is at the scene at the moment but I want you to take over from him right away" said Bell.

"Very good, sir."

"As you can imagine the bloody Press have got hold of it and I dread to think what the papers will print in tonight's late editions" said Bell as he shook his head slowly.

"The usual, I expect, sir."

"Yes, all the gory details and 'what are the police doing about it?' no doubt" said Bell.

"That won't please the Commissioner, sir."

"That's for sure, Hadley, and he'll want some answers over the weekend."

"Yes, sir."

"And with the Americans due to arrive on Tuesday, things couldn't be worse!"

"I must admit, it does all look a bit grim, sir."

"Well, get to it, Hadley and report back to me as soon as you have something."

"Right, sir."

"By the way, have you brought Winters back with you?"

"Yes, sir, he's down in custody."

"Good, he'll have to stay there for while."

"Yes, sir."

"It's a positive move forward to have at least one murderer locked up" said Bell.

"He may not be the killer, sir."

"What?"

"Kelly, the groom has been implicated by Winters in the death of Lady Mortlake…"

"Good God!"

"Winters has changed his story, now denying that he was close to the scene of the incident, sir."

"And blames Kelly?"

"He says that Kelly found her and called out for help."

"Then what happened?"

"Winters heard him and hurried to assist but when he arrived she was already dead."

"Well arrest Kelly immediately, Hadley!"

"I can't, sir…"

"Why not?"

"Kelly has disappeared from Holcot and is on his way to his home in Ireland" said Hadley.

"Good grief, Hadley!"

"We've telegraphed the Liverpool police and requested his immediate arrest, sir."

"Well, he could have come to London first, Hadley, if he intends to travel by express train up to Liverpool to catch the ferry" said Bell.

"Yes, indeed, sir" said Hadley, suddenly aware of the implications.

"So Kelly could have murdered Miss Wells today and now be on his way to Liverpool."

"Yes, he could, sir."

"It's very bad that you let him slip away, Hadley."

"Yes, sir" he replied as he considered it was best not to argue the point.

"I think I've heard enough bad news for the moment, so I suggest you get over to the Savoy and relieve Walters" said Bell as he glanced down at the paperwork on his desk.

The detectives hastened to the Savoy Hotel in the Strand. They were shown up to the room in which Ann Wells had been murdered and were greeted by Inspector Albert Walters.

"Ah, Jim, I'm glad you're here" beamed Albert.

"I'm not sure I am, Albert" replied Hadley.

"As you're one of our top Bobbies, Jim, I think all this is meat and drink to you" replied Albert with a grin.

"Is that why I get all the difficult cases?"

"Probably, Jim. Now, the deceased was found at about a quarter to one this afternoon by the chamber maid, Olive Smith…"

"Where is she now?" interrupted Hadley.

"She's with Mr Simmons, the manager, I've spoken to them both but I'm sure you'll want to interview them."

"Yes, I will."

"The body was examined by the hotel Doctor, and then removed to the Marylebone Hospital."

"Presumably the Doctor is still here?"

"Yes, Jim, I asked him to wait when I knew you were taking over the investigation."

"Thanks, Albert."

"So I'll leave you to it, Jim, and get back to the Yard to finish the paperwork" smiled Inspector Walters before he left the room. When they were alone, Hadley looked at Cooper and said "I just wonder what the hell is going on, Sergeant."

"So do I, sir, but where do we start with this one?"

"With the chamber maid, Sergeant."

Olive Smith was a smart young woman and Hadley was impressed with her composure as he was introduced to her by Mr Simmons in his office.

"Tell me, Miss Smith, exactly what happened today when you went into Miss Wells' room" said Hadley.

"Well, sir, I go into the guests rooms on that floor about lunchtime every day to check the room to see if everything is in order and turn the beds down" she replied calmly.

"Go on."

"I knocked and entered and she was just laying there on the bed, I thought she was asleep, so I said, in a whisper, 'sorry, Madam, I'll come back later' but when I looked closer, her eyes were wide open and her mouth looked funny, so I went up to the bed and realised that something was wrong with her, I mean she wasn't breathing or anything so I touched her hand and it was cold."

"Then what did you do?"

"I came and told Mr Simmons and we went back to the room together and after he had looked at Miss Wells, he said that she was dead, so the Doctor was called and then the police, sir" she replied.

"Well, you acted very properly, Miss Smith" said Hadley with a smile.

"Thank you, sir" she said and she looked at Mr Simmons who nodded his approval.

"Tell me, did you see anybody go into Miss Wells' room today?"

"No, sir."

"Did you see anybody unfamiliar in the corridor perhaps?"

"No, sir."

"On the stairs?"

"No, sir, I didn't see anyone at all today, other than guests."

"Thank you, you've been very helpful, Miss Smith."

"Thank you, sir, may I go now?"

"Yes, of course." The maid bobbed a curtsey and left the manager's office.

"Have you anything to add, Mr Simmons?" Hadley asked the immaculately dressed manager.

"No, Inspector, the events surrounding this tragedy are exactly as Miss Smith told you, I went with her back to the room, realised Miss Wells was dead and immediately sent for Doctor Henderson, the hotel Doctor, who examined her and confirmed that she was dead, probably by strangulation, so the police were summoned."

"Do you know if Miss Wells had any visitors whilst she was staying here?"

"Not to my knowledge, Inspector, but we can ask the front of house manager, Mr Stevens."

"Right, would you kindly send for him?"

"Yes, of course, Inspector."

Mr Stevens duly arrived and looked anxious before he was invited to sit in front of the manager as Hadley introduced himself.

"Do you recollect if Miss Wells had any visitors since she arrived at the Savoy, Mr Stevens?"

"Not to my knowledge, sir."

"And as front of house manager at reception, you would presumably see every guest as they came and went?"

"Yes, Inspector."

"Did you see Miss Wells speak to anyone at all?"

"Well, yes I did, sir, it was yesterday lunch time and I was about to leave reception for my break when Miss Wells entered the lobby from outside and she was closely followed by a tall gentleman who called out to her."

"Then what happened?"

"She stopped and turned to face him, then said something to him, which I couldn't hear, but she looked angry…"

"Go on, Mr Stevens."

"The gentleman got close to her and grabbed her elbow then said something and she shook her self free and came over to ask for her key…"

"Did you say anything to her about the incident?"

"Yes, sir, I asked if the man was bothering her and if she was alright, she said she was fine and when I looked for the man again, he was gone."

"Describe this man if you would, Mr Stevens."

"He was tall and fair haired with a moustache, sir, that's all I can remember I'm afraid."

"Would you recognise him again?"

"Yes, I'm sure I would, Inspector."

"Thank you, Mr Stevens, you've been very helpful" said Hadley with a smile. After Stevens had left the office to return to his duties, Doctor Henderson was summoned and he added little to what Hadley already knew.

"There were bruises around her neck and I believe that she was strangled to death, Inspector" said the Doctor.

"Were there any sign of any other injuries?" asked Hadley.

"Not that I could see, Inspector, but the post mortem will reveal all" replied Henderson.

"Quite so, Doctor."

The detectives left the Savoy and took a Hansom to the Kings Head in Whitechapel. The bar was full as usual and they had to push through the crowd of men who had stopped for a drink on their way home several hours ago and were still drinking, spending their wages from the day's work much to the despair of their wives waiting at home for some money for food. They ordered pints of stout from a harassed Vera and wandered off to find somewhere to sit and wait for Agnes. She and Florrie arrived half an hour later, they made themselves comfortable at the table whilst Cooper struggled through the noisy crowd for their gins.

"I've been asking all the girls down the lane, Jim, about that Lord Mortlake, him that's been kidnapped" said Agnes and Hadley listened carefully.

"Go on, my dear."

"Well, they don't know his name, but he's a good looking gent and it may be him, he's been having two girls at a time, so to speak" said Agnes.

"Has he told any of the girls about himself?"

"No, Jim, but he did say to Iris Meaks and little Jane Howard, when he was having them, like, that he was going to have a very special party and he wanted them to find another two young girls to come and entertain him and a friend, he said he'd send a coach for them and they would have to stay the night up west somewhere."

"Do they know where?"

"No they don't, Jim, but they said they would go whenever he wanted because of the money he promised them..."

"He told them he'd pay them two guineas each!" chipped in Florrie with her eyes wide with amazement at the thought of such a sum.

"He seems to be a very generous man" said Hadley as Cooper

arrived back with the gins.

"Yes, he told Iris, that he was expecting a lot of money soon and he wanted to celebrate with his friend, but Iris said he'd been drinking and was a bit tipsy, so she wasn't sure about that" said Agnes.

"It's all very interesting" said Hadley.

When Hadley eventually arrived home, a little light headed from the late evening in the pub, he told Alice that he would be on duty throughout the weekend. She was not best pleased at that and so she made her feelings known to her husband in no uncertain terms before she packed him off to bed.

Cooper was at his desk when Hadley arrived in the office the next morning and other than greeting one another quietly, said nothing until George made them a pot of strong tea. When Hadley felt sufficiently revived he said to Cooper "we'd best get over to the Marylebone and find out what Doctor Evans has to report, Sergeant."

"Don't you want to question Winters first, sir?"

"No, Sergeant, he'll have to wait, I'm afraid."

"What about Kelly, sir?"

"We can do nothing at the moment except hope that our friends in Liverpool can arrest him before he boards the ferry" replied Hadley.

"And if they can't, sir?"

"It may mean a trip to Ireland, Sergeant, because although the police in Belfast will help, I'm not sure how effective they may be in the time we have left before the Americans arrive."

"We'll never get over there and back before Tuesday, sir."

"Of course not, but we can leave the Chief to deal with the Pinkerton men and hold them off until we return, Sergeant."

"Is that a good idea, sir?"

"Probably not, but it's the only option open to us at the moment" replied Hadley in a resigned tone.

Doctor Evans looked up from his desk as the detectives entered his office and said "morning, gentlemen, I'm surprised to see you so early in the day, you usually call when I'm about to go home."

"Morning, Doctor, it's because this time we are under some pressure for answers that will bring a speedy closure of the investigation" replied Hadley.

"Well, I'm pleased to tell you that my examinations of the two women are complete and show that they were both strangled to death."

"No other factors?"

"No, Jim, come and look at Miss Wells for yourself" replied Evans and they followed him out to the mortuary where the naked body of the young American lay on the cold marble slab. Her body was perfect and she looked as if she were asleep. Hadley peered down at the severe bruising around her lovely throat and felt his anger rise at the senseless killing of the vibrant young woman.

"Her killer simply put his hands around her throat and squeezed the life out of her. You can see his thumb marks quite clearly" said Evans as he pointed to her neck and Hadley nodded.

"What a tragedy" whispered Hadley.

"True, but in life we are always amongst death, Jim" replied Evans.

"Sometimes I think that I've now seen enough of violent death and it's time for me to retire" said Hadley.

"Don't you dare retire, Jim, we need you to catch the perpetrators of these killings and those yet to come, to make sure that they are hanged for what they have done!" said Evans forcefully. Hadley looked at his friend and smiled before giving a little nod.

"Right, Doctor, I'll take your advice. Now, I'll get the Chief to contact the American Embassy and advise them of Miss Wells death" said Hadley.

"I'll wait to hear from you then regarding her body."

"I'm sure her parents will want her returned to America for burial" said Hadley.

"Unlike Lady Mortlake" said Evans.

"I'm not sure if her father will leave her in an English graveyard" replied Hadley.

"I wouldn't blame him for one minute if he had her removed back to America" said Evans.

"Neither would I" said Hadley.

CHAPTER 10

When the detectives returned to the Yard in sombre mood, Hadley went straight up to see Chief Inspector Bell whilst Cooper returned to their office.

"Doctor Evans has confirmed that Lady Mortlake and Miss Wells both died as a result of strangulation" said Hadley to his harassed looking Chief.

"Well it just confirms what we already knew" said Bell.

"Yes, it does, sir."

"Have you any suspects for the murder of Miss Wells?"

"Yes, sir, Mr Stevens the reception manager at the Savoy, saw her being harassed by a man in the lobby yesterday lunchtime, sir."

"Didn't Stevens do anything to stop it?"

"No, sir, apparently the incident was all over in a matter of a few moments and Miss Wells said that she was fine."

"Did she tell the manager who the man was?"

"No, sir."

"Have you got a description of him?"

"Yes, but it is vague, sir."

"Go on."

"He was tall, faired haired with a moustache, sir."

"Well that narrows it down to half the men in London, Hadley" said Bell with a shake of his head.

"Yes, sir, but I think it may have been Lord Mortlake."

"Impossible, the man's been kidnapped!"

"Nevertheless, sir, I believe it could be him" said Hadley.

"What makes you think it's Mortlake?"

"If the kidnap is some elaborate hoax to obtain money and somehow Miss Wells discovered the truth then Mortlake would want her silenced" replied Hadley.

"Good God" said Bell as there was a knock at the door and Cooper entered holding a brown envelope.

"Sorry to interrupt, sir, but this message has just come in from Liverpool and I thought you should see it right away!" said Cooper as he handed the envelope to Hadley.

"Read it out then" said Bell.

"Inspector James Hadley, as per your request, we have arrested Patrick Kelly, Irish citizen, lately employed at Holcot Manor in Northampton, please advise your intentions, regards, Inspector Edward Dunton."

"That's a positive step, Hadley" said Bell with a smile.

"Indeed it is, sir."

"Now get up there right away and bring Kelly back!"

"Couldn't you send another officer, sir?"

"I don't trust anyone else with the prime suspect in such a high profile case, Hadley" replied Bell.

"Very well, sir."

"With two murderers in custody the Commissioner will be relieved and he will be able to placate the Press then have a restful night for once" said Bell with a smile.

Hadley telegraphed his friend Edward Dunton with the news that he and Cooper were leaving immediately and would stay overnight in Liverpool before returning tomorrow with Kelly. George brewed them a quick pot of tea before they hurried off to catch the train from Kings Cross. Cooper bought sandwiches for lunch from a kiosk whilst Hadley checked the time of the next express to Liverpool. He stood in the busy concourse and glanced at his fob watch, it was almost eleven o'clock and the train was due to leave from platform 9 at eleven fifteen.

"Hurry up, Sergeant, we don't want to miss our train!" said Hadley loudly as Cooper strode quickly across the concourse towards him, dodging the other travellers and their cases as they milled about.

"No, sir" replied Cooper as he caught up with Hadley. The detectives then hurried towards Platform 9, anxious to catch the express and oblivious to their fellow passengers. Suddenly Hadley spotted a man in the crowd that he recognised and said "good God, its Mortlake!"

"Where, sir?"

"Over there, Sergeant, he's by the barrier, we can catch him if we're quick!" and they began to run towards the ticket barrier at platform 9. The crowds of passengers and their cases prevented them reaching the barrier before the tall man disappeared onto the platform amongst the other travellers.

"Damn! We've lost him, Sergeant."

"We'll find him on the train, sir."

"Hopefully, Sergeant."

"Are you sure it was Mortlake, sir?"

"Yes, I'm reasonably certain."

"Did you actually see his face, sir?"

"Not quite, but he looked like Mortlake from what I could see of him" replied Hadley.

"Not a positive identification then, sir?"

"Sergeant, you're beginning to sound like me and I don't know whether that's a good thing or not" said Hadley ruefully and Cooper laughed. They showed their warrant cards to the ticket inspector at the barrier and boarded the express, finding two seats on the crowded train in a non smoking compartment. At exactly eleven fifteen they heard the guards whistle being blown accompanied by the sound of doors being hurriedly slammed, followed by the clanking of the couplings and the hiss of steam, as the train moved steadily away from Platform 9. With them in the carriage were two ladies of uncertain years, a vicar and a sailor, which precluded any discussion about the investigation. They sat quietly watching the London suburbs slip by and then the countryside as the express gathered more and more speed.

"I think we'll go and look for our friend now, Mr Cooper" said Hadley.

"Very well, Mr Hadley" replied Cooper with a grin. The detectives left the compartment, went to the rear of the train and began the search for Lord Mortlake. Hadley opened every compartment door on the crowded train and looked hard at each passenger. They found a person who bore a passing resemblance to Mortlake but not the man himself and Hadley was frustrated by his mistake. They returned to their compartment and settled down for the long journey north. The express stopped only at Crewe before making its last dash to Liverpool where they were met on the platform by Inspector Dunton.

"Good to see you, Jim, and you, Sergeant" said Edward Dunton with a broad smile.

"Good to see you too, Edward."

"You seem to be regular visitors to Liverpool these days" said Dunton.

"It's the good policing up here that keeps attracting us back" said Hadley with a smile.

"I'm glad you Scotland Yard boys have realised that at last, Jim!" replied Dunton with a laugh as he slapped Hadley on his back.

"I can't thank you enough for arresting this man, Kelly" said Hadley.

"To tell the truth, Jim, it was more by luck than judgement" replied Dunton.

"Tell me everything once we are in your office and had a cup of tea" said Hadley.

Half an hour later and suitably refreshed, Dunton told the detectives that Kelly became involved with another ferry passenger who was drunk and became belligerent, accusing Kelly of stealing his ticket as they were about to board the ship. A fight ensued and two police constables standing close by watching out for Kelly, arrested both men and brought them into the police station, where Kelly was identified. He was immediately placed in custody despite his protestations of innocence of any crime and demanding to be set free to return to Ireland to see his dying mother.

"So he's down in custody whenever you want to question him, Jim."

"I'll speak to him now, Edward."

"Follow me then."

Kelly was brought from his cell and taken into an interview room where he waited until the detectives were ready to speak to him. When Kelly saw them his face lit up and he said "thank heavens you're here, Inspector, can you tell these stupid policemen to release me straight away?"

"I'm afraid that's not possible, Mr Kelly" replied Hadley as he sat down opposite the anxious man.

"Why, Inspector?"

"Mr Winters has been arrested and under questioning he has implicated you in the murder of Lady Mortlake…"

"That's bloody nonsense!" interrupted Kelly.

"Nevertheless, I must advise you that you are being held under suspicion of murder" said Hadley.

"This is madness! I never would hurt a hair of that lovely woman's head, she was a kind, generous lady who loved horses and she spent a lot of time with me at the stables."

"That may be so, but Winters says that you found her Ladyship and called out for help and when he arrived she was already dead" said Hadley.

"No, sir, that's not true, he found her and then came running back to the stables for me to help her" replied Kelly as the colour finally drained from his face.

"Well, I'm under instructions to arrest you and take you back to Scotland Yard where you will be questioned further" said Hadley.

"Have pity on me, sir and my poor mother, for God's sake, she's dying there in Dundalk with only my sister, Mary there with her" wailed Kelly.

"I'm very sorry Mr Kelly, but I have my orders."

"Oh, God, this is a nightmare" whispered Kelly.

"Tell me, did you go to London to catch the train up here?"

"Yes, sir, it was quicker than taking the train from Northampton and having to change twice" replied Kelly.

"Were you in London at midday yesterday?"

"Yes, Inspector, I caught the two o'clock express from Kings Cross" replied Kelly.

"Did you go to the Savoy Hotel yesterday?"

"No, Inspector."

"Are you sure?"

"Yes, I'm sure, why do you ask?"

"Miss Wells was found murdered in her room at the Savoy…"

"Oh, no, Mother of God, no, this isn't true!"

"I'm afraid it is" replied Hadley as Kelly broke down and wept. The detectives remained silent whilst Kelly composed himself and then he said "listen to me, Inspector, I'm just a poor Irishman who loves horses and managed to get a job that I enjoyed. When Lady Mortlake came to Holcot with Miss Wells I was as happy as any man could be. Both of them were kind and generous to me and they loved riding. They livened the old place up and brought some happiness to us all; except her Ladyship, of course, and Winters and Mrs Noakes, who didn't approve of their friendly ways. 'Not proper' Mrs Noakes used to say, but she's a miserable old witch, she's the one you ought to ask about her Ladyships death, she knows more than she says, I'll tell you!"

"Go on Mr Kelly."

"There's not much else to say, except I'm sad that my dear old mother has to die without seeing her only son. Here, read the letter from my sister, you'll see that mother is close to her end, God bless her" said Kelly tearfully as he took an envelope from his jacket pocket and placed it on the table in front of Hadley. He looked at it for a moment then picked it up, opened the envelope and read 'Dear Patrick, mother is now very weak and Doctor McQuire says that she'll not last long in this world, so can you come home as quick as you can to see her as she keeps asking for you, your loving sister Mary.'

Hadley remained silent and his compassion for Kelly began to infiltrate his thoughts over the validity of the arrest. He found it hard not to believe the desperate Irishman's account of what had transpired in the last two days and was sure that his appreciation of his late mistress was genuine. He reasoned that the groom had no motive for killing either Lady Mortlake or her companion and it was more likely that he would have protected both women if they had been in any danger.

"I'm very sorry, Mr Kelly, but although you have my sympathy regarding your mother, I still have to take you down to London under arrest" said Hadley as gently as he could and Kelly looked down at his clasped hands then nodded.

The detectives returned to Dunton's office where they sat in melancholy mood after Hadley told him what Kelly had said..

"This is going to be the usual dilemma of one man's word against another's" said Hadley.

"Do you believe for certain that either Winters or Kelly murdered Lady Mortlake, sir?" asked Cooper.

"I'm not certain about anything in this investigation, Sergeant."

"Well, at least you've got both of them in custody, Jim" said Dunton.

"That's true, but not much consolation if the real killer of her Ladyship and Miss Wells is roaming free around London,

Edward" replied Hadley.

"Then possibly you are looking for two murderers" said Dunton.

"I've thought of that and it worries me because it certainly would complicate the investigation" replied Hadley.

"I think you should stop worrying and go and have a good meal at the Crown Hotel, where I took the liberty of booking you in for the night" smiled Dunton.

"Thank you, Edward, I do appreciate that" replied Hadley.

"Its northern hospitality so you need not thank me, Jim. When I've finished my paperwork I'll take you to the Crown and you can buy me a pint or two in the bar!" said Dunton and Hadley laughed.

The next morning the detectives collected Kelly from custody and were driven to Liverpool station, accompanied by Inspector Dunton. After farewells on the platform they boarded the train and sat in a reserved compartment for the journey to Kings Cross. Hadley used the time on the train to question Kelly gently on what happened the day that Lady Mortlake was killed. His account did not vary from what he had told Hadley before about the events on that tragic day.

"It was about ten o'clock that morning when her Ladyship came to the stables and said she'd ride Topper so I saddled her up and got her ready whilst her Ladyship chatted to me about riding over to Northampton, so I told her to mind how she went because there's soft ground on the bridle way near the town, then she smiled as she rode off and I attended to the other horses because I thought Miss Wells might ride in the afternoon with her Ladyship" said Kelly and he remained silent as the sad memories came back to him.

"Continue if you would, Mr Kelly" said Hadley.

"About an hour or so later, I suddenly heard someone shouting my name and Winters rushed into the yard and said that her Ladyship had fallen and he needed help, so we went to the house and told Mr Barton but before I could help Winters, I was sent immediately to get Doctor Moore from the village, when I arrived back with the Doctor I went with him to the spot where her Ladyship had fallen, he examined her there and said that she was dead... I couldn't believe it, then Winters and me carried her back

91

to the house and laid her out on a table in the library..." and he paused as the tears ran down his cheeks.

"Then what happened?"

"His Lordship was sent for and the ambulance arrived from the Infirmary and they took her away, sir" Kelly replied.

"Did you see anyone else that day?" asked Hadley.

"What do you mean, sir?"

"Any strangers, anybody you didn't know."

"No, sir, I only saw Winters, Mr Barton and Miss Wells, Mrs Noakes, and the Doctor of course" he replied.

"Tell me about Mrs Noakes" said Hadley.

"She rules the place with a rod of iron, makes everybody's life a misery, especially young Kate, and she hated her Ladyship and Miss Wells."

"Why was that?"

"Well, when her Ladyship arrived she took charge of the place and I heard that she planned to have it done up and made to look nice again..."

"Why should Mrs Noakes object to that?" interrupted Hadley.

"I don't know, sir, but believe me, she hated her Ladyship and did everything she could to spread unkind gossip about her."

"Such as?"

"She was always saying that her Ladyship was too familiar with the servants and that she was 'flighty', if you know what I mean, sir."

"Yes, I do."

"And that she was the wrong woman to have married his Lordship and the marriage would end in tragedy..."

"Go on Mr Kelly."

"She kept on at Winters about her and often said that something should be done about her Ladyship..."

"Like what?"

"I don't know, sir, but soon, Winters was agreeing with her and started on me, telling me that I shouldn't be so friendly with her ladyship because she was going and when she was gone, Mrs Noakes would sack me and wouldn't give me a reference."

"Where did Mr Winters think her Ladyship was going?"

"He didn't say, sir."

"Did you know that Lady Mortlake was unhappy with her

husband and that they frequently argued?"

"Yes, sir, I knew, because I often heard them when I was in the house at meal times."

"I see, so it was common knowledge then?"

"Oh, yes, every time his Lordship came up from London, they had rows and the whole house heard them."

"Do you know what they rowed about?"

"Yes, sir, it was money."

"Did you know his Lordship was in debt?"

"Yes, we all knew."

"What did you think about that?"

"Sad for her Ladyship because it was obvious that he didn't love her and only married her for her money, sir."

"I see."

"And in my opinion, his Lordship is behind the murder of his wife and I think Winters killed her" said Kelly as the train drew into Kings Cross station.

CHAPTER 11

As soon as they reached the Yard, Kelly was placed into Custody. The detectives continued up to their office to discuss the investigation and write notes. Hadley made plans for the next two days and wondered what would happen when the Pinkerton men arrived on Tuesday. He knew that it was unlikely that the investigation would have moved forward to any degree by then and he hoped that the next positive step would be that if the account holder in Geneva was revealed by Mr Moncrieff at the Bank. He planned to call on him first thing on Monday morning followed by a visit to Mr Barrymore to see if the ransom had been paid. If Mortlake was involved in a hoax, then Hadley was sure that once his Lordship re-appeared, 'in depth' questioning, under caution, at the Yard would find flaws in the account of his ordeal and allow prosecution of all those involved. Hadley decided to leave the interview of Winters until the next day and suggested to Cooper that they had done enough.

"I think we have, sir."

"Let's go home now and start again in the morning, fresh and ready for the week ahead, Sergeant."

"Yes, sir, I believe it will be a week to remember."

"I'm sure it will be."

Alice was relieved to see her husband that evening and made sure that he rested after a fulsome dinner, followed by a stout or two. Although they had just enjoyed their holiday, Alice was concerned that, yet again, Hadley was overdoing it and his unremitting work load would eventually affect his health. She begged him to take care and cut back on his daily intake of stout, at which request he nodded and promptly put it out of his mind.

When Hadley arrived in his office on the Monday morning he was feeling fit and ready for the tasks ahead. After sharing a pot of tea with Cooper, he went up to see Chief Inspector Bell.

"I'm pleased you've got Kelly downstairs and if you can get a confession out of him, so much the better" said Bell.

"On the contrary, sir, I've given this some careful thought and I

94

believe the man is innocent, so I want to release him."

"Absolutely not, Hadley!"

"But, sir…"

"I forbid it, Hadley, and until we've got a full confession out of Winters or Kelly for the murder of Lady Mortlake, neither of them will be released, do you understand?"

"I do, sir."

"Good. Now, any sign of Lord Mortlake?"

"Not yet, sir, but if his solicitor, Barrymore, has paid the ransom then we should see his Lordship by the end of the week" replied Hadley.

"Follow that up closely."

"Yes, sir."

"And if you need any help getting information about the Bank account in Geneva, let me know."

"Very good, sir."

"Have you made any further progress with the investigation into the murder of Miss Wells?"

"No, sir."

"Well keep at it, the papers are full of fanciful theories as usual and the Commissioner wants a briefing at three o'clock this afternoon, so make sure you're here if I need you with me."

"Right, sir."

The detectives took a Hansom from Parliament Square to the Banque Suisse Credite in Threadneedle Street and arrived at eleven o'clock. They were shown up to Mr Moncrieff's office very promptly by the aloof receptionist and waved to the seats in front his imposing desk by the anxious Banker. After pleasantries, Hadley asked "Have you had your board meeting, sir?"

"Yes, Inspector."

"And what was the outcome?"

"We've taken steps to request the information that you require from Geneva, Inspector."

"I'm pleased to hear it, sir."

"We have made our request, and advised them that it is a very special and peculiar circumstance that makes it imperative that the name of the account holder is revealed."

"Thank you, sir."

"But a word of caution, in the past when we requested such information, it has been steadfastly refused, Inspector."

"Well just let me know if it is refused this time, Mr Moncrieff" said Hadley in a firm tone.

"You may rest assured that I will, Inspector."

"Good. Now can you tell me if the sum of one hundred thousand pounds has been paid into the account?" asked Hadley.

"Do you know from where exactly?"

"Here in London, sir" replied Hadley.

"If you will give a moment, I will find out, Inspector" said the Banker and he left the office.

"This appears to be progressing well, Sergeant."

"Yes, sir, once we've got the name then we can soon trace the kidnappers."

"The problem will come if the powers that be in Geneva refuse to give the information."

"Do you think that's likely, sir?"

"Anything is possible in this case, Sergeant."

Mr Moncrieff returned within ten minutes and announced "there's been no movement on this account for several weeks, Inspector."

"I'm disappointed to hear that, sir" said Hadley.

The detectives left the Bank and made their way to the offices of Olivier and Barrymore where they were admitted and shown promptly into Mr Barrymore's office.

"Any news of his Lordship, Inspector?" asked the anxious solicitor.

"No, not yet, sir, but I'm sure that once you've paid the ransom, he'll be freed" replied Hadley.

"But I have paid the money, Inspector" said Barrymore nervously.

"Not at the Bank in Threadneedle Street, we've just come from there and there has been no movement in the account for weeks" said Hadley with concern.

"No, Inspector, on my instructions our Bank telegraphed their branch in Paris who paid the money into the Suisse Credite account there."

"Why should they do that, sir?"

"It's because our Bank has no connections in Geneva, Inspector."

"Do you know if the transaction has now been completed, sir?"

"Well, it has certainly left our account and I must tell you that Mr Olivier is very concerned about the whole affair, I mean, this is client's money you know, Inspector."

"I realise that, sir, but needs must when the devil drives."

"Quite so, Inspector."

"Well I suppose we'll have to wait until the transaction has wound its way through the Banking system" said Hadley in a resigned tone.

The detectives left the worried solicitor and took a Hansom to the Kings Head in Whitechapel where they ordered lunch and waited for Agnes. They had just finished eating when Agnes arrived with Florrie.

"Any news, my dear?" asked Hadley whilst Cooper went off to buy their usual sixpenny gins.

"Just a little, Jim" replied Agnes as they sat down at the table.

"Tell me then."

"I've had words with old Sally, she knows everything that goes on down the Lane, and she says that she used to have old Mortlake as one of her regulars because he liked her very special 'specials'…"

"This is interesting" interrupted Hadley.

"D'you mean her special 'specials' are interesting, Jim?" asked Agnes with a twinkle in her eye.

"You know I don't!" replied Hadley as both Agnes and Florrie laughed.

"Well according to Sally, over the years she got quite friendly with the old boy and sometimes he would bring his son along then Sally would find a young girl for him, someone new down the Lane who hadn't been too well used, if you get my meaning…"

"I do."

"And whilst the old man was relieving himself with Sally, his boy was busy in another room with a new girl."

"So old Sally knows what young Mortlake looks like?"

"Yes, she does, and she says he's a good looking fella."

"Can you take me to Sally?" asked Hadley as Cooper arrived

97

back with the gins.

"I can if you want, Jim, but there's no need" Agnes replied before she picked up her glass, nodded to Cooper and took a sip of the clear reviver.

"Why's that?"

"Because I got old Sally to describe the young one to Iris and she says she's sure it's him" replied Agnes.

"You're a little wonder!" exclaimed Hadley.

"Oh, Jim, you're the only man who's ever said that to me" said Agnes in a whisper before she planted a quick kiss on his cheek.

"Now, now, Agnes, let's not get carried away" said Hadley as he blushed slightly.

"Why not, Jim, you know it would do us both some good" she replied with a smile.

"Agnes, that's enough, if you keep on you'll be guilty of diverting police officers in the course of their duty…"

"Police officers, Jim? I only want to divert you, Florrie can take care of Sergeant Cooper" replied Agnes as Florrie laughed whilst Cooper grinned and Hadley raised his eyebrows.

"Will you behave, woman?"

"Only if you say so, Jim" replied Agnes as she enjoyed the moment.

"I do say so…"

"Then I will!" she exclaimed and they all laughed.

"Take me to see Iris tonight if you will" said Hadley returning to the serious subject.

"Alright, Jim, come back at about nine o'clock, she'll be free then before the Toffs come down from their clubs."

"Make sure she knows what it's all about, Agnes."

"I will, Jim."

"Good."

"So are you going to buy us another drink Jim? All this chattering makes a girl very thirsty you know!"

The detectives left the pub and journeyed back to the Yard in the warm afternoon sunshine. They arrived in the office just before two thirty and in time for a pot of George's tea before, as Hadley expected, Mr Jenkins, the Chief's assistant came into the office and advised him that Bell required to see him at once.

Chief Inspector Bell looked more anxious than usual when Hadley entered his office.

"You'll have to come up with me to see the Commissioner at three, Hadley."

"Yes, sir."

"And you'd better have all the answers this time!"

"I'll do my best, sir."

"Well I only hope that's good enough, Hadley."

"Has there been some development, sir?"

"I think you could say that."

"May I ask what, sir?"

"Yes, the American Embassy sent a note to the Commissioner, which he received just before lunch and apparently it quite upset his appetite…"

"I'm sorry to hear that, sir" said Hadley as he tried to hide a smile.

"Now I don't know the details, but it obviously concerns these wretched Pinkerton men" replied Bell.

"Oh, dear."

"Then to make things worse, Reuter's have sent out a telegraph message to all the Press advising them of the American's arrival in London tomorrow."

"Who told Reuter's, sir?"

"I've no idea, Hadley, but I think we'd better get up to the Commissioner's office right away!"

The Commissioner was more than usually ruddy faced, his side whiskers twitching when Bell and Hadley entered his spacious office overlooking the Thames. He stared at them for a moment before he indicated that they could sit before him like naughty school boys.

"Gentlemen, the Mortlake murder and kidnap case, along with the American involvement, has all become much more serious than I could ever possibly have imagined" said the Commissioner gravely.

"Why is that, may I ask, sir?" said Bell nervously.

"Because, Chief Inspector, I am reliably informed by my friend in the American Embassy that not only have the Pinkerton Agents arrived in Liverpool this morning from New York, but they are accompanied by Mr Arthur Riley himself with a considerable entourage which, heaven forbid, includes a native Red Indian!"

"Good God, sir!" exclaimed Bell.

"And they are all staying at the Savoy Hotel!"

"Oh, no, sir, surely the Red Indian is not there as well?"

"Oh, yes, Chief Inspector, a savage at the Savoy and to top it all, Mr Riley has notified the London papers through Reuter's that he will hold a full Press conference at six o'clock tomorrow evening at the Savoy where he will announce his intentions!"

"God help us" whispered Bell.

"So we'd better be ready with some positive answers" said the Commissioner.

"Yes, sir."

"Any news about Mortlake, has he been found?"

"Not yet, sir, but the ransom has been paid" said Hadley and the Commissioner raised his bushy eyebrows.

"Have you any suspects for the murder of the American woman at the Savoy?"

"No, not at present, sir" replied Hadley.

"What about the grounds man from Holcot?"

"He's in custody, sir" said Bell anxious to contribute something positive.

"I know that, Chief Inspector, I told you nervous Nellie's to arrest him!"

"Yes, sir" stammered Bell.

"What I want to know is if you've got a confession out of the blackguard for the murder of Lady Mortlake?"

"No, sir, not yet" replied Hadley.

"Believe me, Inspector, the only way we'll stop these damned Americans causing havoc is to make sure we've got a watertight case against the blackguard!"

"I understand that, sir."

"What about the groom?"

"He was arrested in Liverpool, sir, and we have him in custody" said Bell hoping that he could placate the Commissioner with some good news.

"Has he confessed to anything?"

"No, sir, but I believe he's innocent" said Hadley.

"Well that's as maybe, Inspector, but you'll not release him until I say so" said the Commissioner firmly.

"Very good, sir."

"What about these Jarvis brothers?"

"We have the younger one in custody, sir, and the older brother has gone to Switzerland on business" replied Hadley.

"Are they the prime suspects for the kidnapping?"

"I believe so, sir" replied Hadley.

"When is the brother expected back from Switzerland, if ever, that is?" asked the Commissioner.

"Next Friday, sir" replied Hadley.

"Well, gentlemen, the situation is very far from satisfactory and there will be questions from Ministers at the highest level, so prepare yourselves accordingly."

"Yes, sir" they chorused.

"And Hadley..."

"Yes, sir?"

"Get a confession out of that bloody grounds man before the American Press conference tomorrow" said the Commissioner firmly.

"I'll do my best, sir."

"That may not be good enough, Hadley, so I'm giving you an order!"

"Right, sir."

"I want to see his signed confession for the murder of Lady Mortlake on my desk before six o'clock tomorrow!"

Leaving a worried Chief Inspector pacing up and down in his office, Hadley returned to his. He explained to Cooper what had transpired and the young man looked as concerned as the Chief. After another pot of George's reviver they went down to custody to interview Winters with George following on, carrying pens, paper and a bottle of ink.

The truculent grounds-man was shown into the interview room where the detectives and George were already waiting. Winters sat down opposite Hadley and glared at him for a few moments before lowering his gaze to his clasped hands resting on the table.

"Mr Winters, I must advise you that you are the prime suspect for the unlawful murder of Lady Mortlake..."

101

"I didn't kill her, that bloody Irish liar did!" exclaimed Winters.

"Mr Kelly has been questioned at length by me and his recollection of events on that tragic day, differ from yours" said Hadley firmly.

"Well I know what I know, and I'm telling you that he killed her, not me!"

"Then tell me slowly and carefully exactly what happened the day her Ladyship died" said Hadley calmly. Winters remained silent for a few moments whilst he gathered his thoughts and then he began.

"It was about ten o'clock when I had finished my usual jobs around the place and I set off towards the high meadow with some traps that I wanted to set in Witches Wood, that's what we call the copse up on the hill. I wandered up there thinking about cutting down two elm trees that had died in the Spring, they're far over by Mr Gardner's, he owns the farm that is next to the estate, when I eventually got to Witches Wood I began setting the traps..."

"How long did that take?"

"About twenty minutes or so, perhaps a bit longer, I can't really remember."

"Please continue."

"I had just about finished when I heard a horse at the gallop coming closer to the wood, so wondering who it was, I began to make my way out..."

"And then what did you see?"

"Her Ladyship on her horse, Topper, riding fast towards me, then suddenly the animal stumbled and pitched her from her saddle..."

"What did you do?"

"Ran out of the wood to help her of course, but she had fallen badly and was unconscious, but breathing..."

"Go on" said Hadley as George continued writing furiously, the noise of his pen scratching the paper the only sound in the quiet pauses.

"Then suddenly Kelly appeared..."

"As if by magic?"

"Yes, exactly!"

"Was he on foot?"

"No, he was on Nelson, one of the old horses and must have been following her Ladyship closely…"

"What happened next?"

"He got down and said to me, 'I'll look after her, you go back to the house and get help'"

"And did you?"

"Yes, I ran back and raised the alarm and whilst I was doing that, Kelly suddenly arrived back at the house and he was sent immediately for Doctor Moore in the village."

"So Kelly was alone with her Ladyship for a while?"

"Yes, Inspector, and that's when he killed her!"

"Why should he do that?"

"Because of the money she promised him…"

"What money?"

"I don't know much about it, but Kelly was always boasting in that sly way of the Irish, that he was very close to her Ladyship and she had promised him money to set up a livery stables, breeding fine horses…"

"Then why should he want to murder her?"

"I don't know, perhaps they had a lovers tiff and she changed her mind…"

"A lovers tiff? What are you implying?"

"Well, she spent a lot of time down at the stables alone with Kelly and Mrs Noakes said that she used to come back to the house late in the evening all flushed…"

"That sounds like idle gossip to me" said Hadley.

"There's no smoke without fire, Inspector, and I think Kelly was seeing to her needs whilst the master was away in London."

"Did anyone else suspect that this alleged affair was going on?"

"Yes, everyone knew…"

"How did they know?"

"Because Mrs Noakes told them" replied Winters and on hearing that Hadley decided to end the interview. The detectives returned to their office and whilst George made tea they read his notes and Hadley decided to interview Kelly the next morning.

"It's one man's word against another and I wonder if we'll ever know the whole truth, Sergeant."

"Probably not, sir, but remember, the Commissioner demands a confession from Winters by tomorrow evening."

"Yes, don't remind me, Sergeant."

They spent the rest of the afternoon planning and writing reports before they set off in the early evening to the Kings Head. The pub was unusually quiet, which was very pleasant on a summers evening; they ordered ham, cheese and pickles along with pints of stout. Sitting at a table near the open door they settled down to enjoy the food whilst they waited for Agnes, Florrie and Iris. It was just after nine o'clock that the women arrived and whilst Cooper went off to buy gins and more stout, they sat down with Hadley. After introductions and the return of Cooper, Hadley began to question Iris, who confirmed that she was sure that Mortlake was the Toff who invited her to his planned celebration. She did not know when this would be nor did she know where, but she said that he would send a note which would be left at the bar, telling her when she was required. Hadley asked Iris to let him know immediately she had this information and she promised that she would. After another round of drinks the detectives left the pub and Cooper hailed a cab to take them home.

CHAPTER 12

Hadley was not in the best of moods when he arrived at the Yard the next morning. After a restless night worrying about the complex investigation and the thought of the Americans arriving en masse, along with feeling tired, made him demand strong, sweet tea as soon as he entered his office. Cooper looked pale and only half managed a smile from his desk opposite Hadley's.

"You look as if you've had a rough night, sir."

"It's the worry of it all so just don't speak, Sergeant."

"No, sir."

"Not until after I've had some tea and time to gather my thoughts."

"Right, sir."

George provided two pots of tea, which were consumed in quick succession, before Hadley felt almost human again. He planned to interview Kelly first thing and if he failed to shake the Irishman from his account of events, he knew that he would be unable to force a confession out of either him or Winters. He felt that eventuality would leave him with no option but to tell his Chief that he could not comply with the Commissioner's order. Bell would have to decide what to do next, either charge Winters with murder and then try and assemble enough evidence to make the charge stand or, do the same with Kelly and then inform the Commissioner, which was not a happy thought.

The interview with Kelly failed to give Hadley any reason not to believe the Irish man's original account of the events surrounding the death of Lady Mortlake. It was almost midday when Hadley went to the Chief's office to inform him that he would not have a confession from either suspect.

"But the Commissioner has ordered it, Hadley."

"I know he has, sir, but the fact is…"

"Never mind the facts, we need something to announce before the Americans have their Press conference!"

"I can only suggest that you inform the Commissioner and let him make a decision regarding the suspects" said Hadley.

"Oh, God" whispered Bell.

"I believe that Kelly is innocent and either Winters murdered her Ladyship or a hired assassin from London, who may have also been responsible for the death of Miss Wells."

Chief Inspector Bell put his hands on his head, leaned back in his chair and contemplated the ceiling looking for inspiration. Hadley waited patiently for Bell to say something and after a few moments he announced "I've made a decision, Hadley."

"That's very good, sir."

"We'll charge Winters with the murder of Lady Mortlake and charge Kelly with being an accessory to murder..."

"But, sir..."

"Hadley, that's my decision and I'll inform the Commissioner immediately, so I suggest you go down to custody and prepare the paperwork and advise them accordingly" said Bell.

Hadley returned to his office and told Cooper of the Chief's decision, he had just finished speaking when George appeared.

"Sir, this letter has just arrived for your urgent attention" he said as he handed the envelope to Hadley. The letter was from Mr Barrymore; Hadley read it out aloud.

"To Inspector Hadley, Dear Sir, a note has just been delivered to me stating that the ransom has been received in Geneva and that Lord Mortlake will be released tomorrow in London. I presume his Lordship will go to his home in Connaught Square where you may wish to call upon him for a statement, please advise me accordingly. Yours, Morton Barrymore."

"Well that's good, sir" said Cooper.

"Indeed, we may uncover some useful facts that will help in the murder investigations" said Hadley.

"Anything is welcome, sir."

"Yes, it is, I'll let the Chief Inspector know the good news before we go down to Custody and charge our suspects, Sergeant."

Hadley was in the Chief's office giving him the news regarding Lord Mortlake when he was interrupted by Mr Brackley, the Commissioner's assistant, who announced that the great one wished to see both of them immediately. They followed Mr Brackley up to the office and entered. The Commissioner looked decidedly unhappy and did not invite them to sit.

"Gentlemen, I've just received a note from a Mr Elliot Carter,

106

who apparently is the personal assistant to Mr Arthur J. Riley, advising me that Mr Riley and his entourage have arrived at the Savoy Hotel and that he will call upon me this afternoon before the Press conference!"

"Oh, that's unexpected, sir," said Bell meekly.

"The damned nerve of these Americans!" thundered the Commissioner as his face went red and his whiskers bristled.

"They're very forward, sir" said Bell helpfully.

"It seems that they want to take over everything and tell us what to do in our own country!" said the Commissioner.

"I'm sure you're right, sir" replied Bell in a concerned tone.

"Both of you had better stay in your offices until they arrive, then I'll send for you" said the Commissioner.

"Yes, sir" nodded Bell.

"And Hadley…"

"Yes, sir?"

"Have you got a confession out of that bloody grounds-man yet?"

"No, sir, and to be quite honest, I don't think I'll get one" replied Hadley as Bell's face drained of colour.

"What!" exclaimed the great man as Bell stepped forward and said "but in spite of that, sir, I've taken the decision to charge Winters with the murder of Lady Mortlake and Kelly with accessory to her murder." As he stepped back he hoped that he had appeased the angry Commissioner.

"Well that's a positive move forward, Chief Inspector."

"I thought so too, sir" beamed the exonerated Bell.

"At least that's something to tell Mr Riley and his entourage when they grace us with their presence" said the Commissioner.

"And we can also tell Mr Riley that Lord Mortlake will be released tomorrow, sir" said Bell.

"Ah, you've found him then?" asked the Commissioner.

"Not exactly, sir, but his solicitor received a note saying that the ransom had now been paid and that Mortlake would be set free in London tomorrow" replied Bell.

"Good, but I don't suppose Mr Riley knows of Mortlake's kidnap, Chief Inspector."

"He would have read it in the papers, sir" replied Bell.

"Yes, possibly and of course he'll know of the murder of Miss

Wells" said the Commissioner.

"Yes, sir, and he's bound to be upset at the tragic death of his daughter's close friend" said Bell.

"Indeed, any suspects lined up for that, Hadley?"

"No, not as yet, sir."

"Well, keep at it, Hadley."

"Yes of course, sir."

"Now gentlemen, you may go for the moment and I'll send for you when the Americans arrive."

Hadley returned to his office and told Cooper what had transpired.

"It sounds as if these Americans will cause real problems to our investigations, sir" said Cooper.

"Yes, but two things to bear in mind, first Mr Riley has lost his only daughter in tragic and suspicious circumstances, secondly, with his enormous wealth and power, he intends to get to the truth of what happened to her and who can blame him?"

"I can understand that, sir, but he might use his power in such a way as to cause problems for us" said Cooper.

"Indeed he might, but we must be clever enough to turn everything he does to our advantage, Sergeant" replied Hadley with a sly smile.

"Like what for instance?"

"Wait and see what unfolds before us, Sergeant, but I have the feeling that the arrival of the Americans might be very helpful indeed!"

Mr Brackley arrived a little later and just nodded at Hadley who followed him up to the Chief's office. Bell was waiting anxiously and Brackley said to him "the Americans are with the Commissioner now, Chief Inspector." When they entered the Commissioner's office there were five men, four of them seated and the fifth one standing behind the chair of a distinguished grey haired man with a large droopy moustache. They all stood except the distinguished man as the Commissioner introduced Bell and Hadley to them.

"This is Chief Inspector Bell, who's in overall charge of the case and Inspector Hadley, who is out following up every line of investigation..."

"Only two men on a case as important as this?" interrupted the distinguished man who Hadley knew was obviously Arthur J. Riley.

"That is sufficient, Mr Riley, I assure you" replied the Commissioner firmly.

"Then no wonder there's been so little progress!" exclaimed Riley.

"I can assure you..." began the Commissioner.

"You can assure me of nothing, sir, and it seems to me that we've arrived just in time" interrupted Riley as he turned and looked at two well built young men with broad shoulders dressed in brown, check suits. They both nodded and replied "yes, sir, Mr Riley, sir" in chorus.

"These are my Pinkerton Agents, the best in the business, Mr Edward Morris and Mr Charles Ford" said Riley as he waved his hand at the men who shook hands with Bell and Hadley.

"This is Mr Elliot Carter, my personal assistant, and this is Chief Lone Eagle, who takes care of me" said Riley with a twisted smile. They shook hands with Carter, a tall aloof man, immaculately dressed, but Lone Eagle just stood behind Riley with his arms folded and glared at them. Hadley had only seen pictures of Red Indians and he was intrigued by the man's appearance. He was short in stature but well built with broad shoulders, he had a weather beaten face with piercing black eyes and his dark hair was cut short. He was dressed in a buckskin jacket with a white collarless shirt underneath, his trousers matched his jacket. Around his waist he had a broad belt on which hung a large hunting knife, contained in a leather sheath, decorated with tassels and beads. He gave the appearance of a man not to be trifled with. They sat down and Hadley gained the impression that Mr Riley had taken over the proceedings and was completely in charge of events as the Commissioner looked on helplessly with his mouth half open.

"Now this is how I see it, Commissioner" began Riley as he looked hard at him "Nancy was supposedly killed in a riding accident, but I don't believe that for one damned moment! And do you know why, Commissioner?"

"Well, I, er, er" he stuttered before Riley continued.

"I'll tell you why, Nancy was one of the finest horsewomen

I've ever seen and I understand that she was riding an animal that she was very fond of and rode often, when she supposedly fell off…"

"Before you go any further, Mr Riley, I have to advise you that we now know that your daughter was cruelly murdered" interrupted the Commissioner. Mr Riley sat motionless for a moment before he asked in a menacing whisper "how did my daughter die?"

"The post mortem shows that she was strangled, sir" replied the Commissioner.

"Do you know who did it?" Riley hissed.

"We have the man in custody and he will face a trial in due course."

"Who is this son of a bitch?"

"The grounds-man at Holcot Manor; Winters is his name, sir."

"Why should he want to murder my daughter for Christ's sake?"

"We don't know, Mr Riley…"

"No, no, Commissioner, this doesn't add up, someone else is behind this. I have my suspicions who that person is, and I intend to find out!"

"Who do you suspect, Mr Riley?"

"I'm not saying for the moment, but I'll let you know when my Pinkerton boys have found out for sure, as they will do, you can rest easy on that!"

"I must advise you, sir, that whilst you are in England you and your men will be bound our laws and protocols and you will not interfere with…"

"Don't you sit there and tell me what I may and may not do, Commissioner!" interrupted Riley angrily.

"It is my duty to helpfully advise you, sir, and I also need to remind you that if you have any information regarding the murder of your daughter, you must inform my officers at once, otherwise you will be guilty of withholding information relevant to the case!" said the Commissioner forcefully. For a few moments there was a very uneasy silence and Riley contemplated his hands, Carter cleared his throat whilst Lone Eagle and the Agents remained stony faced.

"I thank you for your timely advice, Commissioner, but I must

110

also tell you that I intend to find out who killed my daughter and I will not be returning home until I see the bastard hung!" exclaimed Riley.

"We all want to see justice done, sir" replied the Commissioner.

"So we do, but I don't hold with your slow, plodding ways, sir, and I'll take any action that I think is appropriate" said Riley.

"Provided it is within the law…"

"The law is an ass!"

"That is not the way we see it in England, sir."

"Now tell me about the murder of little Annie at the Savoy" said Riley.

"Our investigations into that dreadful incident are ongoing…"

"So that means you haven't a clue at the moment" interrupted Riley and Hadley had to hide his smile.

"That is not the case, Mr Riley, for your information a man was seen to accost Miss Wells in front of staff at reception and we are currently searching for him" replied the Commissioner.

"Well that's good to hear, it should be easy to find a tall man with a moustache in London" said Riley in a sarcastic tone.

"How do you know that, sir?"

"My boys have already spoken to the managers at the Savoy, Commissioner, it's the first thing they did when I found out what had happened to that sweet girl" replied Riley.

"I see" murmured the Commissioner, feeling distinctly undermined already.

"Now where's Mortlake, for God's sake?" asked Riley.

"As you may know, he was kidnapped and a ransom has been paid for his release, so I'm pleased to tell you that we have heard from the men responsible and he will be set free in London tomorrow" beamed the Commissioner.

"Good, I'm looking forward to speaking to him" said Riley in a menacing tone.

"We obviously will interview him about his ordeal…"

"Yes, I'm keen to know all about that, Commissioner" interrupted Riley.

"I'm sure you are, sir."

"And I want to know who the hell has got the money that has been paid in Geneva" said Riley to the amazement of the

111

Commissioner, Bell and Hadley.

"How do you know that, sir?"

"That's my secret I'm afraid" replied Riley with a grin.

"I must warn you…"

"Oh, stop warning me about everything, Commissioner, and just do your damned job for Christ's sake!"

"Well, I never…"

"That's as maybe. Now just to let you know, at the Press conference this evening I'll be announcing a reward of half a million dollars for any information that leads to the arrest and conviction of the killer of my daughter and Annie Wells" said Riley and on hearing that the Commissioner sat open mouthed in stunned silence.

"Half a million dollars, sir?" he asked when he had sufficiently recovered from the shock.

"That's what I said, Commissioner."

"Good God!"

"Yes, he is good and I hope he'll help me catch the killer" said Riley with a smile.

"I think that a reward of such magnitude is completely wrong, sir."

"Why's that, Commissioner?"

"You'll have every Tom, Dick and Harry in London scurrying about…"

"That's the idea, Commissioner" interrupted Riley.

"But it will cause confusion, even unrest…"

"So be it, but I've found out in life that money talks and can open locked doors, so as I have plenty, then I'm going to use it for my little girl and her sweet friend, Commissioner."

"I think it very unwise…"

"Think what you like, Commissioner, but I'll have you know that I am a very determined man and I will not be going back to New York until I see the son of a bitch who killed my Nancy and little Annie dangling at the end of a rope!"

"I see…"

"Do I make myself crystal clear, Commissioner?"

"You do indeed, Mr Riley."

CHAPTER 13

After Mr Riley and his entourage had left the Commissioner's office, Bell and Hadley just stood gazing at the dumbfounded head of the Metropolitan Police.

"Well, gentlemen, for once in my life I'm at a loss for words."

"Mr Riley was impertinent to say the very least, sir" ventured Bell.

"Possibly, Chief Inspector, but I do have some sympathy for the man, after all he's lost his daughter and her friend at the hands of a wicked killer" replied the Commissioner.

"Yes, but that is no reason for him…"

"He has every reason, Bell, now I think you both should attend the Press conference with Chief Inspector Burton, our Press officer, he will announce that Winters and Kelly have been arrested and charged with Lady Mortlake's murder, that should steal Mr Riley's thunder and calm things down a little" said the Commissioner.

"But when Mr Riley announces his reward for information, that will surely cast doubt on the validity of the arrest of Winters and Kelly, sir" said Hadley.

"He can offer what he likes but we'll maintain that we have the killers in custody despite what he says" replied the Commissioner.

"I have to say, sir, that I believe Mr Riley may be right in his assumption that there is someone else behind these murders" said Hadley.

"I agree, Hadley, so I want you to continue with the investigation."

"But, surely the case is now closed, sir" said Bell anxiously.

"No, Chief Inspector, I think that it should remain open whilst Hadley delves a little deeper" replied the Commissioner and Hadley smiled with satisfaction.

"Thank you, sir" said Hadley.

"Now if Lord Mortlake appears tomorrow, bring him in here for questioning and hold him if necessary, Hadley" said the Commissioner.

"Very good, sir."

"I want a very detailed report on his recollection of events surrounding his kidnap."

"Yes, sir."

"We need to get to the bottom of that, Hadley."

"Indeed, sir."

"Right, gentlemen, that will be all for the moment."

Bell said little to Hadley as they descended the stairs, only that they would leave the Yard to go to the Savoy at six o'clock.

"Yes, sir" replied Hadley.

"To tell the truth, Hadley, I'm less than pleased with the events of this afternoon."

"I'm sorry to hear that, sir."

"Mark my words, this case is going to become a nightmare of gargantuan proportions before it's over and that damned American goes home!" exclaimed Bell as he reached his office door.

"I hope not, sir."

"Time will prove me right, Hadley" said Bell as he entered his office and slammed the door behind him in anger.

Hadley and Bell accompanied Chief Inspector Burton in a police four wheeler through the busy London traffic to the Savoy Hotel in the Strand. When they arrived the police officers were escorted to the Marlborough Room, which had been booked for the Press conference by Mr Riley. When they entered the elegant room there were a number of reporters that Hadley recognised, some were milling about whilst others were talking inaudibly in small groups. Hadley and Bell sat in the front row of seats whilst Burton sat at the conference table waiting for Mr Riley to arrive. At half past six, Mr Riley, accompanied by the Pinkerton Agents and Lone Eagle, entered the room and walked briskly up to the table, gave Burton a lingering look before he sat down The Press officer introduced himself to Riley who looked less than pleased about his attendance. The Agents and the Red Indian sat alongside Hadley and Bell whilst the reporters settled down, eager to hear what the American had to announce.

"Gentlemen of the Press, I'm Arthur J. Riley of New York, and I'm here in London to investigate the untimely death of my daughter Nancy and her friend, Miss Ann Wells, I'm accompanied by two Pinkerton Agents, Mr Ed Morris and Mr Charles Ford, who will be carrying out a full investigation into the events leading up to the tragic incidents. This afternoon I've had a meeting with the Commissioner of Police at New Scotland Yard, and he has informed me that my daughter and her friend were murdered and that his officers have arrested two men who have been charged with the killing of my daughter, unfortunately the killer of Ann Wells remains at large in London. I have told the Commissioner I believe that at least one other person is involved in the murder of my daughter. I intend to seek him out and see him hang, along with the others already in custody. To encourage the good people of London town to come forward with information I am announcing that I will offer a reward of half a million dollars…" When the audience heard that the assembled press men let out a collective gasp of disbelief.

"Half a million dollars, sir?" queried an incredulous reporter from the second row.

"Yes, indeed sir, half a million dollars, and I'm sure that once you gentlemen have announced it in your papers, useful information will flow in…"

"But your daughter died at Holcot, how can anyone in London know about that, sir?" interrupted a reporter.

"Because, I believe that the murder of my daughter and Miss Wells was committed by the same man, sir, and that man is in London" replied Riley.

"Do you have any idea who it might be, sir?" asked another reporter.

"I have someone firmly in mind" replied Riley.

"Are you going to tell us who it is, sir?"

"Not yet, you'll have to wait until I'm ready."

"Have you told the police who it is, sir?" asked the reporter from the second row.

"No, I haven't."

"Is it a relation of Lady Mortlake, sir?"

"I'm afraid I can't make any further comment at the moment but I promise you that as soon as I have the proof I want, you'll all be the first to know" said Riley.

"Are the police helping you with your investigations, sir?"

"No, but we are working in parallel and I'm sure that Mr Burton here will confirm that" said Riley with a smile as he glanced sideways at Burton, who cleared his throat.

"As you know, I'm Chief Inspector Burton, the Press Officer for the Metropolitan Police…" he began pompously before he was interrupted by the reporter in the second row.

"Yes, we all know that, Charlie, but is it true what Mr Riley has said?"

"I have a statement and it reads as follows" announced Burton ignoring the interruption.

"Two men, James Winters and Patrick Kelly, both of Holcot Manor in Northamptonshire, have been arrested and charged with the murder of Lady Nancy Mortlake in May, they will be appearing in front of Bow Street Magistrates tomorrow, and after the hearing they will be held on remand until their trial at the Old Bailey. The Metropolitan Police are not engaged in the search for any other person or persons with regard to this tragic incident…"

"What about the reward then?"

"The Metropolitan Police believe that the reward offered by Mr Riley is both excessive and wholly unwarranted as the culprits have been arrested and will face a full trial in due course" replied Burton.

"Have the police told Mr Riley that?"

"I can confirm that the Commissioner has informed him of his views on the matter" replied Burton.

"What about the murder of Miss Wells?"

"That is an ongoing investigation."

"Is her murder linked to Lady Mortlake's?"

"No, there is no evidence of any link" replied Burton.

"That's damned nonsense!" exclaimed Mr Riley.

"As I said…" began Burton

"Of course they're linked, it's the same man who's responsible for both murders and my Pinkerton boys will hunt the son of a bitch down and I'll see him hang before I return to New York!" exclaimed Riley with passion as he thumped his fist on the table.

There was a moments silence before Burton cleared his throat and said "I repeat, the Metropolitan Police have two men in custody, they have been charged with murder and will appear before Bow Street Magistrates tomorrow, so that will be the end of the police investigation." On hearing that Riley's face went red before he exclaimed "closing the case is blind stupidity in the face of the facts and this is why I have brought Pinkerton Agents from America to sort this Goddamn mess out!"

"Really, sir" said Burton in disgust.

"You English police with your quaint old ideas don't seem to grasp what's going on" said Riley as he stood up to leave the room.

"What do you intend to do next, sir?" asked a reporter.

"Enjoy a decent dinner and then plan for tomorrow" replied Riley.

"Are you going up to Holcot, sir?"

"Yes, indeed."

"When will that be, sir?"

"In due course, when I'm ready" replied Riley.

The detectives left the Savoy and returned to the Yard in silence. Burton was obviously angered by the American's comments and Bell seemed confused, so Hadley thought it best in the circumstances to say nothing.

"Come up to my office in half an hour, Hadley" said Bell as they entered the building.

"Very good, sir."

After a pot of tea and briefing Cooper before he left for home, Hadley went up to Bell's office.

"Chief Inspector Burton is furious and has gone up to see the Commissioner and report what Riley said at the Press conference" said Bell.

"I'm not surprised, sir" replied Hadley.

"This is going to get right out of hand, mark my words, Hadley."

"Yes, sir."

"And whatever you do, don't get involved with Riley or his agents."

"No, sir."

"I mean it, Hadley, because the man's a menace and his intemperate actions could harm all our careers."

"Yes, sir."

"Riley has too much money and too many friends in high places!"

"Indeed he has, sir."

"It could all become too political for my liking."

"That's true, sir."

"He won't hesitate to use all his power to undermine us and what we are about."

"No, sir."

"I can't get over his offer of a reward of half a million dollars, I mean, it's simply staggering" said Bell.

"Yes, it certainly is, sir."

"Once the Press report that in the papers tomorrow all the low life in London will claim they know something and then only one thing is certain..."

"What's that, sir?"

"More wild goose chases than you can shake a stick at!"

"And we'll be caught up in it all" whispered Hadley.

"Exactly, and the Press will be watching our every move before making lurid and fanciful comments in their papers."

"The Commissioner will not be amused" said Hadley.

"No he won't be, now make sure you're at Bow Street tomorrow to see that things go smoothly and that Winters and Kelly are remanded" said Bell.

"Yes, of course, sir."

"Hopefully once that has happened it will be widely reported and calm the situation."

"I agree, sir."

"Then if Mortlake's kidnappers release him, get him in here for questioning and try and keep him away from Riley" said Bell.

"I'll try, sir."

"I think Riley suspects that Mortlake murdered his daughter and Miss Wells, Hadley."

"I think so to, sir."

"Unfortunately we might never know."

The next morning Hadley and Cooper took a cab to the Magistrates Court at Bow Street and arrived just before ten o'clock. The bench was due to sit at ten thirty and that gave the detectives time to organise their notes and peruse the charge sheets. At precisely the allotted time, a pair of grave and serious magistrates arrived in the court room and took their places. The first case was called, which happened to be Winters and Kelly, but

118

they did not appear from the cells below. Hadley became concerned and he waited impatiently for some explanation from the Court officers. Suddenly a police constable rushed in and spoke in an animated whisper to the senior Court officer who went pale. There was a moments silence as the officer turned to face the bench and said in a calm voice "I regret to report to the bench that the accused men, Winters and Kelly have escaped from custody on their way here..."

"What!" exclaimed Hadley as he immediately stood, red faced with anger.

"How did this happen?" asked the bemused senior magistrate.

"Sir, I am given to understand that the police wagon bringing them here was involved in an accident with a brewery dray on Ludgate Hill, the horses bolted causing the police wagon to overturn..."

"Good heavens!" exclaimed the magistrate.

"It appears that the men escaped from the damaged wagon and made their way through the crowd of onlookers, sir."

"What about the police officers accompanying them?" asked the other magistrate.

"The driver was badly injured, sir, and the escort constable inside the wagon was overpowered by the prisoners and left unconscious."

"This is most regrettable... Inspector Hadley" said the senior magistrate as he looked at the Inspector.

"Yes, sir?"

"I suggest you leave at once and see if you can arrest these dangerous men before they do any more harm!"

"Yes, sir."

The detectives hurried from the court and took a cab to Ludgate Hill, where the damaged police wagon lay on its side with the back door broken open and the side crushed against the cobbled street. The brewers dray was lop-sided with a rear cartwheel missing, several barrels of beer had fallen off and burst open. The smell of beer permeated the air and some of the onlookers made vain attempts trying to recover the stout that ran down the gutter. The dray horses had been removed from their harness and taken back to the brewery in the Stratford Road whilst there was no sign of the police horses, which had bolted after the forceful collision. There were several constables in attendance with one sergeant trying to keep some sort of order.

"What happened, Sergeant?" asked Hadley after he had presented himself.

"I'm not sure, sir, the driver of the dray is over there with one of my constables and as soon as I get a minute, I'll be talking to him" replied the sergeant.

"Is the police driver seriously hurt?"

"It appears so, sir, the ambulance has just taken him and the escort constable to Saint Bart's" replied the sergeant.

"Where are the police horses?"

"I've no idea, sir, apparently they bolted and were long gone when I arrived."

"Dear God, what a mess" murmured Hadley.

"I've sent for more men to help recover our wagon, sir, and the brewery will be sending men out to fix the dray before it is taken away."

"Good, now have you any idea in which direction the prisoners went?"

"No, sir, they had disappeared well before the alarm was raised" replied the sergeant.

"Right, sergeant, we'll leave you to manage this and get back to the Yard to organise searches for the criminals" said Hadley.

"Very good, sir."

As soon as the detectives arrived at the Yard, Hadley sent telegraph messages to all the London police stations informing them of the escape of Kelly and Winters and requesting their help in finding the men. He then went up to report to Chief Inspector Bell.

"This gets worse and worse, Hadley" said the exasperated Chief when Hadley had finished relaying the events of the morning.

"It was a totally unforeseen circumstance, sir."

"That doesn't make it any easier!"

"I appreciate that, sir."

"The Commissioner will go mad, the Press will have a field day and Riley will call us incompetent; it couldn't be worse, Hadley!"

"No, sir."

"What action have you taken?"

"I've telegraphed all the London stations and requested their assistance in recapturing the men, sir."

"Good, and do you think they will lie low here?"

"Possibly, sir, but I think Kelly might make an attempt to escape to Ireland to see his mother."

"How can he do that without any money?"

"I don't know, sir, but he's a resourceful man…"

"He'll probably rob some poor unfortunate person for the fare" interrupted Bell.

"I somehow doubt it, sir."

"Why?"

"Because I think the man is honest…"

"Facing the hangman's noose makes even the most honest of men desperate, Hadley" interrupted Bell as there was a knock at the door before Cooper entered the office.

"I'm sorry to interrupt you, sir, but a message has just come in…"

"Yes, Sergeant?" asked Bell testily.

"Apparently Lord Mortlake has just been found in Hyde Park, sir, and he's badly injured."

"Where is he now?" asked Hadley.

"He's been taken to the Marylebone, sir."

"On your way, Hadley" said Chief Inspector Bell with a resigned sigh.

CHAPTER 14

Hadley and Cooper went straight to the accident admissions at the Marylebone Hospital and were directed to a side ward where Lord Mortlake was recovering from his ordeal. Two police constables were on duty outside the room and they recognised the detectives immediately.

"Who found his Lordship, constable?" asked Hadley.

"A lady and gentleman who were walking in the Park, sir, they called for help and I was close by" replied Constable Woodman.

"Well done."

"Thank you, sir, I saw that the gentleman was badly hurt and covered in blood so I called for an ambulance, Constable Barnes here, assisted me."

"Good work, both of you. Did the couple who found him see anybody with him or attacking him?"

"No, sir, they just found him by the bushes near the Albion Gate" replied the constable.

"The Albion Gate? That's the entrance to the Park just opposite Connaught Square if I'm not mistaken" said Hadley.

"Yes it is, sir."

"When you found him did he tell you who he was?"

"Yes, sir, he mumbled 'thank God you're here, I'm Lord Mortlake, get me to a hospital', so I did. Of course I knew that he had been kidnapped, so I reported it immediately" replied Woodman.

"That's very well done, constable."

"Thank you, sir."

"Now is Lord Mortake alone at the moment?"

"No, sir, the Doctor is with him."

"Right, we'll have to wait then" said Hadley.

Ten minutes later the Doctor emerged from the room and Hadley introduced himself.

"Tell me, Doctor, is Lord Mortlake seriously injured?"

"No he's not, Inspector, much to my surprise."

"May we discuss the matter privately, Doctor?"

"Yes, please come to my room."

The detectives followed the Doctor down the corridor to a

small consulting room where he waved them to sit.

"I realise that you will have to obey the rule of patient confidentiality, Doctor, but I would be obliged if you would answer my questions if you can" said Hadley.

"I'll do my best, Inspector."

"You said that Lord Mortlake was not seriously injured, which surprised you, could you elaborate, Doctor?"

"Well, I hardly am in a position to add much more…"

"Doctor, I am conducting an investigation into kidnap and murder, so please do not withhold information that might be vital in bringing the culprits to justice" interrupted Hadley and there was a silence for some moments as the Doctor considered his reply.

"Oh, very well. After I examined the patient I was surprised to find only slight bruising on the left side of his face, two small cuts on both forearms and two small cuts on both thighs."

"Had he lost a lot of blood?"

"No, but his clothes were well covered, which seemed mysterious to me, Inspector."

"Go on, Doctor" said Hadley in a suspicious tone.

"Well, as I said, he had only small cuts but he claimed that he had been stabbed, tied up for days and beaten badly, but there were no signs of any restraint on his wrists or ankles, or any bruising consistent with beatings."

"What about the blood stained clothes?"

"To be frank, I'm at a loss to explain them, other than to say it's not his blood" replied the Doctor.

"Is he well enough to leave hospital?"

"Yes, but I'll keep him in tonight for observation and then release him in the morning."

"May I question him, Doctor?"

"Yes by all means. To all intents and purposes, Lord Mortlake is quite well, Inspector."

"Thank you, Doctor."

Hadley and Cooper entered the room where the injured Lord lay in bed. He glanced up and said with relief "thank God you're here, Inspector, I've been so close to death these last few days that I hardly know myself."

"You're safe now, my Lord" replied Hadley as he sat at his bedside whilst Cooper remained standing, his notebook and pencil poised.

"It has been a terrible experience, Inspector."

"I'm sure it has, sir, now please take your time and tell us everything."

"Where shall I begin with this nightmare?"

"Did you recognise the two men who kidnapped you from outside your house, sir?"

"No, Inspector, I have never seen them before in my life" replied the Lord.

"What happened to you after they forced you into the coach?"

"The brutes knocked me unconscious, Inspector, and when I came round, they had tied my hands and blindfolded me."

"Have you any idea where they took you, sir?"

"No, Inspector, all I can remember is that the building I was kept prisoner in smelled of fish."

"Did you hear them say anything that might give a clue to who they were or where you were being held?"

"Not really, Inspector, their speech was poor, they were uneducated thugs who were carrying out the orders of their master."

"Obviously they have assaulted you during the time you were captive" said Hadley.

"Indeed they did, I was subjected to frequent beatings and they stabbed me before they brought me to Hyde Park and left me to bleed to death" replied Mortlake. Hadley did not believe a word of it.

"Why did they beat and stab you, sir?"

"I have no idea, unless they derived some perverse disgusting pleasure from seeing me in pain, Inspector."

"Did they ask you anything?"

"No, they didn't, the only thing they said was that 'the master would be pleased'."

"What about?"

"They didn't say."

"Tell me about the food you were given."

"Every day they gave me gruel for breakfast, lunch was a piece of dried bread with a disgusting watery soup of some kind and dinner consisted of cheese or ham with more bread" replied Mortlake.

"And what did they give you to drink?"

"Only water during the day and a bottle of stout at night."

"Were you allowed to wash, sir?"

"No, Inspector."

"You're clean shaven now sir."

"Er, yes, er, the nurse shaved and washed me when I was admitted here" replied Mortlake

"Good, now I understand that the Doctor will release you tomorrow so you may go home…"

"I couldn't possibly leave the hospital, Inspector" interrupted Mortlake.

"Why not, sir?"

"I'm still too weak from loss of blood, I mean you have no idea how I have suffered and I'm only here because the ransom was paid" said Mortlake.

"Quite so, sir."

"If it hadn't been paid then I would be dead by now and my body thrown into the Thames."

"How do you know that, sir?"

"What?"

"That your body would be thrown into the Thames" repeated Hadley.

"The thugs told me, Inspector."

"You just said that they did not tell you anything, sir."

"Well they told me that, Inspector."

"Yes, I see, sir."

"I just can't remember everything - I'm still confused, so please bear with me."

"In that case it's best that you go home tomorrow to recover and I'll call upon you in a day or so to see if you can remember anything that might help the investigation into your kidnap, sir" said Hadley.

"Will I have a police guard, Inspector?"

"I don't think that will be necessary, sir."

"Why not?"

"Because I think the kidnappers have got what they wanted so I'm sure that you are now quite safe, sir" replied Hadley with a sardonic smile.

"I hope so."

"I think it's important that you know that Mr Riley and his entourage have arrived in London and will be in contact with you soon."

"Oh, dear God" whispered Mortlake.

"I advise you to rest and get better as soon as possible."

"Yes, I will, Inspector."

"Good day to you, sir."

The detectives left the hospital and made their way back to the Yard where George gave Hadley a sealed envelope marked 'private' before he went off to make a pot of tea. The note inside read 'Inspector Hadley, please be kind enough to meet me at the Savoy Hotel as soon as possible and please come alone' and it was signed by Arthur Riley.

"Anything important, sir?" asked Cooper.

"Could be, Sergeant, Mr Riley wants me to meet him at the Savoy, alone" replied Hadley.

"Are you going, sir?"

"Yes and you're coming with me."

"He won't like that, sir."

"No, but he won't know because you'll be out of sight, Sergeant."

"Will I, sir?"

"Oh, yes, but we'll keep this unexpected development strictly between ourselves, Sergeant, until we find out what he wants."

"Very good, sir."

After tea they made their way to the Strand where they stopped the Hansom a hundred yards or so from the Savoy Hotel. Hadley instructed Cooper to buy a newspaper, then walk up to the hotel and sit in the reception, reading the paper whilst enjoying a pot of tea. He was to observe everyone arriving and departing whilst Hadley would follow on in about ten minutes and make contact with Mr Riley. This was duly done and some fifteen minutes later Hadley was conducted up to Mr Riley's suite of rooms. The American was alone and he stood, smiled then shook hands with Hadley before he waved him to a seat.

126

"I'm very glad you came, Inspector, because to tell the truth I thought that your superiors may have warned you against such a meeting with me" said Riley.

"They did, sir."

Riley smiled and nodded before he said "you're the very man I can trust and I knew it when I first set eyes on you."

"Thank you, sir."

"I'm sure that you want to get to the bottom of this tragedy as much as I do, Inspector."

"I certainly do, sir."

"I'd like you to work closely with my Pinkerton boys…"

"I'm afraid I can't agree to that, sir" interrupted Hadley.

"Now, hold your horses, Inspector…"

"You must understand my position in all this, sir" interrupted Hadley.

"Dammit man, I just want to see the killer of my daughter and her friend hanged for what he's done!"

"So do I sir."

"Well help me for God's sake!"

"I will, sir, I'll give you and your Agents as much information as I am able but we have to conduct the investigation in parallel, as you rightly said."

"I see."

"Please don't think for one moment that I am being obstructive but I have to answer to the Commissioner" said Hadley.

"Well I suppose that's true enough" said Riley with a nod of his head.

"But that doesn't mean I am unable to assist you as I obey my master" said Hadley with a smile.

"I would appreciate that very much, Inspector."

"Just make sure your Pinkerton boys or Lone Eagle, don't cause me any problems."

"Lone Eagle won't but I can't vouch for the Agents, once they get their teeth into something they never let go, a bit like your English bulldog, Inspector" said Riley and Hadley smiled.

"We have ways of making a bulldog let go, sir" replied Hadley then Riley laughed and said "I think we're going to get along splendidly."

The Pinkerton Agents along with Lone Eagle were summoned

from the adjoining room and they sat attentively whilst taking notes as Hadley briefed them on the facts of the investigation so far. When he had finished he told them that Lord Mortlake had been released by his kidnappers and was in the Marylebone Hospital. Riley raised his eyebrows at that and said "I think it's time I called on him and see what he has to say for himself."

"I would advise you to do that tomorrow, sir, after he has been discharged from hospital" said Hadley.

"Right, do you know where he will go?" asked Riley.

"I'm sure that he will be at his house in Connaught Square, sir" replied Hadley.

"In that case we'll see him there."

"I've told him that you are here in London, sir, so he will be expecting you."

"I'm sure he will, Inspector."

"Finally, sir, when do you intend to go to Holcot Manor?"

"Probably the day after tomorrow, Inspector, but first I want to see if my offer of a reward brings in any information that will be useful to my boys and if it does, I may hold back for a day or so" replied Riley.

"That's understandable, sir."

"Will you be going up, Inspector?"

"Probably not, sir, as you know the investigation is officially over now that Winters and Kelly have been accused of your daughter's murder."

"That's a pity."

"Yes, but I will be staying here in an attempt to arrest them" said Hadley.

"Arrest them? I thought that they were in custody and facing the magistrate this morning" said Riley with a puzzled look.

"They were, sir, but unfortunately on the way to court their police wagon was involved in an accident and they have escaped."

"What!"

"We have alerted all the London police stations and I can assure you that every constable on his beat is looking for them" said Hadley.

"That's no damned good! The sons of bitches could be anywhere!" Riley shouted.

"We'll find them, sir…"

128

"You'd better, Inspector, otherwise they'll be real fireworks!"

"I'm sure, sir."

"What a Goddam mess this is" whispered Riley.

"Can we do anything, Inspector?" asked Charles Ford.

"Not really, sir, but thank you for your offer."

"Well just let us know."

"I will, but I think you'd be best following your own lines of inquiry into Lady Mortlake's murder" said Hadley.

"We will" replied Ford.

"Confidentially, Mr Riley, do you suspect that Lord Mortlake had something to do with your daughter's death?"

"Yes, I'm as sure as I could possibly be about that, Inspector."

"I see, sir."

"And that's why I've got a court injunction preventing him from inheriting Nancy's money, because that's all he was ever after" said Riley in a sad tone.

"I can understand why you took that action, sir."

"Do you think he murdered my girl, Inspector?"

"I have an open mind at the moment, sir" replied Hadley.

As Hadley crossed the reception floor of the Savoy he gave a slight nod to Cooper who joined him outside in the Strand a few minutes later. They hailed a Hansom cab and as it rattled back to the Yard, Hadley told Cooper what Riley had said.

"I want this meeting to be kept confidential for the time being, Sergeant."

"Very good, sir."

"Whilst you were waiting for me, did you see anybody that you recognised or appeared suspicious?"

"No, sir, but did you expect that I would?"

"I'm not sure, Sergeant."

When they arrived at the office George informed Hadley of a report that two men answering the descriptions of Winters and Kelly had stolen a dog cart in the Edgware Road whilst the owner was in an iron mongers. They were seen making off at speed towards the north.

"They're going back to Holcot, I'll be bound" said Hadley.

"Why would they do that, sir? They'd know that we would

look for them there"

"They are taking a gamble that we will be searching for them in London for a while, which will give them enough time to get to Holcot."

"But, sir…"

"They need money and clothes to get away, Sergeant, and they know that Mrs Noakes would help them" interrupted Hadley.

"That's possible, sir."

"I'll send a telegraph to Inspector West at Northampton asking him to arrest them when they arrive at Holcot" said Hadley.

"Are we going to go there, sir?"

"Only to bring them back, Sergeant."

Hadley went up to brief Chief Inspector Bell about the sighting of Winters and Kelly before returning to his office and settling down to report writing and discussion with Cooper with regard to the murders of Lady Mortlake and Miss Wells. The detectives went home late, tired and hungry as they had not stopped all day. Hadley was depressed and moody when he arrived at his house in Camden and it took Alice the rest of the evening to cheer him up. His last thoughts as he closed his eyes were about the hopeful arrest of Winters and Kelly by Inspector Peter West.

CHAPTER 15

When Hadley arrived in his office the next morning he was disappointed to learn that no message had been received from Inspector West with regard to the arrest of the two wanted men. He decided to wait until midday and if he had not heard by then, he would send a follow up telegraph to Northampton. He and Cooper sat and discussed the investigations until just before eleven thirty when George arrived and announced "there's a Mr Ford and Mr Morris here to see you urgently, sir." Hadley sat up in surprise and replied "please show them in, George." The clerk nodded and disappeared for a few moments and returned with the Pinkerton Agents following.

"Hi, there, Inspector" said Ford.

"Good morning, gentlemen" replied Hadley as he waved them to sit.

"Thanks" they chorused whilst nodding to Cooper.

"Would you like some tea?"

"No thanks, Inspector, we haven't any time for socialising I'm afraid" replied Ford.

"Then how can I help?"

"Do you know where Lord Mortlake has gone, sir?" asked Ford.

"I believe that he has probably left hospital and is now at his home in Connaught Square" replied Hadley in surprise.

"Well he's left the hospital for sure but he 'aint at home..." said Morris.

"And his butler says he's not seen him since he was kidnapped, so where is he?" asked Ford.

"I've no idea" replied Hadley.

"I have to tell you, sir, that Mr Riley is awaiting downstairs in his coach and he's hopping mad!" exclaimed Morris.

"I'm sure he is" said Hadley.

"He wants to know where Mortlake is and he thought you might know" said Ford.

"I'm afraid I don't. When I saw his Lordship in the hospital yesterday I advised him to go home and rest and informed him that I would call upon him in a day or so to follow up the investigation into his kidnap" said Hadley.

"Could he have gone to Holcot instead?" asked Morris.

"That's a possibility but unlikely" replied Hadley.

"Well this is all beginning to stink like a barrel of rotten fish" said Ford.

"And Mr Riley is pretty upset, I can tell you" said Morris.

"What can you do to help, sir?" asked Ford.

"Nothing, I'm afraid" replied Hadley.

"Why not, sir?" asked Ford with a touch of anger.

"Because Lord Mortlake has committed no crime and is a free man to come and go as he wishes" replied Hadley.

"I can tell you, sir, that Mr Riley will not be too impressed with your attitude to all this" said Morris.

"That maybe but I have to work within the law, gentlemen and I'm sure that Mr Riley understands that" said Hadley in a firm tone.

"Can you suggest anywhere else in London that Mortlake might have gone?" asked Ford.

"The only other place might be his club" replied Hadley.

"And where is that?" asked Morris.

"He's a member of the Dreyfus Club in Curzon Street" said Hadley.

"Thanks, we'll go there now and see if we can find him but if he's not there, we'll be back" said Ford.

"You can count on it, sir" added Morris. With that the Agents hurried out and both detectives felt as if a whirlwind had just passed through their office.

"Well, what did you make of that, Sergeant?"

"It was quite unbelievable, sir."

"Yes, I think we'd better have a pot of tea to steady us."

"I think that's very necessary, sir."

George was summoned and the tea ordered whilst Hadley racked his brains for an answer to Mortlake's disappearance.

"I wonder if he's gone to seek some comfort with Miss Jarvis?"

"Now there's a thought, sir."

"I think we'll pay her a visit before we have an early lunch."

"That's a very good idea if I may say so, sir." replied Cooper.

Hadley sent a telegraph message to Inspector West at

Northampton and one to Inspector Dunton in Liverpool, in case Kelly attempted to board the ferry to Ireland, before leaving the Yard at midday. The detectives travelled quickly through the traffic to 36 Regents Street where a maid opened the door to them.

"Miss Madeleine is not at home, sir" she said when Hadley asked to see her.

"Do you know where she has gone?"

"No, sir."

"Did she have any callers this morning?"

"Yes, sir."

"Who may I ask?"

"A gentleman, sir."

"Do you know who it was?"

"No, sir, he didn't give his name."

"Well how did you announce him?"

"I didn't sir, when I opened the door he pushed past me as Miss Madeleine came out to meet him in the hall."

"Then what happened?"

"Miss Madeleine just dismissed me and I went downstairs to the kitchen, sir."

"Presumably they went out together?"

"Yes, sir."

"Has this gentleman called before?"

"I don't know, sir, because I'm new here and only started last week."

"I see, now is Mr Jarvis at home?"

"No, sir, I understand that Mr Jarvis and Mrs Jarvis are away on holiday at the moment" she replied.

"Thank you, you've been very helpful" said Hadley and he turned, walked down the steps to the pavement as Cooper followed.

"Do you think that the gentleman caller was Lord Mortlake, sir?"

"Probably, Sergeant."

"What next then, sir?"

"Hail a cab, Sergeant and let's have an early lunch."

The Kings Head was busy as usual and after ordering stout and a ploughman's lunch from a harassed Vera, the detectives found a

133

table in the corner.

"I'm interested to know if Agnes has found out any more about the party that Iris Meaks and her friend have been invited to, Sergeant" said Hadley as he sipped his stout.

"You seem to be fairly sure that it's Mortlake who's having the party, sir."

"Yes, I am, Sergeant, I think he's celebrating his ransom money."

"Who is the other person I wonder, sir?"

"One of Mortlake's unsavoury friends no doubt or the man who has helped him with his bogus kidnap" replied Hadley as Agnes walked into the bar. She looked around and when she saw the detectives she smiled and made her way over to them.

"Hello, Jim…Sergeant" she said as she sat down and Cooper hurried away to get her a sixpenny gin.

"What news, my dear?" asked Hadley.

"I've been thinking of you all morning, Jim."

"That's nice, Agnes."

"Because, would you believe, Iris told me, not an hour ago, that the Toff, who's invited her to his special party, left a message at the bar saying that his coach would collect her and little Jane on Saturday night…"

"That's very interesting, did she say what time?"

"No, only that she must wait in from seven o'clock and make sure that she was clean and tidy" replied Agnes.

"Right, this is very useful information, I want to have a word with Iris before Saturday" said Hadley.

"What about, Jim?"

"I'm going to have the coach followed by two of my men…"

"Oh, no, don't do that, Jim!"

"Why not?"

"If her Toff finds out he won't pay her and little Jane!"

"I'm sorry, Agnes, it is important that I confirm who he is and I can promise you that the Toff will never know" replied Hadley as Cooper returned with the gin.

After a hurried lunch the detectives made their way to the offices of Olivier and Barrymore in Holborn. They were admitted promptly into the office of Morton Barrymore who waved them to sit and asked immediately "have you news about Lord Mortlake?"

"Yes, sir, he was discovered at the Albion Gate in Hyde Park yesterday and two constables were summoned by passersby. An ambulance was called for as his Lordship had been injured..."

"Good God!" interrupted Barrymore.

"He was taken to the Marylebone, where I interviewed him later."

"Is he badly hurt?"

"No, I'm pleased to say that his injuries appear to be superficial and the Doctor informed me that his Lordship would be discharged from hospital this morning."

"That's very re-assuring" said Barrymore.

"Now then, sir, it's obvious that Lord Mortlake has not been in touch with you..."

"No he hasn't, Inspector."

"Have you any idea where he may have gone?"

"Is he missing again?"

"Yes, he left the hospital and has not arrived at his home in Connaught Square" replied Hadley.

"Well, perhaps he's gone to his club" said Barrymore.

"That's what I told the Pinkerton Agents this morning..."

"What!"

"Mr Riley and his Agents are very keen to talk to his Lordship about the death of Lady Mortlake..."

"I trust that these brash Americans are not hounding my client!" interrupted Barrymore.

"I couldn't possibly say, sir, other than that they are looking for him as we speak" replied Hadley.

"That man Riley is so undignified, I read in the Times today that he has offered a preposterous reward of half a million dollars for information leading to an arrest, which is nonsense because you have already got the culprits in custody."

"We did have, sir, but unfortunately they escaped yesterday..."

"Good God, Inspector! How did that happen?"

"An unforeseen accident involving a brewer's dray and the prison wagon on Ludgate Hill, sir" replied Hadley.

"What are you doing about recapturing them, Inspector?"

"Everything that can be done is being done, I assure you, sir."

"I do hope so, otherwise we could all be murdered in our

beds!"

"That's highly unlikely, sir, now if Lord Mortlake contacts you please let him know that I wish to speak to him urgently as I believe that he may be in grave danger of being kidnapped again" said Hadley.

"Oh dear God, I hope not because we can't afford to pay another ransom!" exclaimed the terrified solicitor.

The detectives returned to the Yard where a message had arrived from Inspector West informing Hadley that so far, there had been no sightings of Winters or Kelly, either at Holcot Manor or the train station.

"Where have they all gone, Sergeant?"

"It's a mystery to me, sir."

"Those two and now Mortlake, I wonder who's next?" said Hadley as Jenkins entered the office.

"Chief Inspector Bell would like to see you immediately, sir."

"Right, Mr Jenkins" said Hadley as he raised his eyebrows before following the clerk out of the office.

Hadley noted that the Chief looked decidedly angry as he looked up from his desk and waved a piece of paper.

"I've just received a note from Mr Elliot Carter, assistant to Mr Riley and it says 'Chief Inspector Bell, following the meeting of our Pinkerton Agents with Inspector Hadley this morning, they have been unable to locate Lord Mortlake at the Dreyfus Club as the Inspector suggested and are now anxious to report Lord Mortlake as a missing person so that the Metropolitan police can use their manpower to trace him. Please advise Mr Riley at the Savoy on the progress of the search as soon as possible. Yours etc, Elliot Carter'." There was a deathly hush as Bell glared at Hadley before he asked "well, Hadley, what have you to say for yourself?"

"Only that the Agents came to my office and..."

"Never mind where you met them! I distinctly remember telling you not to get involved with these damned Americans!"

"They came to my office, sir!"

"Well you should have politely told them to bugger off!" replied Bell angrily.

"That didn't seem appropriate, sir."

"Hadley, we are in deep trouble with this, I mean, he talks of police manpower, my God, where do you think we can get that from when we are stretched to bloody breaking point?"

"I don't know, sir."

"I'll have to tell the Commissioner and I don't know what he will say."

"Could you delay that, sir, whilst I try and find Mortlake?"

"Do you think you can?"

"It's possible, sir."

"What makes you think that?"

"I'm sure he called upon Miss Jarvis in Regent Street this morning and provided he hasn't run away with her, she's bound to return home sometime today and she'll know where he is" said Hadley.

"Alright, I'll delay it until tomorrow morning."

"Thank you, sir."

"It's her brother who is employed by the Swiss Bank, is that correct?"

"Yes, sir, and he's expected back from Geneva tomorrow so I will be calling on him" replied Hadley.

"Good, we might find out something about the ransom and who was the master mind behind the kidnap" said Bell.

"Yes, sir."

"Have you any progress to report in the investigation of the Wells murder at the Savoy, Hadley?"

"No, not yet, sir."

"Well keep trying."

"I will, sir."

"And stay away from these Americans!"

"Right, sir."

"I mean it, Hadley."

As soon as Hadley returned to his office he ordered a pot of tea and told Cooper what Bell had said.

"So are we going to wait outside Miss Jarvis' house for Lord Mortlake, sir?"

"We'll call first to see if she has returned and if not, we'll have to wait, because I think it's our only chance of finding him before the morning" replied Hadley.

"It looks like a long night ahead then, sir."

"I hope not, Sergeant."

The detectives hailed a cab and went straight to Regents Street where the maid opened the door to them.

"Is Miss Jarvis at home?" asked Hadley.

"Yes, sir, who shall I say is calling?" she replied and the detectives breathed a sigh of relief.

"Inspector Hadley and Sergeant Cooper."

"Please come in and wait if you would, sir."

They entered the hallway and waited only for a few minutes before they were invited in to the drawing room.

"Inspector Hadley, how good of you to call" said Madeleine Jarvis as she rose to meet them.

"My pleasure, Miss."

"Please be seated, would you like some tea?"

"No thank you."

"As you wish, now how can I help you?" she asked.

"Have you seen Lord Mortlake today?" asked Hadley.

"Yes, Inspector, I have."

"Do you know where he is now, Miss?"

"Yes, he's probably on the train" she replied.

"To Northampton?"

"No, Dover, Inspector."

"Dover, Miss?"

"Yes, he's gone to Geneva, Inspector."

"Geneva?"

"Yes" she replied with a smile.

"Do you know why, Miss?" asked Hadley in alarm.

"He told me that he believed that his life was in grave danger and he wanted to get away from London for a while."

"Do you know his address in Geneva?"

"No, Inspector, he said he would write and let me know as soon as he had settled somewhere safe" she replied.

"Thank you, Miss Jarvis, you have been very helpful."

"Is that all, Inspector?"

"For the time being, Miss."

The detectives left the house immediately and hailed a cab.

"Let's get back to the Yard Sergeant, and telegraph the Dover police, I just hope that we can stop him before he boards the ferry to Calais!"

CHAPTER 16

As soon as Hadley arrived at the Yard he sent a telegraph message to the Dover police giving all the details of the case and requesting the arrest of Lord Mortlake. He then went to report to Chief Inspector Bell who, after hearing the news, paced up and down his office like a demented, caged animal.

"I'll have to inform the Commissioner straight away, Hadley, I've no choice in the matter" he said as he paused mid-way along his worn carpet to glare at Hadley.

"Yes, sir, I understand."

"I know that he will be beside himself with anger over all this."

"I'm sure, sir."

"He'll ask me to explain how this investigation has become confused and completely out of control, Hadley" said Bell as he started to pace once again.

"Yes, sir."

"And what am I to tell him?"

"I really don't know, sir."

"You'd better stay in your office for the rest of the day in case the Commissioner wants to talk to you."

"I had already planned to wait for news from Northampton and Dover, sir" replied Hadley.

"Good, it will give you an opportunity to catch up on your paperwork instead of gadding about round London as usual."

"It will indeed, sir."

"And write me a full report on everything that has transpired since you interviewed Lord Mortlake at the hospital."

"Yes, sir."

"Well, that's all for the moment, Hadley."

"Very good, sir."

"I'll now have to go and face the wrath of the Commissioner, God help me!"

Hadley sat behind his desk trying to gather his thoughts for a moment when Cooper asked "what I don't understand, sir, is that if Lord Mortlake planned to leave London for Geneva, why would he arrange to pick up Iris and Jane on Saturday night?" asked

Cooper.

"Change of plan, Sergeant, I think he's afraid of Riley and his Agents, and they're getting close to him."

"But even so, sir."

"I'm sure that he's somehow involved with his own kidnap and he's gone to Geneva to get his hands on the ransom money, which will do very nicely until Lady Mortlake's inheritance is settled by the court" said Hadley.

"Do you think he'll get her fortune, sir?"

"Yes, I'm sure the court will find in his favour despite what Mr Riley tries to do to stop it."

"I suppose he'll return from Geneva after everything has died down and Mr Riley has gone back to New York, sir."

"That's exactly what will happen, Sergeant, unless our colleagues at Dover can arrest him before he boards the ferry."

"We can only wait and hope, sir."

The detectives spent the afternoon writing reports and re-examining the facts surrounding the murders of the two women and the kidnap of Lord Mortlake. It was five o'clock when a telegraph message arrived from Inspector Bagley at Dover. Hadley read it to Cooper "following up your request to arrest Lord Mortlake, I have to report that I and several officers went immediately to the ferry port to search for him. Unfortunately a ferry boat left the harbour for Calais as we arrived and as there has been no sighting of Mortlake since, I have to assume that we arrived too late to apprehend him. Please advise if you require further police surveillance or if we may stand down. Regards, Inspector Bagley"

"He's slipped the net, sir."

"It seems so, Sergeant" said Hadley wearily.

"What do you plan to do now, sir?"

"Tell the Chief Inspector that Mortlake has escaped, then tomorrow we'll see if Mr Robert Jarvis has arrived back from Geneva and if he has, find out what he has to say for himself" replied Hadley as the telegraph clerk arrived with a message from Northampton.

Hadley opened it and read "no sign yet of either man but will continue surveillance at Holcot and the railway station until ten p.m. tonight when the last train arrives from London, Will

141

continue tomorrow at eight a.m. unless you advise otherwise. Regards, Inspector Peter West."

"Never rains but it pours, sir."

"That's so true, Sergeant."

Hadley went up to Chief Inspector Bell's office and informed him that Lord Mortlake had probably escaped to Geneva, if Madeleine Jarvis was telling the truth.

"Well I'm afraid we can't do much about Mortlake now, so we'll just have to concentrate on catching Winters and Kelly" said Bell in a resigned tone.

"Yes, sir" nodded Hadley.

"Hopefully that'll satisfy Riley and he can sail away to America and leave us in peace" said Bell.

"I doubt if he will do that, sir."

"We all live in hope, especially me, Hadley."

"I'm sure, sir."

"I just hope that you find the killers of Lady Mortlake and Miss Wells before the Commissioner dismisses me and has a seizure" said Bell in an anxious tone.

"I'm confident that will not happen, sir" said Hadley with a smile.

Hadley returned home late and was decidedly worried about the developments of the day. He thought long and hard about the case and was sure in his own mind that Mortlake was linked, if not directly responsible, for his wife's murder and that of Ann Wells. He eventually went to bed and spent a restless night despite Alice's attempts to comfort him.

The next morning was bright and Hadley felt more optimistic about the day ahead as he left his home and hailed a cab to Scotland Yard.

When arrived in the office he spent some time with Cooper planning the day and after a pot of tea they set off to the Banque Suisse Credit in Threadneedle Street, where they were shown up to Mr Moncrieff's office without delay. With an anxious look on his face, Moncrieff invited them to be seated.

"Has Mr Robert Jarvis arrived back from Geneva, sir?" asked

Hadley.

"Yes, Inspector, he is in his office at the moment" replied Moncrieff.

"I'm glad to hear it, sir."

"I presume you wish to speak to him?"

"Yes, in private, sir."

"I'm a little anxious about that, Inspector."

"Why, sir?"

"Because of any implications in your questioning and his answers that may reflect badly on the reputation of the Bank, Inspector" he replied.

"You need not be concerned, sir."

"But I am and so are my fellow directors, Inspector."

"Very well, sir, then if you understand clearly that the conversation with Mr Jarvis must remain strictly confidential…"

"Yes, yes, of course, Inspector" nodded Moncrieff pleased that he had been able to force Hadley's agreement.

"Before we speak to Mr Jarvis, may I ask if your Head Office have released details of the account in Geneva where the ransom for Lord Mortlake was deposited?"

"Yes, Inspector, and I must say that your request has caused much disquiet in Geneva" replied Moncrieff.

"I'm sorry about that, sir, but I'm sure that the powers that be in Geneva will get over it in due course" said Hadley.

"Your cavalier attitude to this grave matter is not welcome, Inspector!"

"Now listen to me, Mr Moncrieff, I'm investigating the murders of two women and the kidnap of a Lord of the realm, so that makes any 'disquiet' in Geneva of little importance to me!"

"Really, Inspector!"

"And if you have any complaints regarding me or my investigation, please take the matter up with the Commissioner himself, who, I might add, is actively commanding the investigation day by day!" said Hadley as he watched Moncrieff's jaw drop. There was a few moments silence before Hadley asked "so may I have the details, sir?"

"Yes, yes, of course, Inspector, I have them here" replied the anxious Banker as he shuffled through a small pile of folders. He opened one and then announced "the account in Geneva is held by an Englishman, Mr Mortimer Holcot of 36, Regents Street, London."

"That's very interesting, sir" replied Hadley.

"Presumably you will be speaking to him as part of your investigation?"

"You may rest assured, sir" replied Hadley.

"I would urge you to keep this information confidential and not cause Mr Holcot any un-necessary distress, as he is a customer of the Bank and we are duty bound to protect our customers" said Moncrieff.

"I'm sure you are, sir."

"Your co-operation is welcome, Inspector."

"Will you please send for Mr Jarvis now, sir?"

"Yes, Inspector."

Robert Jarvis looked tired and a little pale as he was introduced to the detectives before being invited to sit.

"Mr Jarvis, Inspector Hadley wishes to ask you some questions as part of his investigation into the kidnap of Lord Mortlake and the murder of his wife" said Moncrieff.

"Yes, sir" nodded Jarvis.

"Please help him all you can and be assured that I am here to support you and I give you permission to divulge any Bank information that he may require" said Moncrieff.

"Very good, sir" replied Jarvis.

"Thank you, Mr Moncrieff" said Hadley and the Banker smiled then gave a little nod.

"How can I help, Inspector?" asked Jarvis.

"Have you recently opened an account in Geneva for a Mr Holcot of Regents Street?" asked Hadley and he watched Jarvis turn very pale. There was silence as he tried to compose himself then Jarvis looked at Moncrieff and asked "surely that is confidential information, sir, and I am not at liberty to answer."

"You may answer, Mr Jarvis" replied Moncrieff.

"Well, I, er, er, I'll have to consult my records…" he began.

"Come, come, Mr Jarvis you must remember Mr Holcot, he has the same address in Regent Street as your parents and your sister Madeleine" interrupted Hadley and he watched as Jarvis went deathly pale and Moncrieff's jaw dropped once again.

"Yes, I do remember" he whispered.

"You'd better explain yourself, Jarvis!" exclaimed Moncrieff.

"Yes, please do" said Hadley with a curious smile. They all waited whilst Robert Jarvis gathered his thoughts and composed himself.

"Mr Holcot is a close friend of my family…" he began.

"Also known as Lord Mortlake if I'm not mistaken" interrupted Hadley and Jarvis looked terrified then nodded.

"Good God Almighty!" exclaimed Moncrieff.

"I'm sorry, sir, I was only trying to help him and my sister begged me to do it" said Jarvis.

"Go on, Mr Jarvis" said Hadley.

"I opened the account for him because he said he had some money which he wished to divert away from tax liability here…"

"And you thought that was a proper thing to do, Jarvis?" demanded Moncrieff.

"I didn't think it would do any harm, sir."

"You're a disgrace to yourself and the Bank, make no mistake you will be dismissed from your post as soon as the investigations into this scandalous affair have been completed" said Moncrieff forcefully and Jarvis bowed his head.

"Did you open the account here or in Geneva?" asked Hadley.

"In Geneva, Inspector."

"When was that?"

"I did it on my last trip in March" Jarvis replied.

"About two months ago" said Hadley.

"Yes, Inspector."

"Did you open the account with a payment?"

"Yes, one hundred pounds."

"Which Lord Mortlake gave you?"

"He gave me fifty and my sister gave me the rest" Jarvis replied.

"What a disgrace!" exclaimed Moncrieff.

"Mr Jarvis are you complicit in the hoax kidnap of Lord Mortlake?" asked Hadley.

"No, Inspector, I knew nothing of it until I read it in the papers" replied Jarvis forcefully.

"Is that really the truth, sir?"

"Oh, my God, you must believe me, Inspector" Jarvis wailed.

"I'll leave my option open on that for the time being but I warn you that you may face arrest in due course" said Hadley.

"The absolute disgrace of it all, Geneva will be inconsolable when they learn of what has been going on here in London" said Moncrieff and Jarvis looked as if he was about to cry.

"I need not detain you any longer, gentlemen, you have both been very helpful in my investigations" said Hadley as he stood up to leave.

"Oh, Inspector, I'm glad…" began Moncrieff, slightly startled.

"Good day to you" said Hadley as he left the office, followed by Cooper.

The detectives hurried to 36, Regent Street, where they were admitted into the presence of Madeleine Jarvis, who was surprised to see them. After pleasantries Hadley said "I've just come from a meeting with your brother Robert, at the Banque Suisse Credit, and he informs me that you gave him fifty pounds to open an account for Lord Mortlake in Geneva, can you confirm that, Miss?"

On hearing that, Madeleine went pale before she managed to stammer "yes, Inspector, that is so."

"Are you complicit in the hoax kidnap of Lord Mortlake, Miss?"

"No, no, Inspector, of course not, I knew nothing of the kidnap until I read it in the papers" she replied.

"Do you intend to join Lord Mortlake in Geneva, Miss?"

"No, well that is…"

"Yes, Miss?" asked Hadley as he realised that she was uncertain.

"Perhaps, that is if Andrew is forced by circumstances to remain there for a while" she replied.

"What circumstances are those, Miss?"

"I don't know, Inspector, he hasn't told me" she replied in an agitated tone.

"How will you know when to join him?"

"Andrew has promised to write as soon as he is settled somewhere safe" she replied.

"Do your parents know of all this?"

"No, Inspector, and I beg you to keep this conversation

confidential" she replied.

"I can't promise you anything, Miss, and I have already advised your brother that he may face arrest and you may do so too."

"Oh my God" she whispered.

"I advise you, Miss Jarvis, for your own good to remain here at home for the time being whilst I conduct further inquiries into this serious matter."

"Yes, Inspector, I will" she whispered.

The detectives left Regent Street and Hadley decided to take an early lunch, so they took a cab to the Crown Inn in the Strand. The bar was quite busy and they had to wait to be served with their stout followed by pork pies with pickles. They sat and discussed the morning's developments and Hadley felt that at last the investigation was gathering momentum.

On arrival back in the office George presented Hadley with a telegraph message from Inspector Dunton in Liverpool. He read it out aloud "pleased to inform you that Patrick Kelly was arrested this morning as he attempted to board the ferry to Belfast. I wait your instructions, yours etc, Inspector Dunton."

"That's the news we've been hoping for, sir" said Cooper.

"Indeed it is, Sergeant, please ask George to make a pot of tea whilst I go and inform the Chief Inspector!"

Bell's face wrinkled into a relieved grin as Hadley told him the good news.

"Thank God for that, Hadley."

"Yes, indeed, sir."

"I'll tell the Commissioner whilst you get away up to Liverpool and bring the blackguard back!"

"Right, sir."

"And don't hold back when you question him about Winters, because he's sure to know where that murderer is hiding."

"I won't, sir."

"If you leave now you will be back first thing tomorrow with Kelly, then hopefully we'll find Winters" said Bell in a triumphant tone.

147

CHAPTER 17

Hadley telegraphed Inspector Dunton, informing him that he and Cooper were on their way, before they left the Yard for Kings Cross station. They caught the five o'clock express and arrived in Liverpool, where Dunton was waiting for them.

"I can't thank you enough for arresting Kelly, you've really saved my bacon, Edward" said Hadley as he shook hands with Dunton at the ticket barrier.

"Glad to be of service, Jim, now come back to the station and tell me everything."

Over a cup of tea Hadley explained the unforeseen accident that allowed Kelly and Winters to escape and Dunton was sympathetic when Hadley told him of the American involvement.

"Everything is so political today, Jim, I can't be doing with it all."

"I agree."

"Roll on my retirement, that's what I say" said Dunton.

"Sometimes I do wonder if it is all worth it" said Hadley.

"I share your thoughts, Jim, now tell me, do you want to interview Kelly tonight or leave it until the morning?" asked Dunton.

"It's late now so I'll leave it and question him on the train to London, Edward."

"Very good, Jim."

Inspector Dunton had booked two rooms for the detectives in a small but comfortable lodging house close by the police station. By eight o'clock the next morning they were back at the station and were interviewing Kelly briefly before they were due to catch the nine o'clock express to London.

"I can't believe what's happened to me, sir, it's like a terrible nightmare" said Kelly.

"I'm sure it is" said Hadley.

"I never killed her, you must believe that, sir" he pleaded.

"I am under orders, direct from the Commissioner to arrest you and bring you before a magistrate charged with Lady Mortlake's murder" replied Hadley.

148

"I know that, sir, but I think you believe that I never killed the sweet lady" said Kelly.

"If evidence comes to light that proves your innocence, Kelly, I will be pleased."

"Bless you, sir, and I hope that you find something soon so I can get home to see my dying mother."

"So do I Kelly, now after your escape from the prison wagon, did you and Winters stay together?"

"Yes, sir, for a while, I was anxious to get home and Winters just wanted to get away somewhere" replied Kelly.

"Do you know where he's gone?"

"No, sir, after we took a dog cart we travelled to Aylesbury and stayed the night with a friend of his, then he went off the next morning with the cart, he didn't say where he was going" replied Kelly.

"He left you stranded?"

"Yes, sir, and when I told his friend that I wanted to get home to Ireland to see my mother, he lent me the money for my fare."

"He was trusting as well as generous then?" said Hadley.

"Yes, sir, he was."

"I presume you caught a train from Aylesbury to Liverpool?"

"I did, sir, and was arrested as I tried to board the ferry."

"Well, we can discuss everything in detail on the journey to London, Kelly."

"I'm sure we can, sir."

On the return journey to Kings Cross, Kelly answered every question that Hadley put to him and never stopped talking. Cooper struggled to keep up as he made copious notes of the groom's replies. Hadley was convinced that the man was innocent of the murder of Lady Mortlake and was sure that Winters had carried out the dreadful deed. He suspected that Winters had returned to Holcot and although he asked Kelly repeatedly, he was unable to confirm this.

On arrival at the Yard, Kelly was taken to custody and Hadley went straight up to Bell's office to report in detail.

"I'm relieved you're back with him, Hadley" said Bell with a grin.

"So am I, sir."

"Now we just have to find Winters."

"Yes, sir."

"Did Kelly tell you where he had gone?"

"No, sir, they parted company at Aylesbury and Winters went off in the stolen dog cart leaving Kelly with a friend" replied Hadley.

"Get all the details, Hadley."

"I already have them, sir."

"Good, because Mr Riley and his Agents arrived half an hour ago and are with the Commissioner now" said Bell.

"That's not good, sir" said Hadley with a sigh.

"No, it isn't, so I suggest we get up to the Commissioner's office, give him the news that you're back with Kelly and pour some oil on troubled waters."

When they entered the Commissioner's office he looked relieved to see Hadley, which was in contrast to Mr Riley, the Agents, Elliot Carter and Lone Eagle.

"I'm sorry to disturb you, sir, but I thought you should know immediately that Inspector Hadley has arrested Kelly and he is now in custody down stairs" announced Bell with a smile.

"I'm pleased to hear it, Chief Inspector" said the Commissioner and turning to Riley, he added "so you see Mr Riley, in spite of what you say about our policing methods, we do get results."

"I'm not too impressed, Commissioner, there's still one of the killers loose as well as the man behind it all, so in my book, one out of three sure 'aint good enough for me!" replied Riley angrily.

"Well, er, er…" stammered the Commissioner.

"You're too damned well easily satisfied and complacent, that's why my Agents are here" interrupted Riley.

"I can assure you, sir, that we…"

"You can't assure me of anything, Commissioner, and tomorrow we are going up to Holcot and we'll tear the damned place apart and everyone in it until we get some answers, you may depend on it!" exclaimed Riley now red faced with anger.

"I must advise you, sir, to be very careful and not take the law into your own hands as I will not hesitate to arrest you and your Agents, if you transgress in any way" replied the Commissioner.

"Don't you ever threaten me with arrest sir, I am an American citizen with all the right connections; I could have you replaced at the drop of my hat!"

"That might be possible in America but I would remind you that you are in Queen Victoria's England and we obey the law here, sir!" There followed a deathly silence for some moments before Riley gave a half smile then nodded and said "very well Commissioner, I'll make sure that my Agents do nothing that disturbs your quaint old fashioned ways."

"I'm obliged to you, Mr Riley" replied the relieved Commissioner.

"Before I go today, I want to see this man who's accused of my daughter's murder" said Riley.

"I'm afraid that's not possible, sir" replied the Commissioner.

"Why not?" asked Riley.

"Well, because he's been remanded in custody pending his appearance at Bow Street Magistrates…"

"If you've got him under lock and key how can it hurt to see him?" interrupted Riley.

"It's not ethical…"

"To hell with ethics, I want to talk to the man!" interrupted Riley angrily and the Commissioner blushed and gave in as he realised that Riley would not be content.

"Can we organise that Chief Inspector?" asked the Commissioner wearily.

"Of course, sir" replied Bell.

"Then if you would like to accompany Chief Inspector Bell down to custody, Mr Riley, he will arrange for you to see Kelly" said the Commissioner.

"Thank you" said Riley as he stood up.

"Perhaps you other gentlemen would care to wait in the Chief Inspector's office whilst Mr Riley is down in custody?" mused the Commissioner.

"Yes, they can wait there but Lone Eagle comes with me" said Riley as Bell's face clouded with apprehension.

"Why do you require your Red Indian gentleman to go with you, Mr Riley?" asked the Commissioner.

"Because he knows instinctively when a man is telling lies and I want to make sure that I hear the truth from Kelly" replied Riley in a firm tone.

"I see" said the Commissioner as Riley followed by Lone Eagle and the others left the office escorted by Bell and Hadley. As they descended the stairs, Bell said to Hadley in a whisper "get Cooper up to my office to keep an eye on this lot whilst we're in Custody."

Hadley nodded and went to his office as Bell guided the party of Americans into his. When everything had been arranged, Bell and Hadley accompanied Riley and Lone Eagle down to custody where Kelly was brought from his cell into an interview room. He looked nervous as he sat down opposite Riley and with Lone Eagle standing behind his master Hadley was not surprised that the man looked nervous.

"This gentleman is Mr Riley, and he is the father of Lady Mortlake" said Bell.

"I recognise you, sir" said Kelly as he smiled at Riley.

"How do you know me?" asked Riley.

"From photographs that your daughter showed me, sir" he replied.

"Why should she do that?"

"She often talked of her home in New York and said how she missed you and her mother, sir" replied Kelly and Riley lowered his head and looked down at his clasped hands resting on the table.

"Did she now" whispered Riley.

"Yes, sir." There followed a few moments of silence whilst Riley composed himself before he said in a firm tone "I'm going to ask you a direct question Kelly, and I want a truthful answer."

"Yes, sir."

"Did you murder my daughter?"

"No, sir, I did not!" he replied instantly.

"Do you know who did?"

"I think Winters killed her, sir."

"Anyone else involved?"

"Not in the actual killing, sir."

"Explain what you mean, Kelly."

"I think that she was hated by several people at Holcot, sir, and I'm sure that if Winters wasn't carrying out orders to do it, he knew that he would be protected if he did, if you see what I mean, sir."

"I'm not sure I do, but you could be telling me all this to shift the blame from yourself" said Riley.

"Oh, no, sir, not at all, I thought the world of your daughter and Miss Wells. They were kindness itself to me and they both loved horses, as I do."

"Nevertheless, Kelly…"

"Let me tell you, sir" he interrupted.

"Go on."

"I knew that her Ladyship was very unhappy in her marriage…"

"How did you know that?" interrupted Riley.

"Because she told me, sir, she said that she planned to leave Holcot with Miss Wells and return to America where she intended to breed thoroughbred horses on a ranch somewhere, I think she said in Kentucky."

"My God" whispered Riley.

"And she said that when she had everything arranged, she would send for me to go out to Kentucky and work for her as her head groom and manager, she said that she thought I had a good eye for horses" said Kelly and Riley looked stunned at what he had said.

"Did Lord Mortlake know about all this?"

"I don't know, sir, but all I can say to you is this, your daughter was giving me the chance to go to America and breed horses, so ask yourself why would I want to kill a lovely, kind lady who was offering me, a poor lad from Ireland, the golden chance of a lifetime? I tell you Mr Riley, I would have given my own life to save hers!" When Riley heard that, tears began to run down his cheeks and he whispered "I do believe you're telling me the truth, Mr Kelly."

"So when they hang me, they're hanging the wrong man for sure" said Kelly.

"I'm sure they won't hang you and I'll help you all I can" said Riley.

"Don't waste your time on me, sir, I tell you they plan to hang me in any case because the English hate the Irish, there's no doubt about it" said Kelly firmly.

"You're not dead yet, Mr Kelly" said Riley.

"It's only a matter of time to be sure, sir" came the swift reply.

Riley remained silent for some while thinking about what Kelly had said to him.

"I think I've heard enough, Mr Kelly, so thank you for your time" said Riley as he stood up to leave.

"I'm glad I've had the chance to tell you to your face that I didn't kill your daughter and how kind she was to me, sir" said Kelly and Riley nodded his thanks as he left the room.

The party returned to Hadley's office where Riley sat down and looked at Lone Eagle for a moment before he asked him "what do you think?"

"Horse man Kelly tells you truth" the Indian replied.

"Are you as sure as I hope I am?"

"Yes, it is plain to see that he cared for Nancy daughter and would have protected her" replied Lone Eagle.

"Then if that's what you think, I believe him to be innocent" said Riley.

"This is good" nodded the Indian.

"Chief Inspector, I want you to release Kelly and I'll stand surety for him whatever the cost" said Riley.

"I'm afraid that's impossible, sir" replied Bell hastily.

"Nothing is impossible in my book, Chief Inspector" replied Riley.

"I'm sure the Commissioner won't allow it, sir."

"Never mind about him, I'll guarantee that Kelly doesn't escape…"

"And how can you guarantee that, sir?" asked Bell firmly.

"I'll get Lone Eagle to look after him night and day, Chief Inspector" said Riley with a smile.

"With all due respect…"

"Save your respect, I can promise you that there is no man alive who can escape from Lone Eagle" said Riley and the Indian beamed with pride.

"That's your opinion, sir."

"He's the son of a Cheyenne Chief as well as the greatest and fastest tracker imaginable and I can assure you he's deadly quick with that hunting knife of his, that's why he became my personal scout and bodyguard when I built my railroad across America" said Riley.

"His skills may be entirely suitable for the plains of America but hardly proper and acceptable in England, sir" replied Bell.

"Listen to me, Chief Inspector, I think that Kelly can help me find Winters and when we have him, we'll find the son of a bitch who planned the murder of my daughter!"

"You may believe that…"

"I do, Chief Inspector, now fix it will you?"

"I can't promise anything, sir."

"Does your answer mean I've got to spend more of my precious time arguing with that pompous fat arse upstairs?" asked Riley angrily as Hadley lowered his head to hide his smile.

"Your remarks are becoming offensive, sir" replied Bell, now red faced with indignation.

"I'm sure that you'll get over it in time, Chief Inspector…"

"Really, sir, you go too far!"

"That's how I get results" said Riley with a grin.

"I'll ask the Commissioner if he will agree to bail prior to Kelly's appearance before the Bow Street Magistrates" said Bell in a resigned tone.

"That's fine, and be sure to tell him that I'll post any amount of money as surety, Chief Inspector."

"I will, sir, you may rest assured" replied Bell curtly.

"It's getting late so I'm going back to the Savoy now with my people and you can send word to me when Kelly is free, then I'll send Lone Eagle for him with the surety, Chief Inspector."

"Very good, sir."

"So I wish you good afternoon, gentlemen, and don't let my little intrusion into your 'proper world' stop you from searching for Winters" said Riley with a smile.

"Nothing will deter us from our duty, I can assure you, sir!" said Bell angrily.

"That's good, now we're off up to Holcot tomorrow and I am willing to bet that we find Winters before you do, Chief Inspector."

"I doubt it, sir."

"Let's go and find the others Lone Eagle, we've work to do" said Riley as he stood up and with a nod at the policemen he left Hadley's office followed by the Indian. Bell looked at Hadley for a few moments and said "the nerve of that bloody American, it fair takes one's breath away!"

"It does indeed, sir."

"God knows what I'm going to say to the Commissioner, Hadley."

"You'll have to use all your powers of persuasion, sir."

"Yes I will, but thank God, I'm very good at persuading people of importance, Hadley."

"You are, sir."

"And my paperwork is always very precise."

"It is, sir."

"The Commissioner also says that my man management is very good."

"He's right, sir" said Hadley trying not to smile.

"As he always is, Inspector."

"Of course, sir."

"That's why he is the Commissioner."

"Yes, sir."

"Sometimes I do thank God for my humility" said Bell in a vacant tone.

"That's very wise, sir" replied Hadley as he tried but failed to hide a wry smile.

"Now, I think you had better get up to Holcot before Riley arrives there with his entourage, they're bound to wreak havoc and upset everyone and that could well affect our lines of inquiry."

"Do you want me to go tonight, sir?"

"No, go first thing tomorrow morning, we must save on hotel expenses, Hadley."

"Yes, of course, sir."

"Make every attempt to find Winters before Riley does."

"You think he may be there, sir?"

"Possibly, but if he isn't then you can be certain that someone at the Manor will know where he is. Make sure you are armed when you go, Hadley, I think Winters could be very dangerous when cornered."

"Very good, sir."

"Now I'll go and try and persuade the Commissioner to free Kelly."

When Cooper returned to the office, Hadley told him what had transpired before he sent a telegraph message to Inspector West informing him of their impending arrival the next day. Then the detectives went down to the armoury and signed out two .45 calibre revolvers and twenty four rounds of ammunition before they went home for the night.

CHAPTER 18

The detectives arrived in Northampton at ten o'clock the next morning and made their way to the police station where they were shown up to Inspector West's office. Over tea, Hadley explained what had happened in London and plans were made to go immediately to Holcot Manor and search for Winters.

"I think it advisable to bring a sergeant and a constable, just in case we find Winters and he becomes violent" said West.

"Thank you, Peter, although we are armed I would appreciate the extra help in the search" replied Hadley.

"You're welcome Jim. I must say that I doubt if he is there, my men have had the road to Holcot under surveillance ever since I received your message" said West.

"I'm sure you have, but he's a wily old fox and he knows that we are looking for him, so if he is there, you can be sure that he would have come across country to the Manor" replied Hadley.

"That's always a possibility."

The five policemen set off in the warm June sunshine to Holcot Manor. Hadley wondered how long he had to find Winters before the Americans arrived on the scene. He thought that the Commissioner might have objected to Kelly's release on bail and that could have held Riley and his entourage in London for the time being, so each moment was precious to him. When they arrived at the Manor, Barton opened the door and was taken aback at the sight of the number of policemen.

"Good morning, gentlemen, can I help you?"

"Good morning, Mr Barton, would you inform her ladyship that we are here and wish to see her?" asked Hadley.

"I will, sir, would you please come in and wait in the hall?"

"Thank you" replied Hadley and he strode past the butler into the gloomy hallway, followed by Cooper and the others. Barton disappeared into the door at the far end of the hall and re-appeared some moments later.

"Her Ladyship will see you now, Inspector, but only you, sir, she has requested that your colleagues remain here" said Barton with a gentle nod of his head. Hadley smiled and replied "very well, Mr Barton." The butler led Hadley into the drawing room where Lady Mortlake sat in her winged chair peering out of the window.

"Inspector Hadley, Milady" announced Barton as the old woman glanced up at Hadley.

"I'm surprised to see you again" she said curtly.

"Good morning, your ladyship" replied Hadley ignoring her remark.

"Well, what do you want now?"

"I'm anxious to trace Mr Winters" replied Hadley.

"Trace him? I thought you arrested him some time ago, Inspector" she said with disdain.

"Indeed we did, Milady, but due to an unforeseen accident he escaped custody along with your groom, Kelly" said Hadley

"An accident, what sort of accident?"

"There was a collision between the police vehicle carrying the prisoners and a brewer's dray, on the way to Bow Street Magistrates, Milady" replied Hadley.

"How very remiss, Inspector, I trust that no one was seriously hurt in the incident."

"One constable was taken to hospital, Milady, but as I said, both of them escaped, however, we have recaptured Kelly but Winters remains at large…"

"And you think he may have come back here?" she interrupted.

"Yes, Milady."

"Well you are mistaken, Inspector, I can tell you with absolute certainty that Winters is not here" she said firmly.

"I hear what you say, Milady, but I must insist that I interview all your servants and search the house and grounds…"

"You'll do no such thing, Inspector!" she interrupted angrily.

"Please do not make my duties any more difficult than they already are, Milady."

"I'm not interested in your duties, I assure you!"

"Milady, I and my officers will search with or without your permission as I have a warrant and if you allow us to proceed immediately it will save you from an even worse experience" said Hadley.

"And what do you mean by that, Inspector?"

"Sometime today, Mr Arthur Riley and his entourage will

arrive here from London and he will…"

"Riley, the American? My son's father-in-law is coming here?" she interrupted in a horrified tone.

"Yes, with his entourage which includes a Red Indian, Milady" replied Hadley with a mischievous smile.

"Oh, God no! Not Riley and a savage at Holcot!"

"I'm afraid so, Milady."

"Why are they coming?" she asked anxiously.

"To look for Winters, Milady."

"Can't you stop them?"

"Well only if I can find Winters before they arrive" replied Hadley.

"I've told you, he's not here but you must satisfy yourself of that fact before Riley gets here" she said anxiously.

"Thank you, Milady."

"Then you can tell Mr Riley that he has had a wasted journey so he may return to London straight away!"

"Indeed, Milady."

"I don't want Americans, especially savages, wandering about the place disturbing everybody, they're so uncouth you know" she said disparagingly

"I couldn't possibly comment, Milady."

"Quite so, you're only a policeman" she said in a condescending tone.

. "That is true. One last thing, Milady."

"Yes, what is it?"

"Do you know where Lord Mortlake is at present?"

"I imagine he is now at his London home in Connaught Square attending to important business matters, Inspector" she replied.

"I have been informed by a close friend of Lord Mortlake that he has in fact left the country and gone to Geneva" said Hadley.

"What nonsense, Inspector, I can assure you that if my son had decided to go abroad he would have informed me first" she replied in a dismissive tone.

"That's what I thought, Milady."

"Now I must not detain you, Inspector."

"No, Milady."

"Barton, gather all the servants in the kitchen and tell them that the Inspector wishes to question them" she said firmly.

"Very good, Milady" replied Barton with a slight nod.

"And tell Mrs Noakes to come and see me immediately before the Inspector speaks to the servants, Barton."

"Yes, Milady" said Barton before he left the room.

"So Inspector, if you would like to organise your men into a search party, you are at liberty to go where ever you wish in your fruitless search for Winters" she said.

"Thank you very much for your co-operation, Milady."

"I only give you permission in the hope that you will be satisfied and stop the Americans invading my home" she said.

"I will be mindful of that, Milady."

"Good. You may go now" she said as she returned her gaze to the window that over looked the untidy garden.

In the hallway Hadley gave his instructions to his colleagues.

"We have her ladyship's permission to search the place, so I suggest Peter that you take your men and cover the out-buildings whilst Cooper and I search the house."

"Very well, Jim."

"If Winters is here, let's hope we find him before the Americans arrive" Hadley smiled before he turned to make his way to the kitchen as West made for the front door. As the detectives crossed the hallway, Barton appeared from the corridor leading to the kitchen followed by Mrs Noakes. She gave them an icy stare followed by a nod of recognition as she flounced by.

"She's not too happy to see us, Sergeant" whispered Hadley as they made their way along the corridor and Cooper grinned.

Entering the kitchen, they found Mrs Chambers, the cook and Kate, the maid, already sitting at the long table. Hadley wished them 'good morning' and sat at the head of the table with Cooper by his side.

"We're just waiting for Mrs Noakes and Mr Barton to join us before I speak to you all" said Hadley.

"What about Mr Mathews and Mr Hopton?" asked Mrs Chambers.

"Who are they?" asked Hadley.

"Mr Mathews is the new grounds-man and Mr Hopton is the new groom, sir" replied Mrs Chambers.

"I'll speak to them later" replied Hadley as Barton appeared.

"Mrs Noakes will not be long, sir" said Barton as he sat at the opposite end of the table.

"Thank you, Mr Barton." It seemed an age of embarrassing silence before Mrs Noakes finally entered the kitchen and sat alongside Barton.

"As you may all know, Mr Winters and Mr Kelly have been arrested and charged with the murder of her Ladyship" said Hadley as he gazed at the stony faced servants.

"They didn't do it" said Mrs Noakes but Hadley ignored her remark and continued "due to an unfortunate accident on the way to the court, both men escaped from police custody, Mr Kelly was re-arrested but Mr Winters remains at large…"

"Good for him" said Mrs Noakes.

"We are here today to try and find him, so do any of you know where he might be hiding?" asked Hadley. They all looked at one another and slowly shook their heads.

"He's not here, Inspector, and I think it very unlikely that he would ever return to Holcot" said Mrs Noakes and Barton nodded in agreement.

"Why do you say that, Mrs Noakes?"

"Because he must know that the police are looking for him and Holcot is the most obvious place you would search, Inspector, so he's clever enough to stay well away" she replied.

"Do any of you know if he has friends or relatives locally?"

"He has no family and his only friends are seated at this table, Inspector" replied Mrs Noakes firmly.

"Is that your opinion too, Mr Barton?" asked Hadley.

"Oh, yes, sir, what Mrs Noakes says is quite right" replied the butler.

"Very well, if none of you have anything to add, I will begin my search of the house, Mr Barton, will you please accompany Sergeant Cooper and me?" Barton looked horrified and he glanced at Mrs Noakes, who gave a slight nod, before he stammered "yes, sir."

Barton gave the detectives a guided tour of the Manor, starting with the attics followed by the servant's quarters and finally the main rooms of the house. The whole place appeared melancholy and in need of restoration. The search failed to find any trace of Winters and Barton suggested that as he had his living quarters over the stables along with Kelly, it was hardly surprising that

162

there was no sign of him in the house. Hadley smiled and said "Mr Barton, when a fugitive is hiding from the police they frequently turn up in the most unexpected places, especially if someone is assisting them."

The detectives left the house and went in search of West and his men. They found them in the stables talking to a man Hadley did not recognise, he assumed it was the new groom, Mr Hopton. West introduced Hadley to the groom who confirmed that he had only started working there two days before and knew nothing of any relevance. The stables and all the out buildings had been searched to no avail and Hadley was disappointed at the outcome. As they made their way back to the house they heard the sound of an approaching coach and horses. Hadley feared that it was the Americans and he was right. The coach suddenly appeared from the long drive at some speed with Lone Eagle and Kelly sitting beside the driver. The Indian smiled as he caught sight of Hadley. The coach stopped by the Tudor entrance then Lone Eagle sprang down from his seat and opened the coach door for Mr Riley, Elliott Carter and the Agents. When they were all standing, gazing at the façade of the Manor, Hadley approached with the others.

"Good day, Mr Riley." The American turned and smiled and said "I guessed you would be here before me, Inspector, but no matter, I'm glad to see that you are as keen as I am to find Winters."

"You can be sure of that, sir, now might I have a word in private with you?"

"Certainly, Inspector" smiled Riley and he followed Hadley away from his entourage. The two men walked a short distance to the trees that lined the driveway and stood for a few moments whilst Riley gazed back at the house.

"It's exactly as my daughter described in her letters, a broken down pile of old bricks, God, why were we all fooled by that 'no good' man" he whispered.

"Because he's a person who has made an art out of deceiving people, sir" replied Hadley.

"You're right, Inspector, and it cost my lovely daughter and her friend their lives."

"I am truly sorry about that, sir" said Hadley.

"I believe you are" replied Riley.

"I have a daughter, sir, and I know how distraught I would be if anything happened to her."

"You have to be a doting father to understand, Inspector, and I think you do" replied Riley with a smile.

"Yes, sir."

"Now what do you want to talk to me about?"

"We've searched this place from top to bottom and there's no sign of Winters, sir" said Hadley.

"And so?"

"There's nothing for you and your Agents to do here, sir."

"Inspector, I've come all the way from America to find the killer of my daughter and this God forsaken place is top of my list to tear apart looking for answers!"

"I see, sir."

"I'm glad you do, because believe me, I'm going to leave no stone unturned!"

"Lady Mortlake and her servants will be as unhelpful and obstructive as you can imagine."

"Listen to me, they can have it the hard way or the easy way, the easy way is to tell me what I want to know, the hard way, well, we'd better not speak about that, but be assured Lone Eagle and my Agents have ways of persuading even the most reluctant people to talk!"

"I must remind you of what the Commissioner said about taking the law into your own hands, sir." Riley smiled and replied "thanks for reminding me, Inspector, I'll bear it in mind."

"I hope that you will, sir, because I do not want to take any action against you or your people" said Hadley.

"Are you threatening me with arrest, Inspector?"

"Yes, sir, if you break the law" replied Hadley and Riley laughed.

"I admire you Inspector, you're a man after my own heart."

"I'm pleased to hear it, sir" Hadley replied with a grin.

"Now if there's nothing more, Inspector, I'm going to go into this dusty old place with my boys and start asking questions that Lady Mortlake and her servants might find difficult to answer."

"You're free to carry on, sir."

"That's what I like to hear" said Riley with a smile. The

American turned away and walked towards the house, Hadley had noticed that Lone Eagle watched them closely all the time they were in conversation. When Riley joined his entourage he spoke for a few moments and then nodded to Carter who knocked at the front door. When Barton opened it the horror showed on his face at the sight of the Indian and Hadley smiled to himself as he made his way to his colleagues standing close by.

"Gentlemen, as you will have noticed, Kelly has been freed on bail to assist in the search for Winters and I think we'd better stay for a while just in case Mr Riley and his Agents get carried away with their investigations and go too far" said Hadley with a smile and they all nodded.

"We'll take another walk around the buildings in the meantime, Jim, just in case we missed something" said West.

"A good idea, Peter" replied Hadley. After West and his men had set off in the direction of the stables, Hadley said to Cooper "do you remember when we interviewed Mrs Noakes for the first time?"

"Yes, sir, I made notes and have them here" replied Cooper.

"Remind me, Sergeant, did she say that Lady Mortlake or Miss Wells had suggested that Lord Mortlake's mother should move out of the Manor and go and live in the old gate house?"

"I believe she did, sir, and I think it was probably Miss Wells who suggested it."

"Sergeant, I don't remember seeing a gate house when we drove in here, do you?"

"No, sir, I noticed that there are just gates at the entrance."

"That's what I think, so there must be another entrance to this place" said Hadley.

"And if there is, you'd like to search the old gate house, sir."

"Correct, Sergeant, I'm glad to see that you're following my thoughts more closely these days."

"I am indeed, sir" grinned Cooper.

"But don't follow them too closely!"

"Why not, sir?"

"Because you'll end up in serious trouble with either the Chief Inspector or the Commissioner!" replied Hadley and Cooper laughed out loud.

"Come on, Sergeant, let's make some inquiries about the old

gate house" said Hadley as he strode towards the front door of the Manor.

Barton opened the door and just raised his eyebrows but said nothing so Hadley asked "Mr Barton, can you tell me if there is another entrance to Holcot Manor?"

"There is, sir, but it hasn't been used for years and it is now all overgrown" replied Barton.

"Is there a gate house by this entrance?" asked Hadley and on hearing that Barton looked anxious.

"I believe so, sir."

"How can we get to it?" asked Hadley.

"It's nigh impossible, sir."

"Why is that?"

"As I said, it is so overgrown and the trees have made it an impenetrable obstacle" replied Barton.

"We're used overcoming obstacles, both natural and manmade" replied Hadley firmly.

"I don't advise you to go there, sir" said Barton anxiously.

"Why not?"

"There's nothing to see except an old ruined building, sir."

"Nevertheless, Mr Barton, I will see it, so please tell me how I get to it" said Hadley in an angry tone. Barton stepped back and his face went quite pale before he stammered "I'm not sure, sir, I've only been there once, when I first came to Holcot many years ago and I've forgotten where it is."

"Perhaps Mrs Noakes can tell us" said Hadley.

"Oh, she won't know, sir."

"I think Mrs Noakes does know, because she told me that it was suggested that Lady Mortlake should move there after Lord Mortlake came to Holcot with his wife"

"I know nothing, sir, nothing at all, you'll have to ask Mrs Noakes" he flustered and Hadley knew that the man was terrified.

"Very well, Mr Barton, please tell Mrs Noakes that I wish to speak to her right now!"

CHAPTER 19

As the detectives waited in the gloomy hallway for Mrs Noakes to appear Ed Morris wandered down the stairs and smiled when he saw Hadley.

"This is some old place, isn't it, Inspector?"

"It certainly is, Mr Morris."

"They say that Queen Elizabeth slept here one night, can you believe that?"

"Yes, I can and I expect she may have stayed more than one night."

"Is that so?" Morris asked as he reached the bottom of the stairs.

"It's more than likely" replied Hadley.

"It looks as if nothing been touched here since then" said Morris.

"You could be right, Mr Morris" replied Hadley with a smile as Charles Ford appeared at the top of the stairs and followed his companion down to the hall way.

"This place gives me the creeps" said Ford when he arrived.

"Yeah, it's got a kinda sad and lonely feel to it" nodded Morris as Mrs Noakes arrived in the hall followed by Barton. She glared at the gathering of detectives and turned to face Hadley with her eyes blazing with anger.

"What's this I hear about the old gate house?" she demanded and Hadley waited for some moments before he replied, which angered her even more so.

"I intend to search it, Mrs Noakes…"

"Whatever for?" she interrupted.

"I need to satisfy myself that Winters is not hiding there" replied Hadley.

"Well I can tell you for certain that he's not!"

"How can you be so sure Mrs Noakes?"

"Because you can't get to the place, it's all overgrown now and no one has been there for years" she replied.

"That makes it the very place to hide."

"I'm afraid you're wrong as usual, Inspector."

"I don't think so, Mrs Noakes" replied Hadley. She then turned to the Agents and asked "have you now finished disrupting the household looking for Winters?"

"Yes, Ma'am, we have, for the time being that is" replied Ford.

"For the time being? What's that supposed to mean?" she asked angrily but before either of them could reply to her, Hadley asked firmly "Mrs Noakes, where is the old gate house situated?" She glared at him and replied "it's miles away on the far side of the estate and I don't know how you get to it from here."

"Well, as a gate house it must obviously be close to a passing road, so I'd be obliged if would tell me what road it is on" persisted Hadley.

"I don't know, Inspector!"

"Then we'll have to drive round all the roads until we find it" said Hadley.

"That's unlikely" she retorted.

"Why is that, Mrs Noakes?"

"Because it's set way back from the road and as I've told you already, it's so overgrown that it is impossible to see" she replied. At that moment the sound of raised angry voices came from the drawing room followed by the door opening. Barton rushed towards the drawing room as Riley, Carter and Lone Eagle came out into the hall followed by Lady Mortlake who was shouting abusive language at them.

"Get out of my house you bloody Colonials!" she screamed and continued "I want you all out and that includes you Inspector!"

"Only when I'm ready to go, Milady" replied Hadley firmly.

"I will not endure this harassment any longer and I'm warning you all right now, get out of Holcot or I'll see to it that you'll all regret it!"

"Please calm yourself, Milady..." began Hadley.

"Don't you tell me to be calm, you insolent, impudent fellow you!" she exclaimed and before Hadley could reply, Mrs Noakes started on them all.

"You heard what Milady said, now get out and stay out!" she said, her eyes blazing with anger.

"Barton, show these dreadful people out of my house!" exclaimed Lady Mortlake.

"Very good, Milady, this way if you please gentlemen" said

Barton politely as he hurried towards the front door. There was a moments silence before Riley looked at Hadley who nodded and they all left the house.

When they had gathered outside Riley said "well, what do you make of that, Inspector?"

"I expected it, sir. I think we're getting close to the truth here and it's the reaction of desperate people with something to hide."

"Yeah, you could be right, Inspector, and I can tell you that the old woman went crazy when I told her that her son would not get a single penny of Nancy's money."

"I can believe that, sir" replied Hadley in a surprised tone.

"It's my daughter's inheritance they wanted, and not her, which breaks my heart" said Riley with a tear in his eye.

"I'm sure that's true, sir, and I'm very sorry" replied Hadley.

"Yeah, but I guess it's the way of the world, Inspector."

"I'm afraid it is, sir" said Hadley and the two men remained silent for a few moments, both deep in thought.

"So, what's next, Inspector?" asked Riley.

"I want to search the old gate house for Winters and Mrs Noakes is doing all she can to dissuade me, so I'm sure she knows that he's either still there or has been recently" said Hadley.

"Right, let's go find it" said Riley.

"Nobody seems to know where it is…"

"Kelly will know" interrupted Riley.

"That's true, and where is he?" asked Hadley slightly alarmed at his disappearance.

"He's gone to the stables to see the horses and talk to the new groom" replied Riley.

"I see" said Hadley in a concerned tone.

"Don't worry about him, Inspector, I told the Commissioner that I would keep him close and Lone Eagle is making sure that Kelly goes nowhere without my say so" smiled Riley.

"That's re-assuring, sir."

"I keep to my word, Inspector, now let's go find Kelly" said Riley and Hadley nodded.

The entourage found Kelly talking amiably to Hopton at the stable door and the two men stopped their conversation as soon as

Hadley and Riley approached.

"Morning, Mr Kelly."

"Morning, Inspector."

"It appears that as far as you're concerned Mr Riley is a very persuasive gentleman" said Hadley with a smile.

"Yes, sir, he is to be sure and I'm very grateful to him for my release" replied Kelly.

"You should be because it is not often that the Commissioner changes his mind about suspects in custody."

"I'm sure, sir."

"Well it's good you're here because you're the very man who can lead us to Winters."

"I'm not sure I can, sir and I've already told Mr Riley that" replied Kelly.

"That's true but I have confidence in you, Mr Kelly and I'm sure you'll think of something that will lead us to him" said Riley.

"Thank you, sir, but if you've searched the place and he's obviously not here, well I don't see how I can help" said Kelly.

"We haven't looked in the old gate house yet" said Hadley and Kelly's eyes widened when he heard that.

"Yes, sir, that would be a very good place to hide out, because nobody ever goes there!"

"Exactly, now do you know where it is?" asked Hadley eagerly.

"It's over the far side of the estate, sir, I'm not really sure where because I only went near the place when I first came to Holcot but I remember it's in a dense wood" replied Kelly.

"But you know roughly where" persisted Hadley.

"Oh, yes, sir."

"Can we get there by road?"

"We'd do better going across the estate, sir" replied Kelly.

"Right, then that's what we'll do, Mr Riley may I suggest that Mr Carter remains here and the rest of us ride over to the gate house" said Hadley.

"Good idea, Inspector" replied Riley.

"Mr Hopton, will you please saddle up horses for all of us?"

"Certainly, sir."

"Mr Kelly would you give him a hand?" asked Hadley.

"Oh yes, sir, I'd be delighted to!"

"Are your Agents armed, Mr Riley?"

"Yes they are, Inspector."

"Good and so are we."

"Do you expect trouble from Winters?"

"I'm not sure, sir but it's always better to be armed than not, just in case" replied Hadley.

"It makes good sense, Inspector." Just then Inspector West appeared with his men and Hadley told him what he planned to do and asked him to wait until they returned from the old gate house.

"Yes of course, Jim and that will give us time to search some more outbuildings we've spotted further away from the house, they look dilapidated and over grown, this place is certainly run down" said West.

In a short while seven horses were saddled up and Kelly suggested that Mr Riley should ride his daughter's favourite horse, Topper. Riley smiled as he was helped up into the saddle by Lone Eagle who then sprang up onto his own horse.

"Right, is everybody ready to go?" asked Hadley from the back of a large grey mare. They all chorused 'yes' and Hadley said "then lead on Mr Kelly." The party moved off out of the stable yard and onto the rolling green pastures of the Holcot estate.

The magnificent seven rode quickly across the open countryside before they reached, then followed, a tree line that led up to high ground. As they progressed the trees became more and more dense then, after about a mile, Kelly stopped and dismounted before peering through the wood which looked impenetrable to Hadley.

"I think it's somewhere through here, sir" said Kelly.

"Right, let's dismount and see if we can find a way in" said Hadley. After Riley had dismounted he said to Lone Eagle "see if you can find a way in that someone has used recently." The Indian nodded and immediately began to jog along the tree line looking for tell tale signs. Hadley smiled and said to Riley "I think we'd do well to let Lone Eagle discover the way."

"Believe me, Inspector, there's no better man for the job" replied Riley.

"I'm sure, sir."

"He's been a wonderful and faithful companion to me,

Inspector."

"I can see that, sir."

"Whenever I go someplace, he leaves his Reservation and comes with me as my bodyguard" said Riley with pride.

"How did you meet him, sir?"

"It was when we were pushing the railroad through the Dakotas and I decided it would be beneficial all round if we tried to make friends with the local Indians instead of fighting them all the time."

"That's good sense, sir."

"I thought so but some Army officers just wanted to fight the Indians for every stretch of land but that's not my way, so with the help of my scouts I made contact with a Cheyenne tribe, Lone Eagle is the youngest son of their Chief and he spoke a little English."

"He was your interpreter then?"

"No not quite, but he did help a hell of a lot, making sure his father understood what we were about."

"Go on, sir."

"Then we made a sort of peace pact but it was an uneasy standoff, they're proud people you know, Inspector."

"Yes, I'm sure."

"Then tragedy struck them in the bad winter of '75 when many of them caught pneumonia and other diseases because of lack of food, when I heard what was happening I sent a medical team to help them and wagon loads of good food."

"That was very generous of you, sir."

"If you've got plenty of money then I reckon that if you can help some folks who are in real trouble by spending a little, you should do it, I think it's part of trying to be a good Christian" replied Riley and Hadley was impressed.

"That's true, so then what happened, sir?"

"The Chief was grateful for the help and he said I had saved his tribe, I doubt that really, nevertheless, as my reward he made Lone Eagle my bodyguard for life."

"How remarkable, sir."

"It is, but he won't take any salary so I pay his money to the Chief so he can buy food and medicines when they need them, it all works very well, Inspector."

"Yes, I can see that, sir."

"He often causes quite a stir when I turn up with him and his presence sets some snooty folks back on their heels, I can tell you" said Riley.

"I can believe that" replied Hadley.

"And I must admit that I enjoy it" said Riley with a wry smile.

They stood and watched Lone Eagle as he continued to move along the tree line, then he stopped suddenly and bent down close to the ground.

"I believe he's found something, Inspector" said Riley.

"It looks like it, sir."

Lone Eagle took some time in studying the ground then stood up, looked at Riley and nodded.

"Told you so" said Riley as he began to walk towards the Indian followed by Hadley and the others. When they were all grouped around the Indian he said to Riley "somebody is going through here, Chief."

"Well done, Lone Eagle, you lead the way and we'll follow" said Riley.

"I go ahead and you follow quietly in a short while" said the Indian.

"Alright, but you watch yourself, we think there's a dangerous man in there" said Riley.

"I much more dangerous than him, Chief" smiled the Indian.

"I'm sure you are, but I don't want you take any chances" replied Riley and the Indian smiled then nodded his appreciation for Riley's concern before stepping through into the tangle of overgrown bushes that surrounded the trees.

"I suggest that we follow him next and you bring up the rear, sir" said Hadley.

"Inspector, I promise you that I've faced many difficult situations in America and…"

"But you're in England now, sir, and I think I would be failing in my duty if I did not take your personal safety into account, so let Sergeant Cooper and I go next, followed by Mr Ford and Mr Morris, remember, sir, we are all armed and trained professionals" said Hadley and Riley smiled then nodded.

"You'd better get going then, Inspector otherwise Lone Eagle will be wondering where you all are!"

"Right...Mr Kelly will you stay here with the horses?" asked Hadley.

"Yes, sir" replied Kelly.

"And look after my hat" said Hadley as he handed his battered top hat to Kelly who smiled.

"Follow me, Sergeant, and Mr Morris, Mr Ford, Mr Riley if you will."

"We're right behind you, sir" replied Cooper

"Then let's go and see if we can find Winters" said Hadley as he pushed through the bushes and into the wood.

Hadley found the going difficult and the thick undergrowth pulled at his clothes but he could see where Lone Eagle had gone. After a short distance, Hadley found the Indian crouched down by a tree holding a finger to his lips for silence. Hadley stopped in his tracks, holding his hand up to warn Cooper and the following Americans. They all waited motionless for the Indian to make the next move. Then Lone Eagle waved Hadley forward to his side and whispered to him "I hear someone close, you stay here but come quick if I call."

"Right" whispered Hadley. The Indian nodded then moved silently but cautiously off into the tangle of overgrown bushes. Cooper and the others moved closer to Hadley and in a whisper he relayed what Lone Eagle had said. They all nodded but remained silent straining their ears for any sound that might indicate what was happening. It seemed an age before they heard the rustling of bushes and someone approaching slowly. Hadley reached for the revolver in his pocket and Cooper did the same as their hearts raced with anxious anticipation. Suddenly Lone Eagle appeared with a smile and they all breathed a collective sigh of relief.

"Old place not far away and someone is there" whispered the Indian.

"Good, now lead us to it" replied Hadley. Lone Eagle nodded and turned, making his way back through the undergrowth. They struggled on for some distance behind the Indian before Hadley glimpsed the top of a dilapidated stone building. When they got closer and could see more of the gate house through the trees, Lone Eagle stopped and crouched down.

"Look, I see man at window" said Lone Eagle and Hadley

followed his outstretched arm with his finger pointing at a small casement window. Hadley glimpsed the face of Winters for a moment before he disappeared from view.

"He's there!" he hissed with excitement.

"You were right, sir" whispered Cooper.

"Yes I was for once, thank God" murmured Hadley. Cooper relayed the good news to the Americans crouched down behind him and they all smiled with satisfaction.

"Lone Eagle, try to lead us as close as you can without the man seeing us" said Hadley.

"Then you must be patient and wait for me to call you" he replied.

"We will be" said Hadley.

"It takes time to move without being seen" said the Indian.

"I'm sure, so we'll be patient" replied Hadley and Lone Eagle nodded then moved forward into the undergrowth.

"Sergeant, we'll get as close as we can to the building, hopefully without being seen by Winters."

"Right, sir, then how do you plan to get in if the door is locked?"

"I'm not sure, we might have to rely on brute force and if that fails then we'll have to shoot the lock off" replied Hadley.

"That might persuade Winters into giving himself up without a fight, sir."

"I doubt that, Sergeant."

"Why, sir?"

"Because he knows he faces the hang man, Sergeant, and my guess is that he would rather die here than on the scaffold in London." As Hadley finished speaking they heard a gentle whistle.

"Come on, but be as quiet as you can" whispered Hadley as he moved slowly forward. When they reached the spot where Lone Eagle was crouched, they could see that there was a narrow track in front of him that led up to the gate house.

"We must not go on path, otherwise man will see us" whispered Lone Eagle.

"Right" nodded Hadley.

"I go round another way" said the Indian.

"Yes, we'll wait for your call" whispered Hadley and Lone Eagle nodded and disappeared into the undergrowth once again.

"I'm afraid this is going to take some time, Mr Riley" said Hadley.

"No matter how long it takes, Inspector, I want the man who killed my daughter" replied the American.

"Quite so" said Hadley and the party remained silent listening for the Indian's call. It came some while later and they set off slowly in the direction of Lone Eagle. This time they were positioned in a place that was not overlooked from the gate house and the Indian said "now we move forward quick." Hadley nodded as the Indian hurried through the sparse undergrowth up to the stone wall at the end of the gate house. When they had all caught up, Hadley said "we'll try the door, but if it's locked we'll have to break it down."

"Don't let's waste our breath doing that, we'll just shoot the goddamn door open!" said Ford.

"We've got enough fire power to do that so damn quick and Winters won't know what's hit him!" said Morris.

"Very well, gentlemen" said Hadley realising that it would be the quickest and easiest way in the circumstances. They moved around the side of the building and approached the front door, which looked like solid oak that had gone grey with age. Hadley reached out for the door handle and gently tried to open the door but it did not move, then he put his weight behind it but to no avail.

"Let's shoot the damn door open" said Morris as Ford produced a heavy revolver from his shoulder holster. Morris followed suit and said "We're ready, Inspector."

"Right, gentlemen, I'll let Winters know we're here so he has a chance to give himself up" said Hadley.

"What!" exclaimed the Agents in unison.

"Its standard police practice" replied Hadley.

"You English are so unbelievably correct!" exclaimed Ford.

"I reckon stupid more like" said Morris.

"We've crept all this way so Winters won't know we're here and now you want to Goddam announce yourself!" said Ford.

"Listen to me, gentlemen…

"Shoot the damned door!" exclaimed Morris once again and Ford fired his revolver at the key hole below the handle. The wood splintered as the first bullet struck and then as Morris opened fire the area around the door lock it disintegrated in showers of splinters. The Agents fired all twelve rounds from their revolvers into the door before it gave way then Hadley rushed forward and pushed it open. Once inside he drew his own revolver as Winters appeared at the top of the stairs holding a shotgun.

"Winters, you're under arrest!" shouted Hadley.

"Not yet, you meddling bastard!" he replied and then he pointed the gun at Hadley and fired. Hadley threw himself instantly to the stone floor as the blast passed over him and peppered the wall by the doorway. Fortunately Cooper was outside with the others and none of them were hit by the shot. Hadley fired his revolver in Winters direction but missed as the man scampered back along the upstairs landing. Within a second Cooper was helping the Inspector to his feet as the Agents were frantically re-loading their revolvers.

"Are you hurt, sir?"

"No, Sergeant, just angry that I missed him!"

"We'll get him now, sir."

"Yes, come on gentlemen, he can't get away" said Hadley.

CHAPTER 20

Hadley raced up the stairs followed by Cooper and the others. As he stepped onto the narrow, dark landing he heard a door shut at the far end. He proceeded cautiously along towards the door with his revolver cocked to fire. When he reached the door he listened carefully but could hear nothing from the room beyond. He tried the door handle and pushed at the door but to no avail.

"I think we'll have to shoot our way in again, Sergeant" he whispered and Cooper just nodded.

"Here, let us have a crack at it, Inspector" said Ford.

"Just wait a moment, if you will, Mr Ford" whispered Hadley.

"Don't tell me you're going to try and sweet talk this lunatic into giving himself up?" said Ford.

"No, I just want to try and picture in my mind what he's doing" replied Hadley.

"I'll tell you what he's doing, he's waiting in there with a loaded shotgun to blow your head off!" exclaimed Morris.

"Damn right" added Ford.

"Let my boys do it, Inspector" said Riley and Cooper, fearing that Hadley would get shot, nodded his approval.

"Very well, gentlemen, go to it, but try not to kill him, I want some answers before he appears in court and is hanged" said Hadley.

"Leave it to us, Inspector, we're used to winging a suspect and not getting hurt" said Ford, Morris nodded.

"Go ahead then" said Hadley. The Agents tried the door handle once again before they stood back and fired point blank into the area of the lock. The muzzle flashes from both revolvers lit up the dark landing as the bullets thudded into the stout door. Within five or six shots it gave way and Ford rushed into the room followed by Morris and the detectives. Hadley and Cooper stood with them looking at the empty, untidy room, searching in vain for Winters.

"Where the hell has he gone?" asked Ford.

"He's gotta be somewhere here" said Morris.

"But where, for Chrissake?" asked Ford as he continued to glance anxiously around the room. Then Riley and Lone Eagle entered, both looking around for Winters.

"Don't tell me that the son of a bitch has got away?" asked Riley angrily.

"He won't get far, sir" said Hadley.

"I hope you're right, Inspector."

"There must be a way out, perhaps behind the panelling, look carefully gentlemen" said Hadley. They all searched the panelled room and Cooper found what appeared to be an uneven gap in the oak panels adjacent to the fireplace.

"Look at this, sir" he said and Hadley came over and peered at the gap. There seemed to be no way of prising open the panels and as the others joined the detectives Hadley said "Lone Eagle, could you use your knife to see if you can open this up?" The Indian nodded and drew his large hunting knife from its moccasin sheath. He placed the point of the blade into the gap and traced it all round the panels and down to the floor. He looked down at the floorboards and noticed that they showed signs of wear up to the oak panelling.

"Man has gone through here" he said.

"How the devil do we get this open?" asked Riley.

"Blow the damn thing to bits!" said Ford.

"Then go to it, boys" said Riley just as Lone Eagle held up his hand to stop them. They waited patiently for a few moments as the Indian probed more deeply with his knife, suddenly there was a click and then a small panelled door swung back to reveal a very narrow dark staircase.

"My God, it's a Priest's hole" said Hadley.

"A 'what'?" queried Ford.

"A Priests hole. In Tudor times, Catholic family's had secret stairways built for visiting Priests to either escape or hide when the King's men came looking for them" replied Hadley.

"Why should they do that?" asked Morris.

"Because King Henry the Eighth was busy arguing with the Pope about his marriage to Katherine of Aragon, which led to his excommunication..." said Hadley.

"Let's leave the history lesson for the moment, gentlemen" interrupted Riley. Then Lone Eagle made as if to go down the stairs but Riley stopped him and said "let the Agents go first, he may be down there waiting with his damn gun." Lone Eagle nodded and stood back, making way for Ford and Morris to enter the narrow confine. Hadley, then Cooper, followed by Lone Eagle and Riley made their way cautiously down the stone staircase behind the Agents in the dim light. The stairs came to an abrupt end and then turned at right angles into an even narrower space and continued downwards. Hadley had to turn sideways as his shoulders were brushing against the stone walls making his progress slow.

"I'm getting too old for this, Sergeant" he whispered.

"No you're not sir. I'm sure you'll be doing this sort of thing for years to come" replied Cooper.

"Steady, Sergeant, always remember that I could have you replaced with someone more sympathetic towards me" replied Hadley and Cooper smiled to himself. At last they made their way down to the foot of the stairs and Hadley could see more clearly the stone corridor as it became lighter. Suddenly the Agents stopped and listened in silence. Morris turned to Hadley and said "we're coming to the end of this, Inspector."

"Thank God."

"We've just got to make sure that our friend is not waiting outside for us with his gun."

"Mind how you go" whispered Hadley and Morris nodded before he moved forward behind his colleague. The Agents hesitated for a moment and then Ford stepped out into the day light through a small open door followed by Morris. Both men instantly stood back to back then pointed their revolvers around in a sweeping arc and Hadley was impressed by their co-ordinated action so he made a mental note to use the same procedure when confronted with a similar situation. When it appeared safe, he strode out to join them followed by Cooper and the others.

"Well, it seems he's got clean away" said Morris.

"Only for the moment" said Riley then he turned to Lone Eagle and said "find which way he went and follow him, we'll be right behind you." The Indian nodded and smiled before he started looking down at the ground for traces of Winters. Like a Bloodhound he suddenly stopped, sniffed the air for a moment and then set off through the tangled undergrowth.

"Keep up with him boys" said Riley and the Agents nodded then plunged into the bushes followed by Hadley and Cooper. Lone Eagle moved quickly and purposefully through the trees and the others struggled to keep up with him. Hadley noticed the look on his face when Riley told him to follow Winters, it was an absolute pleasure for him to take on the mantle of a hunter once again and it was obviously second nature to the man. Hadley looked back and saw that Riley was struggling to keep up and he said to Cooper "stay back, assist Mr Riley and make sure he's alright, Sergeant."

"Right, sir."

"We don't want anything to happen to him" said Hadley as they followed Lone Eagle into a small clearing which was in the middle of the dense foliage. Hadley saw the Indian suddenly crouch as if he sensed danger and he looked anxiously around. Then Winters stepped out from behind a tree and fired both barrels of his shotgun at them. Ford and Morris were both hit, they spun round and with cries of pain, fell to the ground as Hadley raised his revolver and returned fire. He missed and Winters instantly disappeared into the bushes. Lone Eagle then let out a war cry that was loud and shrill, which sent an icy shiver down Hadley's spine. The Indian drew his hunting knife and raced across the small clearing then plunged into the bushes after Winters.

"Stop him, Inspector, he'll scalp that son of a bitch in a second for this!" exclaimed Riley. Hadley glanced at the American and saw that he was clutching his arm.

"Have you been hit, sir?"

"Yes, but it's nothing, now just get after that bloody man will you?"

"Sergeant, stay here and look after everybody!"

"Yes, sir."

As Hadley raced into the bushes he heard another shot being fired followed by an agonising scream. He blundered through the undergrowth to where Lone Eagle stood with his blood soaked knife looking down at Winters. The petrified grounds-man was staring wide eyed up at the Indian who began to whoop and wave his knife at his injured prey. Winters was bleeding profusely from a cut right across his forehead as well as stab wounds in both arms close to his shoulders.

"Save me from this bloody savage" he moaned to Hadley as Lone Eagle suddenly crouched down and grabbed a handful of Winter's hair before making cutting motions round his scalp with his knife all the while whooping. It was a terrifying sight and Hadley did not know quite what to do for the best.

"Steady if you please Lone Eagle, leave this man to me and go and help Mr Riley, he's been injured" said Hadley and when the Indian heard that he pointed his knife at Winters head then made another quick cut above his forehead, whooped loudly as Winters screamed, before he rushed away through the undergrowth back towards the clearing.

"Oh, God help me, I'm going to bleed to death" whimpered the injured man.

"No you won't, I'm going to make sure that you are saved for your appointment with the hangman" replied Hadley as he bent down to examine the wounds. He wiped the blood from his face with his handkerchief and then tied it tightly around Winter's right arm where the bleeding was more profuse.

"Have you anything that I can tie around your other arm?" asked Hadley.

"Yes, my belt."

Hadley undid Winters belt and tightened it around his left arm. Picking up the shotgun, which was close by, he broke it open and removed both cartridge's, putting the live one in his pocket, before snapping it shut.

"Do you think you can walk back?" Hadley asked.

"Yes, I think so" murmured Winters as Hadley bent down and helped the injured man to his feet. His forehead was still bleeding quite badly and Hadley said "I think we'd better be as quick as we can." Winters nodded and stumbled forward into the bushes followed closely by Hadley carrying the shotgun. When they reached the clearing Cooper and Lone Eagle were attending to the Agents on the ground whilst Riley was leaning against a tree clutching a blood soaked handkerchief to his arm. Hadley sized up the desperate situation quickly and said to Riley "we need help urgently, will you ask Lone Eagle to guide Cooper back to where Kelly is waiting with the horses?"

"Yes indeed, Inspector" replied Riley and he called to the Indian. Hadley then crouched down beside Cooper and said "Sergeant, go back with Lone Eagle, find Kelly and get him to ride to the village for the Doctor, tell him what's happened and summon an ambulance from Northampton, then let Inspector West know what has happened."

"Right, sir."

"Be as quick as you can because if I'm not mistaken, we've only a little time left."

"Yes, sir, I think you're right, Mr Morris is bleeding quite badly and so is Mr Ford, I've not been much help to either of them I'm afraid" replied Cooper in an anxious tone.

"Leave them both to me Sergeant, now go quickly with the Indian and get help." Cooper nodded and stood up as Lone Eagle was already striding towards the bushes. Hadley gazed at the pale faces of the two Agents as they lay side by side on the blood soaked ground and he feared that if the Doctor did not arrive soon then both men would die from loss of blood.

"Can I help at all, Inspector?" asked Riley as he crouched down alongside Hadley.

"I don't think so, sir, I'm afraid we'll just have to be patient and pray for the Doctor" replied Hadley gloomily. Riley stood up and glanced at Winters, who was leaning against a tree, his pale face streaked with blood.

"If my boys' die, I'll kill you myself, you son of a bitch!" Riley exclaimed and Winters hung his head in shame.

Hadley spoke encouraging words to both Agents and they responded with weak smiles and gentle nods.

"It seems crazy that we've come all the way to England to get shot when we could have been shot back home with no problem at all" said Morris with a grin.

"You can say that again" said Ford in a whisper and Hadley smiled but feared inwardly that Ford would die as he had taken the full force of the shotgun blast in his left shoulder and was still bleeding profusely. There was little that Hadley could do except keep talking to the men and trying to take their minds off their injuries. He told them all about Agnes and Florrie, which seemed to delight them and they both said that they would like to meet them before they returned to America. Hadley was glad to hear their positive comments and he promised that he would arrange a long evening over pints of stout with the two women. He told the Agents that the women would be pleased to meet them and he said it would be a night to remember.

It seemed an age before Hadley heard the sound of people

approaching through the undergrowth, then suddenly a smiling Lone Eagle appeared, followed by Cooper, Doctor Moore and a woman. The Doctor went immediately to the Agents and quickly examined them both as the woman opened a large canvas bag she was carrying and took out rolls of bandages. The Doctor called for assistance to ease Ford into a sitting position so that he could bandage his chest and shoulder. Hadley and Cooper obliged and as soon as Ford sat up the Doctor and the lady went to work stripping off his blood soaked shirt, cleaning the wounds with spirit then bandaging the wounded man. When they had finished they gently lay Ford back down, his head resting on his blood soaked jacket. They then turned their attentions to Morris and did the same for him. Cooper stood back and told Hadley that the lady was the Doctor's wife.

"Thank heavens that they are here" murmured Hadley.

"Yes, indeed, sir."

"What about the ambulance, Sergeant?"

"The Doctor has sent for it, sir, and Kelly will go and wait for it at the entrance to the house then guide it over here" replied Cooper.

"That's good, Sergeant. Is Inspector West coming?"

"He said he would wait for the ambulance and then come over with it, sir."

"Very well."

Doctor Moore then attended to Riley and after he was examined, bandaged and comfortable, he turned his attentions to Winters. When the Doctor had finally finished, Hadley surveyed the scene and he thought that it looked like a photograph of the aftermath of a bloody battle somewhere in the Empire. The Doctor approached him and said "we must get these men to hospital as soon as possible, Inspector."

"I realise that, Doctor."

"Time is of the essence Inspector, the two badly injured men have lost a lot of blood and they both need immediate surgery."

"We'll give you all the help you need, Doctor" said Hadley.

"Thank you" replied the Doctor as his wife administered water from a bottle to all the injured men.

They waited patiently for the arrival of the ambulance as Hadley, along with Cooper, tried to keep the wounded Agents in light conversation. After about an hour, the Doctor looked at his fob watch and said "the ambulance should be here by now, can someone go and guide the men through the wood?" Riley nodded and asked Lone Eagle to meet them, he smiled then disappeared in an instant into the bushes and Hadley hoped that he would not scare the ambulance attendants too much.

A little later Lone Eagle arrived followed by Kelly, Inspector West and two bewildered looking attendants carrying a stretcher.

"Thank heavens you're here at last" said Doctor Moore as the attendants placed the stretcher on the ground beside Ford. They lifted him with care, assisted by the Doctor and Kelly, onto the stretcher.

"God, Jim, what a mess" said West.

"Yes it is, Peter, and it's all Winters bloody fault."

"He'll pay for this then" said West.

"He certainly will."

"Are you alright, Jim?"

"I'm fine thanks."

"Is there anything I can do?" asked West.

"Perhaps you and your men could escort the ambulance back to the Infirmary and keep Winters under close arrest whilst he's being seen by the doctors?"

"Of course."

"Can we have some help please in getting to the ambulance?" asked the Doctor. Kelly and Lone Eagle immediately led the way, holding back the undergrowth for the attendants to struggle through, followed by the Doctor and his wife. When they had gone, Riley said to Hadley "I only hope that we're not too late to save them."

"We can only pray that we're not, sir."

"What are you going to do with Winters?"

"Arrest him and take him back to the Yard after he's been to the hospital for treatment, sir."

"Does he need treatment?"

"Yes, I'm afraid Lone Eagle has made quite a mess of him as you can see" replied Hadley.

"He deserved it!"

"He probably did, sir, but now the law must take its course and Inspector West will remain with him to make sure he doesn't escape and I will take him back to London."

"Don't worry, with Lone Eagle keeping a close eye on him, he's going nowhere" said Riley.

The attendants arrived back quite quickly with the Doctor and lifted Morris away with the help of the others.

"If you would like to come now, gentlemen" said the Doctor to Riley and Winters. They nodded and followed him into the bushes as Hadley looked about the clearing, sighed and said to Cooper "what a damned mess, Sergeant."

"It is, sir, but we've got Winters and that's who we came for."

"Yes, but a high price has been paid for his capture, Sergeant."

"Are you coming back now, Jim?" asked West.

"No, not for the moment, Peter, I want to look around the gate house and see if I can find anything of interest" replied Hadley.

"Right you are."

"Ask Kelly to leave our horses tethered up and we'll ride back later to the Manor" said Hadley.

"Are you coming back to Northampton tonight?"

"Possibly, but if I decide not to, we'll stay in the village."

"Right, I'll see you due course no doubt" he smiled and then followed the others through the bushes.

"Now, Sergeant, let's see what we can find in the gate house!"

CHAPTER 21

The detectives entered the gate house through the front door which had been blasted open by the Agents. They looked carefully around the downstairs rooms which contained nothing but dusty old furniture then they made their way up the stairs to the dark corridor. Hadley opened the first door on his left and glanced round a dusty room where the furniture had been piled up in an untidy heap. Then he opened the first door on his right and stepped into a large, clean but cluttered room with a sofa, small writing bureau and single bed.

"It seems Winters was living quite comfortably, sir" said Cooper as he gazed around the spacious room.

"Yes, it would appear so" replied Hadley as he glanced over at the bureau with its ink pot, pens, writing paper and envelopes. His curiosity was aroused and he wondered why Winters would require writing implements so he went to the bureau but found no trace of anything written. He then opened the drawers, they were empty, except for the bottom one which contained a loaded 45 calibre revolver. He picked the gun up and turned to Cooper.

"Look what we have here, Sergeant."

"That's a surprise, sir, I could only imagine Winters using a shotgun."

"Me too Sergeant, let's search this room thoroughly and see what else it reveals." They went about the search carefully but discovered nothing of interest. Hadley found a few clothes in a small wardrobe that were old and shabby along with a pair of stout boots and a top coat that had seen better days.

"Well there is nothing here except what I would expect to find in a hideout, Sergeant."

"But the revolver is a bit puzzling, sir."

"Yes it is" replied Hadley thoughtfully as he looked at the gun for a moment before placing it in his pocket.

"Shall we continue searching the place, sir?"

"Yes."

They left the room and went along the corridor to the doorway of the room from which Winters escaped. It was cluttered with old furniture, untidy, with a pile of blankets on the floor in a corner and a small table in the centre of the room. There was an opened packet of biscuits, some tea in a caddy, a large cup and several plates along with various pieces of cutlery spread across the table. In the fireplace there was evidence of a recent fire along with a kettle, several pots, one of which contained what looked like the remains of a stew.

"He obviously was cooking his meals in here, sir" said Cooper.

"It seems so, but there's something not quite right about this place, Sergeant."

"And what's that, sir?"

"I have a feeling that Winters was not alone here."

"Well if that's true then whoever it was has long gone, sir."

"Possibly, Sergeant."

"Or do you think that he might be hiding in another priest hole, sir?"

"I doubt it, Sergeant."

"What do we do now, sir?"

"Wait patiently, Sergeant."

"Wait, sir?"

"Yes, we may be being watched so we'll leave and make our way back to the horses and return later."

"If you say so, sir, but I thought you would have been more anxious to return to London with Winters."

"After what the Indian did to him, I don't think he's in any fit state to travel at the moment, Sergeant."

"Will you be charging Lone Eagle for his attack, sir?"

"There's no point, he will claim that his actions were in self defence when Winters fired his shotgun at him" replied Hadley.

"I suppose so, sir" replied Cooper and they remained silent as they had a last look round.

"There's nothing to be gained by staying here Sergeant, so let's leave now."

They made their way back through the wood to where the horses were tethered and Hadley smiled when he saw that Kelly had left his top hat on the saddle of his grey mare. He placed his battered hat on his head, un-tethered the horse and mounted her. They rode silently across the pastures towards the Manor in the late afternoon sun.

"This is very pleasant, Sergeant."

"It certainly is, sir."

"I think it would be even more agreeable if we had something to eat."

"Yes, it would, sir."

"So we'll ride on to the village and see if we can find something tasty in the pub, Sergeant."

"That's a very good idea, sir."

"All my ideas are good, Sergeant" replied Hadley and Cooper smiled.

They eventually arrived at the Bunch of Grapes pub in Holcot, tethered the horses by a water trough and went into the pub's cool interior. When they had ordered pints of stout and a ploughman's lunch, Hadley asked the landlord if he had rooms for the night.

"Yes, sir, we've got three as a matter of fact."

"We just require two, thank you" said Hadley.

"Just for tonight, sir?"

"Yes, thank you."

"Will you be wanting dinner, sir?"

"Yes we will."

"Very good, sir, we serve it at eight o'clock."

"That will be most convenient" said Hadley.

"Now begging your pardon, sir, but are you two gentlemen policemen?" asked the landlord.

"Yes, we are."

"I thought as much, are you here to investigate the shooting at the Manor, sir?"

"Yes, we are."

"Terrible business, the whole village is talking about it, they say there are several dead and they were taken away by ambulance to the Infirmary."

"I can tell you that everyone involved in the incident was alive when they were taken in the ambulance" said Hadley.

"Oh, that's a relief, sir."

"It is."

"I hope you catch who's ever responsible, sir."

"We've already got him under lock and key" replied Hadley with a smile.

"Thank God for that, you never know who's wandering about these days, do you, sir?"

"Indeed you don't" replied Hadley with a smile.

They rested in their rooms for a while before making notes on the day's developments and then went down to dinner at eight. After a delicious meal of jugged hare with a selection of the season's vegetables followed by apple pie and custard, the detectives felt ready to face the possibility of a long night ahead. They left the pub, mounted up and rode sedately through the quiet village towards Holcot Manor in the dusk of a warm summers evening. It was dark by the time they reached the drive of the Manor but as it was a clear night and the Moon had risen, their way was lit by a beautiful silvery glow that settled over everything. They made their way past the house and out onto the pastures and eventually arrived at the wood. After tethering the horses they pushed into the undergrowth, moving slowly in the eerie darkness until at last they reached a vantage point where they could observe the gate house. Immediately they could see the glow of a candle from one of the small latticed windows upstairs.

"You were right, sir" whispered Cooper.

"Yes, fortunately."

"Do we wait, sir?"

"No, we'll go in now and confront whoever is there, Sergeant."

"Right, sir."

"Have your revolver ready in case you need it."

"Yes, sir."

They crept forward slowly to the front door which appeared closed but as Hadley touched the handle it opened and swung back easily. They moved silently into the hallway and up the stairs which occasionally creaked, causing them to stop, wait and listen. There was no other sound and Hadley wondered if anybody was actually in the house. When he reached the door to the spacious room, he grabbed the handle, flung it open and stepped in. Sitting at the bureau writing a letter by candle light was Lord Mortlake who jumped with shock and then scrambled for the revolver in the bottom drawer.

"I have it here, your Lordship" said Hadley with a smile as he held up the gun before he pointed it at the pale faced Lord.

"Good God, Inspector, you startled me" stammered Mortlake.

"I'm sure, sir."

"I wondered who it was for the moment."

"Yes, I can imagine, sir."

"You can't be too careful these days, Inspector" said Mortlake as he tried to recover his composure.

"Very true, sir, now if you don't mind, I've a lot of questions to ask and now would be the appropriate time for you to answer them truthfully" said Hadley.

"Yes, of course, please sit down, Inspector and you too, Sergeant" replied Mortlake anxiously as he waved them to the sofa. They smiled and Hadley put the revolver in his pocket as Cooper took out his notebook and pencil.

"What are you doing here, sir?"

"I'm trying to keep out of the way of kidnappers, Inspector."

"I suspect that it is more likely that you are hiding from me" said Hadley.

"That's simply not true, Inspector."

"I was given to understand by Miss Jarvis that you had gone to Geneva, sir."

"Ah, yes Inspector that was a little ruse on my part" replied Mortlake with a grin.

"Why sir?"

"Well to be perfectly honest, Miss Jarvis was becoming a bit of a nuisance with her silly romantic ideas and her conduct was becoming intrusive, so I told her that I was leaving for a while."

"I understand that her brother opened a Bank account on your behalf in Geneva, can you confirm that, sir?"

"Ah, yes, yes he did" nodded Mortlake.

"Why do you require a Bank account in Switzerland, sir?"

"Well, I shouldn't really tell you, Inspector, but I will."

"Thank you, sir, that's very wise."

"I was advised to do it for tax reasons."

"You propose to evade paying tax, sir?"

"No, I plan to avoid having to pay it, Inspector."

"The ransom money for your kidnap was paid into your account in Geneva, explain that if you will..." Just then Hadley heard a sound outside and he reached for his revolver as the door burst open and a tall, bearded man carrying a shotgun stepped into the room and shouted "don't move or I'll shoot!"

"Thank God you're here, Mathews!" exclaimed Mortlake.

"I saw them coming across to the wood so I followed them, sir."

"Well done, Mathews."

"Are they the police, sir?" asked the grounds-man.

"Yes, they are."

"They can't be trusted then, sir."

"Quite right" replied Mortlake as he stood up and said "Inspector, your weapons if you please." Hadley gave him a hard look and as he handed over his revolver and Mortlake's he said "what makes you think that you can possibly escape from justice?"

"My well thought out plans, Inspector, now give me yours too, Sergeant." After Cooper had given his gun to Mortlake, he smiled and said "now, I think we'll put you in the downstairs room with all the old furniture and by the time you get out of there, if ever you do, I'll be long gone and you'll never see me again, Inspector."

"That's what you hope, but the reality is that we will find you and bring you to justice, then you'll have to face a court and answer for your crimes" replied Hadley.

"What crimes are they, Inspector?"

"First, the murder of your wife…"

"Winters took the opportunity to strangle the silly creature when she fell from her horse and he did that of his own accord because he knew I hated her."

"How despicable!"

"And as you already have him under arrest, you can hang him at your leisure, Inspector" said Mortlake.

"We will, make no mistake!"

"That's what I like about you, Inspector, you're so predictable."

"Then you murdered Ann Wells in London…"

"Yes, I had to do that because she spotted me in the Strand when I was supposed to be kidnapped" interrupted Mortlake with a grin.

"You are a cruel murderer who will hang one day…"

"Only if you can catch me, Inspector" interrupted Mortlake.

"It will be a race between Riley and me to find you and I can assure that I will never stop looking, whilst he will spend his entire fortune hunting you down using Pinkerton Agents wherever you try and hide in the world" said Hadley and he watched Mortlake's face grow pale at that.

"We'll see" Mortlake hissed.

"And you'll never escape from Lone Eagle" said Hadley.

"Enough!" exclaimed Mortlake and Hadley knew that he had rattled the man.

"You know what I say is true" said Hadley calmly with a glint in his hard blue eyes.

"Take them down to the room, Mathews."

"Come on you two" said the grounds-man as he waved his shotgun at the detectives. They made their way down to the hallway and waited for Mortlake to join them. He came down the stairs carrying a candle and opened the door into the large room full of furniture. He handed the flickering candle to Hadley and waved them into the room. Once they had entered he slammed the door behind them and they heard the key rattle in the lock. They looked at each other in the light and Cooper said "it's going to be a long night, sir."

"That's not necessarily so, Sergeant."

"How do you plan to escape, sir?"

"You can start by trying to pick the lock with your special little tools whilst I plan our next move once we get out, Sergeant." Cooper smiled and produced his leather wallet containing the hard steel instruments. Hadley pulled up a dusty chair and sat and watched Cooper at work, trying to open the lock. Time ticked by as Cooper struggled to undo the un-yielding mechanism. Age, along with rust and dust in the lock all played a part in making his task very difficult and he was forced to take a rest.

"Here, let me try" said Hadley and Cooper handed him the tools but it was to no avail. After a short while, the Inspector sat back on his chair and tried to think of another way out of their prison but he was unable to do so. The candle was close to burning out when Hadley looked at his fob watch in the flickering light and said "it's nearly midnight, Sergeant, so try again if you would." Then Cooper's perseverance paid off and he managed to click the lock mechanism open as the candle fluttered and died leaving them in darkness.

"Well done, Sergeant."

"I knew I would do it in the end, sir" replied Cooper as he opened the door to the hall. Stepping outside they listened for any sound but there was none. They left the building and made their way back through the wood to where the horses were tethered. Hadley knew that as Mortlake and his grounds-man had left the gate house they would have taken the horses, so it was no surprise to find them gone.

"It's a long walk ahead of us to the village, Sergeant."

"Yes, sir, but as it's a nice moon lit night and we can see where we're going, perhaps we can cut across the fields."

"A good idea, although it'll mean we'll have to scramble through ditches and over hedges, Sergeant."

"If we move quickly, sir, it'll be good exercise."

"I think you're enjoying this, Sergeant!"

"Speed is of the essence if we're to catch Mortlake before he gets too far away, sir."

"You're beginning to sound more and more like me, Sergeant, and that's worrying!" exclaimed Hadley as he strode away in the direction of the village.

CHAPTER 22

It was two hours later when Cooper hammered loudly on the front door of the Bunch of Grapes pub. Eventually the landlord appeared holding a candle and looked bemused when he saw the bedraggled detectives.

"Good heavens, gentlemen, I'd given you up for the night."

"I'm sure you had" said Hadley.

"Come in, come in" said the landlord as he stepped back and opened the door wide for them.

As Hadley entered the pub he said "we need to get to Northampton immediately, do you have a small trap we can use?"

"Yes, sir, would you like me to drive you?"

"That would be very helpful."

"Where do you want to go to in the town, sir?"

"The police station."

"Right, please wait while I get dressed."

Twenty minutes later the horse and trap carrying the detectives was hurrying on its way to Northampton. Hadley was anxious to alert West and his colleagues to the situation. The journey in the moonlight seemed to take forever and Hadley was impatient. He hardly spoke to Cooper all the way and only commented once when the lights of Northampton came into view.

When they arrived outside the police station, Hadley thanked the landlord for all his help and gave him two guineas for the rooms and evening meal.

"That's very generous of you, sir, but your bill doesn't come to that" said the land lord.

"Never mind, your help is appreciated, so thank you and I wish you good night" replied Hadley as he and Cooper stepped down from the trap.

The desk sergeant looked up and recognised the detectives as they entered the station.

"Good morning, Inspector."

"Yes, I suppose it is now, can you contact Inspector West immediately, sergeant?"

"I can send a constable round to his address, sir."

"Would you do that please, it is urgent that I speak to him."

They waited in West's office until he arrived some half an hour later.

"Morning, Jim… Sergeant."

"Morning, Peter."

"This must be urgent."

"It is, we discovered Mortlake at the gate house…."

"Good heavens, where is he now?" interrupted West.

"I've no idea, after his man, Mathews, threatened us with a gun, we were locked in a room by Mortlake who then escaped" replied Hadley.

"When did this happen?"

"Just before midnight, Peter."

"No time to lose then!"

"No."

"I'll organise surveillance on the Holcot Road and at the station."

"Thank you, Peter and tell your men that Mortlake is armed with our revolvers."

"Right, I'll make sure that some of my constables are armed then."

"That's a very necessary precaution."

"I suggest that we search the Manor for him as soon as possible."

"Good, now tell me, how is Mr Riley?" asked Hadley.

"His wounds are not serious but the Infirmary kept him in for observation."

"And the Agents?"

"Ford is in a serious condition, they've operated on him but he's lost a lot of blood, Morris is recovering quite well after his operation" replied West.

"What about Winters?"

"They've kept him in and I've got him under police guard, not that my men are needed with the Indian prowling about and occasionally peering in at Winters and frightening him half to death" replied West and Hadley smiled.

"I bet the Indian caused a stir when he first arrived at the hospital."

"He certainly did, Jim, now you both look all in, so I suggest

196

you have some tea and then have a rest while I get everything organised" said West.

"Thanks Peter, that's appreciated."

The detectives slept in adjoining cells for the rest of the night and were woken at eight by the duty Sergeant carrying steaming mugs of tea.

"Inspector West says he would like you to join him in his office when you're ready, sir."

"Thank you, Sergeant" replied Hadley as he took the mug of tea. By half past eight they had washed and were present in West's office ready for the day ahead.

"I've deployed armed men on both sides of the village and on the Holcot road north as well as the railway station, Jim" said West.

"That's good, Peter."

"Now I'll get a warrant to search the Manor thoroughly, in case he's still there, as well as arrest warrants for him and Mathews."

"I have a feeling that they're both still there."

"You could be right, Jim."

"Before we go out to the Manor I'd like to see Mr Riley and his people" said Hadley.

"Yes, of course, Jim, if you go to the Infirmary now, I'll have the warrants ready by the time you get back."

A police four wheeler took the detectives to the Infirmary where they were admitted to Mr Riley's private ward. Elliot Carter sat close to the bed, whilst Lone Eagle stood by the door with his arms folded.

"Morning, gentlemen, how are you?" asked Riley with a smile as Carter helped him to sit up in bed.

"Very well thank you, sir, but more to the point how are you?" said Hadley.

"Okay, they've taken good care of me here, but I'm worried about my boys, they're seriously hurt" replied Riley.

"Yes, I believe they are, sir."

"I've told the doctors here if they need any help from surgeons in London, I'll willingly pay their fees and expenses, I've told them that my boys must have the very best care and attention" said

Riley.

"That's good to hear, sir, I'm sure they will make a speedy recovery."

"I damned well hope so, Inspector, I feel kinda responsible for what happened."

"Don't for one moment blame yourself for what Winters did, sir."

"Well, perhaps not if you say so, Inspector."

"I do, sir. Now, I have some news for you…"

"Yes, what is it?" interrupted Riley.

"Sergeant Cooper and I went back to the gate house late last night and found Mortlake there…"

"Good God! Did you arrest him?"

"We did, but he escaped, sir."

"How the devil did that happen?"

"His new grounds-man, Mathews, was armed and he foiled us. We were locked in a room until we managed to escape" replied Hadley.

"So now what?"

"Inspector West has posted armed officers in the village, on the Holcot road and the railway station" replied Hadley.

"Well that's something I guess."

"The Inspector is now organising warrants for the Manor and we will be going there to look for Mortlake immediately we leave you" said Hadley.

"That's good, is there anything I can do to help, Inspector?"

"Yes, sir, would you give your permission for Lone Eagle to accompany us?" There was a moments silence before Riley said "yes, Inspector, if you think he can help."

"I do, sir, as you said 'no man can escape from him' and I'd like to have him with us to catch this murderer."

"So I was right, he is a murderer."

"Yes, he claims that Winters killed your daughter and he admitted murdering Miss Wells, sir."

"The low down son of a bitch! I'll see he hangs for what he's done!"

"They'll both hang, I assure you, sir."

"Then go to it, Inspector and take Lone Eagle with you!"

"Thank you, sir."

"Chief Riley, I should stay with you" said the Indian in a concerned tone.

"Don't worry about me, Lone Eagle, I've got Elliot here and I'm safe enough, you go and help the Inspector catch the other murderer."

"If you say so, Chief Riley" said the Indian.

"And when you find him, make sure you don't kill him, Lone Eagle, that's the hangman's job!" said Riley and the Indian grinned then nodded.

By the time the detectives and Lone Eagle returned to the police station, West had his search and arrest warrants, and he and his men were ready to go.

"I've six constables and two Sergeants, Jim, I think that should be enough don't you?"

"Yes, Peter, how many are armed?"

"Both Sergeant Timkin and Woods are armed and of course I'm carrying a revolver" replied West.

"May we sign out two for us, please?"

"Of course, Sergeant Timkin will take you to the armoury."

"Then we can go and see if Lord Mortlake is still at his country estate" said Hadley with a smile.

The detectives, West and Lone Eagle travelled in the police carriage which was followed by a wagon carrying the rest of the force. They stopped and checked with the officers on surveillance duty in the Holcot road who reported that there had been no sign of Mortlake. Hadley was both apprehensive and excited as the four wheeler turned into the long drive up to the Manor. He hoped against hope that Mortlake had stayed at the house and he was determined to search every part of the decaying, gloomy place for the confessed killer. As soon as they arrived, West instructed Sergeant Timkin and his men to search the stables whilst Cooper knocked at the door. Barton opened it and frowned when he saw the officers, then his eyes widened as he noticed Lone Eagle, before he glanced to heaven for divine help.

"Good morning, Mr Barton, would you please tell her Ladyship that we are here with a warrant to search the house but before we begin I'd like to have a few words with her" said Hadley firmly.

"Please come in gentlemen, and kindly wait in the hall whilst I inform her Ladyship" replied Barton. They all entered the hallway and as soon as Barton had disappeared Hadley said "Peter, would you ask your men to round up all the servants in the kitchen and then begin the search up stairs?"

"Right away, Jim...Sergeant, please take your constables and do as Inspector Hadley has asked."

"Very good, sir" replied Sergeant Woods before they hurried away. Barton returned a few moments later and announced that her ladyship would see them now. They followed Barton to the drawing room where she sat, impassive with an angry look.

"Well, what is it this time?" she asked.

"We have a warrant to search the house..." began Hadley.

"Whatever for?" she interrupted.

"We're looking for your son, is he here?"

"No he's not, Inspector and whatever makes you think that he is?"

"Because, your Ladyship, he imprisoned myself and Sergeant Cooper in the old gate house last night."

"Did he indeed, well if he did I'm sure you deserved it" she replied haughtily.

"After Mathews threatened us with a shotgun" said Hadley, ignoring her remark.

"So you say, Inspector."

"If your son is here we'll find him, make no mistake and he'll be arrested for the murder of Miss Ann Wells..."

"What nonsense, I think you are deluded and for the sake of my peace and quiet, I suggest you leave my house immediately and take that savage with you!" she exclaimed as she pointed at Lone Eagle.

"Your obstructive and unhelpful remarks are noted your Ladyship..."

"Good, now leave!"

"Before we begin the search can you tell me if the house has a priest's hole?" asked Hadley and he noticed how she paled at that.

"Not that I know of, Inspector."

"Thank you" replied Hadley before he turned and abruptly made his way out of the room followed by the others.

"Show them all out, Barton" she called to the perplexed butler

200

who just nodded.

Once in the hallway, Hadley said "we'll talk to the servants individually and find out what they know." When they entered the kitchen all the staff were seated at the long table, they gave Hadley glaring, hostile looks as Barton joined them. He told them that there was a search warrant in place and they were looking for Lord Mortlake. Their faces showed no emotion as Mrs Noakes said forcefully "he's not here."

"You told me that before, Mrs Noakes, but Sergeant Cooper and I met him last night in the old gate house" said Hadley.

"I don't believe you" she replied.

"As you please, Mrs Noakes, now I want to talk to you one by one in the library whilst the constables are searching upstairs" said Hadley.

"It'll do no good because he's not here and we've nothing to say" said Mrs Noakes.

"And I'll start with you, Mrs Noakes" said Hadley firmly.

"Why me for heaven's sake?"

"Because you're the housekeeper and along with Mr Barton, you will know what has been going on here" replied Hadley. She stood up, gave a hard but knowing look to the others at the table before Hadley, Cooper and Lone Eagle followed her out of the kitchen while West stayed with the servants. Once in the library, Hadley asked the angry woman "is there a priest hole in this house?" She went pale and said "why do you ask?"

"Because if there is one then I think that I need to look there first for Lord Mortlake" replied Hadley.

"Well there's not one here" she said firmly.

"You seem very sure, Mrs Noakes."

"I am, Inspector" she replied and Hadley nodded then waited a few moments before he asked "when did you last see Lord Mortlake?"

"Before he was kidnapped" she replied quickly.

"And you've not seen him since?"

"No, I was given to understand that after he had been released by those vile people, he was staying at Connaught Square, Inspector." Hadley remained thoughtful and then said "thank you, Mrs Noakes, you may go now and would you please ask Mr Barton to come to the library?" She nodded and left the room looking relieved.

"That old woman tells you lies, Chief Hadley" said Lone Eagle.

"Yes, I'm sure she does" replied Hadley.

Barton appeared a few minutes later and stood before them looking anxious and perplexed. Hadley felt some sympathy for the old man because it was obvious that her Ladyship was difficult and Mrs Noakes was a bully, which would make his life somewhat unbearable as he tried to serve two mistresses.

"Mr Barton, I want you to tell me the truth about his Lordship" said Hadley.

"Oh, of course, sir."

"And what you say to me now will remain in the strictest confidence."

"Very good, sir."

"Do you know if he is here?"

"Well I couldn't say for sure, sir" replied Barton nervously.

"What do you mean by that?"

"He may be here, but I wouldn't necessarily know, sir."

"Explain why not."

"Because if his Lordship is here, sir, only her Ladyship and Mrs Noakes would know."

"Why is that, Mr Barton?"

"I'm only the butler, sir, Mrs Noakes organises everything and has the last say in all matters, as you may have noticed."

"Yes, I have, and tell me how she managed to rise above you to her exalted position."

"Simply put, sir, Lord Rupert promoted her during their long and close relationship whilst he was alive" replied Barton, looking relieved that he had at last said what must have been on his mind for many years.

"Did they have an affair?"

"Yes indeed they did, sir, much to my disgust and I felt great disappointment for her Ladyship who endured the affront without complaint" replied Barton.

"When Lord Mortlake died why didn't her Ladyship dispense with Mrs Noakes?"

"Because Lord Andrew insisted that she should remain here with all the same advantages."

"Why would he do that?"

"Because Mrs Noakes was attending to his physical needs from the time that he was old enough to enjoy the pleasures of the flesh, Inspector" Barton positively beamed as he said it.

"I see" said Hadley in surprise.

"Did Lord Rupert know of this affair?"

"Yes, sir, not only did he know but he encouraged it."

"Good heavens" whispered Hadley.

"And when Lord Andrew was not in congress with Mrs Noakes because Lord Rupert was here relieving himself with her, he was busy forcing himself on Kate" said Barton now feeling free of any inhibitions regarding his employers sexual proclivities.

. "I see" said Hadley somewhat bemused.

"Lord Andrew called them 'his country comforts', much to my disapproval, sir" said Barton in a dismissive tone.

"I can imagine" said Hadley.

"Now will that be all, sir?" asked Barton to a surprised Hadley.

"Before you go, do you know if there is a priest's hole in the house?"

"I'm not sure, sir, but I would not be surprised if there was one, the Catholic Tudors were very keen to hide the priest's away when the King's men came to search" replied Barton.

"Indeed they were, Mr Barton."

"Who would you like me to send next, sir?"

"Kate if you please" replied Hadley and Barton gave a slight bow and left the room.

"Well, what do you make of that, Sergeant?"

"Quite unbelievable, sir."

"Barton tells you the truth, Chief Hadley" said Lone Eagle.

"Yes, I'm sure he does."

Kate arrived soon after and looked apprehensive as she sat down on the edge of a chair.

"Miss Kate please answer my questions truthfully if you please" said Hadley with a smile.

"I'll try, sir" she whispered nervously.

"Anything you say to me will remain in strict confidence."

"Yes, sir."

"Do you know if Lord Mortlake is here?"

"I don't know for sure, but I think he is somewhere in the

house" she replied.

"What makes you say that?"

"Because late last night I woke up and heard Mrs Noakes talking to a man and it sounded like him, sir."

"Thank you very much Kate that will be all" said Hadley as he smiled.

CHAPTER 23

Hadley sent Cooper to ask West and his men to join him in the library. When they were all assembled Hadley said "I think that Mortlake is definitely here in the house and is probably hiding in some obscure secret place, so I want us to search each room for hidden doorways, loose floorboards, false ceilings and the like."

"Do you want us to search in two teams, Jim?" asked West.

"Yes, if you go with one of your Sergeants and his constables, we'll look with the others" replied Hadley.

"Right, we'll start in the attic"

"Leave nothing to chance, Peter, he's here and we have to find him" said Hadley.

They searched the old house carefully from top to bottom but could find no sign of a hiding place or Lord Mortlake. Hadley was confident that the murderer was somewhere close and he asked Lone Eagle for his thoughts when they had finished the search and were all standing outside in the driveway in the warm mid morning sun.

"He has gone from house but is not far away, Chief Hadley" said the Indian.

"Then we must search the stables and out buildings once again" said Hadley.

"But we've already looked, sir" said Sergeant Timkin.

"I realise that, but we must look again, Sergeant" replied Hadley.

"Right, men, let's get on with it" said West in a resigned tone. As Timkin and his men headed for the stables, West said "I think our bird has flown, Jim and we're now wasting our time."

"I don't know what to think, Peter."

"We've not found Mathews either, so it's obvious that they have both escaped together" said West.

"Yes, I agree that's possible."

"I suggest that after we've finished this search, we call a halt, return to the town and concentrate on the train station" said West. Hadley thought for a moment and replied "very well, Peter."

West nodded and then strode away after his men. Hadley looked at Cooper and asked "what do you think, Sergeant?"

205

"I think he's right, sir, we've searched high and low for both men and there's no trace of either of them" replied Cooper as Mrs Noakes appeared at the open front door. She glared at the detectives and Lone Eagle before she called out "I told you he wasn't here but you wouldn't listen to me!" Hadley smiled and replied "we'll be leaving soon, Mrs Noakes, please let her Ladyship know."

"It'll be my pleasure, Inspector" she replied as she slammed the large door shut with a resounding crash.

"Old woman still lies" said Lone Eagle and Hadley nodded. They walked slowly towards the stables to oversee the search and as they arrived in the yard, Kate suddenly appeared round the corner of the house and approached quickly, she bobbed a curtsy at Hadley.

"Sir, begging your pardon, sir, can I have a word in private, sir?" she asked nervously.

"Of course" Hadley smiled as he took her arm, nodded at Cooper and walked a few yards away from him and the Indian.

"What is it, Kate?"

"I think I know where they are, sir."

"Tell me where, Kate" said Hadley his eyes glinting with anticipation.

"They're hiding in the old ice house, sir."

"What makes you think that, Kate?"

"We keep some cured bacon sides in there and eggs and suchlike, because it's cool, and when Mrs Chambers asked me just now to go and get some ham to boil, Mrs Noakes told her off and said that no one should go there until you had all gone, sir."

"Tell me where the ice house is, Kate."

"It's on the other side of the Manor, sir."

"Take us there right away!"

"Oh, I couldn't do that, sir."

"Why not?"

"There'll be hell to pay if Mrs Noakes found out I was even talking to you, sir, no, you must go there on your own" she replied.

"Alright, Kate, tell me how to get there." When Kate had finished giving directions she hurried away back to the rear of the house as Hadley rejoined Cooper and Lone Eagle.

"She says that they're hiding in the ice house, get everybody together, Sergeant" said Hadley.

"Right, sir."

When they were all assembled Hadley gave them the news and instructed them to proceed with caution and be prepared to use their weapons if necessary. Hadley and West led the force around the back of the house into the walled kitchen garden and through a wrought iron gate. Beyond was a narrow path which meandered through overgrown bushes until it separated and following Kate's directions, Hadley took the right hand fork through even more dense undergrowth. Suddenly he came across the steps down to the entrance to the old ice house. This was a red brick construction built into the ground. Ice was collected and stored in winter months then used during the summer for the preservation of food and the cooling of wines. Hadley, West and Cooper drew their revolvers before cautiously descending the narrow steps to the door of the ice house. Hadley listened for a moment but could hear nothing, then he tried the door handle which gave easily and he opened the door then peered into the cold, gloomy interior.

"Stay back or I'll blast you!" said a voice from the darkness which Hadley recognised.

"Don't be a fool, Mathews, the game is up and you are under arrest" said Hadley.

"Stay back I say!"

"If you fire at me, you'll be dead in moments" said Hadley.

"I'm warning you!"

"We're all armed and ready to use lethal force against you, so give yourself up Mathews."

"I'm not giving up!"

"Your certain death will be unfortunate and will accomplish nothing" said Hadley as his eyes grew accustomed to the gloom and he could see Mathews hunched up at the far end of the ice house, clutching his shotgun.

"I've told you, I'm not giving up!"

"Where's Mortlake?" asked Hadley hoping to both distract the man as well gaining vital information.

"He's long gone" replied Mathews.

"Where to?"

"Somewhere far away and where you'll never find him."

"In that case there's no point in you holding out" said Hadley.

"I've told you, I'm not giving up!"

"Listen to me Mathews, put the gun down and come out now" said Hadley.

"Bugger off, you interfering bastard!"

"I'm going nowhere and neither are you" replied Hadley.

"Then we'll stay here forever" replied Mathews.

"I'm afraid not my friend and I promise you that it's only a matter of time before the final inevitable outcome."

"Oh, and what's that?"

"Your surrender, Mathews, because armed officers will stay out here until you either starve to death or give yourself up" replied Hadley.

"That's what you think!"

"That's what I know for certain, Mathews, good day to you!" said Hadley as he stepped back and slammed the door shut. He followed Cooper up the steps and said to the assembled officers "we'll have to mount a guard until this fool gives himself up."

"But he could be in there for days, Jim" said West anxiously.

"I realise that, Peter, but we have no other option unless we risk death by trying to rush in and over power him." West thought for a moment and then said "I'll call my men in from the village and the Holcot road then set up a duty rota."

"Thank you, Peter."

Whilst West was organising his men, Hadley, Cooper and Lone Eagle went to the kitchen door of the house and entered.

"I want to speak to Mrs Noakes immediately, please get her" Hadley said to Barton who looked totally shocked by their un-announced arrival in the kitchen. The butler nodded and hurried off as Hadley sat at the table and Mrs Chambers asked "I've just made a pot of tea, would you all like a cup while you're waiting?"

"That would be very nice, Mrs Chambers" Hadley replied with a smile as Cooper and Lone Eagle sat down with him. Tea had been served when Mrs Noakes arrived followed by Barton.

"What is the meaning of this, Inspector?" she demanded.

"Mrs Noakes I wish to talk to you about…"

"I thought you said that you were leaving which was obviously another lie or a hopeless mistake on your part!" she interrupted. Hadley said nothing but picked up his cup of tea and sipped it which drove Mrs Noakes mad with anger.

"Answer me you insufferable wretch of a man!"

"I will, Mrs Noakes when you moderate your tongue and stop interrupting me" he replied before he took another sip.

"Oh my God, must this be endured?" she whispered.

"I'm afraid so, Madam. Now, we have found Mathews in the old ice house, he is armed and refuses to give himself up."

"So what has that got to do with me, Inspector?"

"I believe that you knew he was there…"

"Utter nonsense" she interrupted.

"And what's more, I think you know where Lord Mortlake is hiding" said Hadley.

"You're totally wrong as usual, Inspector" she replied.

"No Mrs Noakes, I'm not, and I suspect that you are withholding vital information from me."

"I've nothing more to say except finish your tea, leave my kitchen and take this savage with you!" she said as she glared at Lone Eagle, who smiled and said to Hadley "old woman still lies to you, Chief Hadley."

"I know she does, Lone Eagle."

"I've never been so insulted in my life!" she said before she turned and stormed out of the kitchen.

"Sergeant, we'll arrest her for obstructing the police in the course of a murder investigation" said Hadley.

"Very good, sir."

"We'll ask Inspector West to take her back to Northampton when he goes." On hearing that Barton smiled a curious smile and Mrs Chambers went pale.

When Hadley finished his tea he arrested Mrs Noakes in the servant's parlour and she was speechless with indignation. Cooper escorted her to the police carriage and left the angry woman in the care of a young constable before he joined Hadley back at the ice house. When he arrived, Hadley and West had descended the narrow steps to the door with drawn revolvers. Hadley opened the door slowly and then said "Mathews, I'm giving you one last chance to come out and give yourself up."

"Go to hell!" said Mathews.

"It will save a lot of unpleasantness later."

"Are you deaf or something? I said go to hell!"

"It's your last chance, Mathews."

"Before what?"

"You'll see."

"You can't bluff me."

"I don't intend to, do you still refuse?"

"Bugger off!"

"Right…Inspector West, seal up this door and place armed officers outside indefinitely until Mathews is dead or agrees to give himself up" said Hadley in a loud voice.

"Very good, Inspector" replied West with a grin as he slammed the door shut.

"Get a hammer and some nails from the stables and nail the door up, when he hears that he will not be so cocky" said Hadley.

After the door had been nailed up, Sergeant Timkin and a constable were stationed at the top of the steps whilst the rest of the officers followed Hadley back to the entrance to the house. West assigned the officers to the duty roster of two hours on with four off on a continual basis and then said to Hadley "I suggest we return to my office now and plan the search for Mortlake."

"You go on, Peter and get Mrs Noakes into custody, I'll stay here for a while with Cooper and Lone Eagle" replied Hadley.

"You're wasting your time Jim, he's not here" said West.

"You may be right, but on the other hand…"

"Alright, Jim, I'll send the carriage back for you at the end of the afternoon" said West with a smile before he climbed into the four wheeler and sat opposite a stony faced Mrs Noakes. Hadley nodded and gave him a little wave as it moved off down the long drive. They watched its progress for a while and then Cooper asked "what do we do now, sir?"

"We think, Sergeant."

"About what, sir?"

"The whereabouts of Lord Mortlake."

"Well we know he's not here, sir."

"Do we know that for certain, Sergeant?"

"Yes, sir."

"We didn't think Mathews was here but he was found hiding in the ice house."

"Yes, sir."

"And if Kate hadn't told us we would have left this place none the wiser, Sergeant."

"That's true, sir, but it doesn't follow that because we've found Mathews, Mortlake is still here."

"This is a game of bluff and double bluff, being played by a man with gambling instincts which are second nature to him and that makes it so hard to predict what he plans to do next."

"So do you believe he's somewhere here, sir?"

"Yes I do, Sergeant, what do think Lone Eagle?"

"I think you are right, Chief Hadley" replied the Indian.

"Let's take a stroll and try and guess where Mortlake could be hiding, gentlemen" said Hadley with a smile before he walked away towards the lawn that bordered the long drive.

"He could be anywhere on the estate, sir" said Cooper as he caught up.

"Yes, so all we have to do is to try and put ourselves into his twisted mind, Sergeant" said Hadley.

The afternoon sun shone as they wandered along the drive way discussing where they should start the search for the missing Lord. Eventually Hadley said "I think we should return to the gate house."

"It's the obvious place that we would look for him so he wouldn't hide there because he knows that."

"Precisely, Sergeant."

"I believe that Mathews was telling the truth when he said that Mortlake was far away and we'd never find him, he's probably in London making plans to escape to Geneva whilst we're wasting time here, sir."

"That's possible, Sergeant, but nevertheless, we'll go and search the gate house before the carriage arrives to take us back to Northampton" replied Hadley.

Hopton saddled up three horses and they rode out across the estate to the thick wood that surrounded the gate house. When they arrived they dismounted and the detectives followed Lone Eagle silently through the undergrowth to the ruined old place. As they approached, Hadley whispered to Lone Eagle "will you go and listen for any movement before we rush in because if he's there, I don't want him to get away from us this time." The Indian just nodded and move silently forward whilst the detectives waited and watched the windows for any sign of movement. Lone Eagle crept up to the door and gently opened it before he disappeared inside.

"Be ready to run, Sergeant."

"Yes, sir."

"And have your revolver to hand just in case."

"Right, sir" replied Cooper as he drew his revolver and slipped off the safety catch.

Suddenly Lone Eagle re-appeared and nodded vigorously to them as he pointed upwards.

"My God, he's there!" exclaimed Hadley before he rushed forward with Cooper following and struggling to keep up. They reached the doorway as Lone Eagle silently raced up the stairs but unfortunately the noise the detectives made alerted the person in the house. Lone Eagle drew his hunting knife and flung the door open before he leapt into the room. The detectives heard the shot ring out as they reached the top of the stairs and Hadley's heart sank at the thought of the Indian in mortal danger. As Hadley reached the open door another shot rang out and he raised his revolver ready to fire without hesitation. The sight that met him was distressing, the Indian lay on the floor with blood pouring from his arm whilst Mortlake, white faced with a transfixed stare, was clutching the hilt of Lone Eagle's knife which was buried deep in his shoulder close to his neck. When he saw Hadley he dropped his revolver and said "God help me" as he fell to the floor. The detectives rushed into help both men, Hadley attended to Mortlake as Cooper did what he could to staunch the Indian's wound with a tourniquet made from his belt.

"Best leave the knife where it is" said Hadley to the wounded Lord.

"Am I going to die?" whispered Mortlake.

"Eventually, but it will be by the hang man's rope, so I hope that's of some comfort to you at the moment, sir" replied Hadley.

"You bastard" whispered Mortlake.

"Sergeant, ride as fast as you can back to the Manor and get help, tell Holcot to summon Doctor Moore from the village and then get the police wagon over here!"

"Right, sir!" replied Cooper as he rushed away.

Whilst they were waiting, Lone Eagle made no sound but Mortlake groaned occasionally and cursed God then all the saints. Hadley moved between both wounded men and tried to comfort them. When he was with the Indian he whispered to Hadley "if I die, tell Chief Riley what happened and promise me that you will see that I go back to my people for them to bury me."

"You're not going to die, Lone Eagle."

"But promise me if I do."

"I promise you, Lone Eagle."

"You are a good man, like Chief Riley."

"I hope so."

CHAPTER 24

It seemed an age before Cooper arrived back with the Doctor, his wife and two constables.

"Thank heavens you're here at last, Doctor" said Hadley.

"If you carry on having these violent skirmishes I think I'd better set up a field hospital to try and cope, Inspector!" replied Doctor Moore as he immediately went to Lord Mortlake leaving his wife to attend to the Indian.

"Doctor, I promise you that this is the last" replied Hadley.

"Don't forget we've still got Mathews to sort out, sir" whispered Cooper.

"Yes, don't remind me, Sergeant."

Doctor Moore examined the wounded men carefully and he looked anxious when he said to Hadley "we have to get them to hospital for surgery as soon as possible, Inspector."

"We'll take them in the police wagon, Doctor."

"Right, but you'll have to be very careful with Lord Mortlake, the knife is in a very dangerous position and under no circumstances must it be knocked or jarred."

"We'll be careful, Doctor."

"It would be better to take Lord Mortlake to the wagon first of all and I will stay with him whilst you bring the other man" said the Doctor.

"Very good, Doctor...constables please help the Doctor get his Lordship to the wagon."

"Yes, sir" they nodded and moved forward before helping Mortlake up from the floor, assisted by the Doctor, who remained close as they half carried him from the room, down the stairs and out of the gate house.

"Your turn now, Lone Eagle" said Hadley as he and Cooper helped the Indian to his feet.

"I can walk by myself, Chief Hadley."

"As you wish, but we'll be close just in case" replied Hadley and the Indian nodded his thanks.

When the injured men, Doctor Moore and his wife were all aboard the police wagon it set off slowly across the estate on its journey to the Northampton Infirmary. Hadley and Cooper returned to the room in the gate house, recovered Mortlake's revolver and discovered their own revolvers in the bottom drawer of the bureau.

"Now we have to tell her Ladyship that her precious son has been found, is injured and under arrest for murder, Sergeant."

"Will you tell Mathews, sir?"

"Oh, yes" replied Hadley with a smile.

The detectives went to the Manor and were admitted to her Ladyship by a relaxed Barton who announced them with a smile "the police again, Milady."

"I thought you'd gone away so what is it now, for God's sake?" she asked angrily.

"Your Ladyship, I have to inform you that we have found your son hiding in the old gate house…"

"Have you now" she interrupted.

"Unfortunately he has been injured resisting arrest…"

"If you've hurt Andrew I assure you that you will face…"

"Never mind what I will face, Milady, your son has confessed to the murder of Ann Wells and will be charged with her murder…"

"You're mad!" she interrupted.

"Out of courtesy I must inform you that Lord Mortlake has been taken to the Northampton Infirmary for treatment before I take him to Scotland Yard under arrest and so, as I have nothing more to say to you, I wish you a good afternoon Milady" said Hadley then he gave a little nod and strode out of the drawing room, followed by Cooper.

The detectives went to the ice house and informed Sergeant Timkin what had happened at the gate house. Hadley went down to the door and knocked on it.

"Mathews, I've come to tell you that we've found Mortlake in the gate house and he's now been taken away to Northampton."

"I don't believe you!" shouted Mathews.

"As you please, good bye."

"Where are you off to?"

"To Scotland Yard in London, with Mortlake."

"Oh."

"Don't worry, Inspector West will be here to charge you with the attempted murder of police officers and aiding and abetting a confessed murderer if you're not shot first, so goodbye Mathews."

"Wait a minute…"

"Yes?" asked Hadley and he waited patiently with a smile.

"I may have been a bit hasty…"

"Yes, I think you were" replied Hadley.

"I was angry…"

"That's very true Mathews."

"If I come out, can we talk?"

"Of course" replied Hadley and he nodded to Timkin who descended the steps with a claw hammer.

"Listen to me, Mathews, the door will be opened in a few minutes and I want you to be standing close to it without your shotgun, do you understand?"

"Yes, sir."

"I warn you that if you threaten us, I will shoot you instantly, is that clear?"

"Yes, sir."

"Right, Sergeant, prise the nails out" said Hadley as he drew his revolver, slipped off the safety catch and pulled the hammer back ready to fire. After Timkin had removed all the nails he stood back, then Hadley opened the door to reveal Mathews standing with his hands up and blinking in the bright afternoon sunlight.

"Come on out, Mathews" said Hadley and the grounds-man stepped out of the ice house. He was escorted to the kitchen garden where Hadley said "the only talk we're going to have is me telling you that you're under arrest for threatening police officers with a weapon, abducting and imprisoning them as well as aiding a murderer to escape then you will reply 'I understand'." Mathews looked hard at the Inspector and replied "as I said before, you can't trust the police."

"That's your opinion… Sergeant, take him away and keep him safe until the wagon arrives back."

"Yes, sir" replied Timkin and he escorted Mathews out of the garden with the duty constable.

"Well that's a relief, sir" said Cooper.

"Certainly is, Sergeant."

"I had visions of another episode needing the Doctor once

again."

"I must admit that I did too, Sergeant."

They returned to the drive in front of the Manor to await the arrival of the police carriage. Hadley looked at his fob watch as he was anxious to leave the gloomy place. They stood for a while and then a four wheeler appeared from the stable yard with Hopton driving it. As he pulled the horses up to a halt outside the house, Barton opened the front door and Lady Mortlake appeared, descended the steps then waited for Barton to open the carriage door for her. After the butler had helped her in, he closed the door and stood back as Hopton slapped the reins and the coach moved off. Barton stood for a few moments watching the coach as it gathered speed down the drive and then he wandered over to the detectives.

"Her Ladyship has gone to the Infirmary to see Master Andrew" he said with a smile.

"Thank you, Mr Barton" said Hadley.

"I trust that he is not seriously injured, sir."

"I don't know exactly how serious his injuries are, Mr Barton, but be assured he is receiving the best medical attention available" replied Hadley. Barton gave a nod of his head and remained silent for a few moments as he watched the carriage disappear out of the drive into the road.

"Then you're taking him to London under arrest, as I understand, sir."

"Yes, Mr Barton, Lord Mortlake has confessed to the murder of Miss Wells."

"Do you know who killed Lady Nancy, sir?"

"I believe that Winters was responsible."

"That doesn't surprise me, sir."

"Why do you say that, Mr Barton?"

"He hated her because he knew the Master hated her and Winters is a peculiar man, an opportunist always anxious to please the Master in the hope of some reward" replied the butler.

"I see" mused Hadley and he gave Cooper a knowing glance.

"And what of Mrs Noakes, may I ask, sir?" enquired Barton.

"She will be interviewed by me and then I will decide what charges she will face" replied Hadley.

217

"Is she likely to go to prison, sir?"

"She might if she's found guilty of obstruction."

"How very appropriate" smiled Barton.

"You think so?"

"Yes I do, sir, Mrs Noakes has made all our lives a misery over many years and when Lady Nancy and Miss Wells arrived, she became even more obnoxious."

"I see."

"Those two lovely young women brought hope for a bright future in this place but Mrs Noakes, Master Andrew and her Ladyship did everything to obstruct and stifle them" said Barton with some feeling.

"Please go on" said Hadley.

"I know that as Americans they were perhaps a little too headstrong for our ways at first, but they were kind, generous and considerate to everyone and if Master Andrew had treated his wife with love and affection, I'm sure that Lady Nancy would have given him everything that he wanted to be a successful and popular man in society. But, he squandered her affections and ignored her, pursuing his low life activities in London instead, much to his disgrace."

"Why are you telling me all this, Mr Barton?"

"Because I believe you and Sergeant Cooper to be good upstanding men, doing their duty and I want you to know the truth before I leave" replied Barton.

"You're leaving?"

"Yes, sir, I have had it in mind to retire for some while and now I think it is time I did so."

"Where are you going?"

"I'm going to live with my brother and his wife in Dorset, they have a small farm near the coast where they live quite comfortably, sir."

"That sounds very pleasant."

"Yes, they've asked me for some time to stay with them and now I'm looking forward to it, sir."

"Does her Ladyship know that you are leaving?"

"Not yet, sir, I plan to inform her when she returns from Northampton" replied Barton.

"So then you'll leave Kate and Mrs Chambers to the tender

mercies of her Ladyship?"

"Kate has told me in confidence that she and Mr Hopton intend to marry and move back to the village where he was employed by the blacksmith before he was asked to take Kelly's place, sir" replied Barton.

"Her Ladyship will only have Mrs Chambers to look after her?"

"I'm sure Milady will find others that she can put upon and when Mrs Noakes eventually returns, all the servants will be bullied into submission as usual, sir" replied Barton as the police four wheeler arrived and swung into the drive.

"Well, it's time for us to go, Mr Barton, I thank you for your thoughts and wish you the very best for the future" said Hadley as he held out his hand to the butler.

"Thank you very much, sir" replied Barton with a smile as he shook hands with the Inspector and then Cooper. The police carriage arrived then swung round and stopped. Sergeant Timkin came out of the house when he heard the sound of the horses and was told by the driver that the wagon was on its way to collect him and his constables. The detectives climbed aboard the carriage and waved as it sped down the drive away from the Manor and back to Northampton.

Inspector West was the first to greet the detectives when they arrived at the Infirmary.

"I've got to hand it to you, Jim, if you'd been as hasty as me to get back here, then Mortlake would have got clean away" said West as they walked up to the ward where Riley and his Agents were recuperating.

"Don't be too hard on yourself, Peter, I promise you that I was only following my instincts, which are often completely wrong" replied Hadley.

"I don't believe that, Jim."

"Just ask Cooper here, he'll tell you about my instincts and wild goose chases!"

"I wouldn't dare, sir" said Cooper with a grin and Hadley laughed before he asked "how is Mortlake?"

"Still in surgery, Jim" replied West.

"And Lone Eagle?"

"Would you believe, all bandaged up and sitting with Mr Riley!"

"Yes I would believe it, that man is as tough as they make them" replied Hadley.

"Luckily it was a flesh wound and the bullet went straight through his arm" said West.

"I'm relieved to hear it" said Hadley as they reached the American's private ward. Hadley knocked then entered and Riley smiled as he looked up from his chair.

"I'm glad you're back safely, Inspector."

"Yes, sir, thanks to Lone Eagle here" replied Hadley and the Indian beamed.

"I've heard all about it" said Riley.

"That's good, but I wonder if Lone Eagle told you everything about his bravery?"

"I don't expect so because he's kinda modest when he doesn't have to be" replied Riley.

"Well before I tell you what he did, may I ask how you are, sir?"

"I'm fine, thank you."

"And your Agents?"

"They're both much better, thank you, the Doctors say that it will be a little while before Mr Ford is alright but Mr Morris should be fit and ready to travel fairly soon" replied Riley.

"Will you be leaving then?"

"No, I won't leave until they are fully recovered. When the Doctors say that I'm free to leave here, Elliot will book a suite in the Excelsior Hotel and we'll stay there until everybody is fit to travel back to London" replied Riley.

"Very good, sir."

"And of course I won't be going back to New York until after the trial, Inspector."

"Yes, of course, sir."

"Now, all of you, please sit down and tell me everything" said Riley. "Elliot, would you kindly ask that pretty nurse outside to organise some tea and biscuits for us?"

"Yes, sir" said Elliot with a smile.

Over tea Hadley went into great detail of all the events at Holcot

220

Manor and Riley smiled with satisfaction at the end.

"Well, I must say that you've done everything possible to bring these murderers to justice, Inspector, and I will be telling the Commissioner in no uncertain terms of my regard for your professionalism" said Riley.

"Thank you very much, sir, but I must also say that without Lone Eagle's help we would not have succeeded so quickly in arresting Mortlake and Winters."

"Well, let's say that you all made contributions to the case and the outcome is exactly what I hoped for, Inspector" said Riley.

When the detectives left the Americans, Mortlake was out of surgery and recuperating in a side ward, with his mother by his bedside. Next door was Winters and both murderers were under a heavy police guard. The Doctor informed Hadley that Winters would be well enough to travel to London in a day or two but it would be at least a week before Mortlake could be discharged from the Infirmary.

The detectives went with West back to his office where Hadley composed a detailed report of the events at Holcot which was telegraphed to Chief Inspector Bell. He then interviewed Mrs Noakes, who proved to be awkward and obstructive as usual. Hadley charged her with attempting to pervert the course of justice before releasing her on police bail, pending her appearance at the County Court.

"What do you plan to do now, Jim?" asked West as Hadley sat down in his office.

"Stay here until Mortlake and Winters are fit enough to travel back to London" replied Hadley.

"Take a break from the investigation and have a well earned rest then?"

"Only after all the report writing, Peter" replied Hadley. West smiled and said "it never ends does it?"

The detectives booked into the Excelsior Hotel and other than a daily visit to the Infirmary to check on the condition of all concerned in the case, relaxed and enjoyed sampling the local beer in various pubs around Northampton. When Hadley was advised that Mortlake had made a speedy recovery and he, along with Winters, were well enough to be discharged, arrangements were made with West for a prisoner escort of a Sergeant and three constables. Hadley sent a telegraph message to Chief Inspector Bell informing him of their arrival time at Kings Cross and requesting a police wagon with escort to meet them and convey them to the Yard. By this time Mr Riley and his entourage had been discharged from hospital, with the exception of Mr Ford, and were now in suites of rooms at the Excelsior Hotel, where the wealthy American entertained the detectives and West to lavish dinners on their last two nights at the hotel.

Sergeant Timkin with his three constables provided the prisoner escort to London and when the train eventually pulled into Kings Cross, Hadley was relieved. As soon as they arrived back at the Yard, Mortlake and Winters were charged and placed in the care of the Custody Sergeant then Hadley went with Cooper up to Chief Inspector Bell's office to report.

"I'm pleased you're back with the suspects" said Bell as he waved them to a seat.

"We're glad to be back, sir" said Hadley.

"There has been a lot of pressure from the Americans you know."

"I'm sure, sir."

"The Commissioner was more than usually worried by the whole affair, Hadley."

"I can believe that, sir."

"Yes, it all became very political and we were concerned that you might not have an early arrest."

"So was I, sir."

"The papers in London have been having a field day with the whole damned affair and that stoked up the Americans even more" said Bell in an anxious tone.

"The Press has a lot to answer for, sir."

"Indeed it has, but when I received your telegraph informing me that you'd arrested Winters and Mortlake, well, I was much relieved."

"I'm pleased to hear it, sir."

"We issued a press statement with all the facts, which calmed down the papers and the Americans, then I was able to sleep at night, much to Mrs Bell's relief."

"That's good to know, sir."

"Yes it is. Now the Commissioner says that he wants to see you both, in due course, to commend you" said Bell with a smile.

"Thank you, sir."

"Probably after Mr Riley arrives back in London with his entourage."

"Very good, sir."

"Have you any idea when that will be, Hadley?"

"I'm sure that it will be quite soon as Mr Ford is making a very speedy recovery from his injuries, sir."

"That's good, now all you have to do is prepare the case against the two suspects and I'll pass it to the Crown Prosecution office and let's get these murderers in front of a judge and hanged" said Bell firmly.

"Right, sir."

The detectives spent the next two days preparing their case notes for Bell and other than early lunches at the Kings Head, where they relayed some of the story, which had already appeared in the Press, to a wide eyed Agnes and speechless Florrie, they completed the task diligently. Mr Riley and his complete entourage arrived back in London and took up residence in the Savoy Hotel once again. Hadley and Cooper were invited to dine with them the night before the meeting that had been arranged with the Commissioner. The detectives learned that Mr Riley had offered the job of assistant head groom to Kelly at his ranch in Kentucky where he planned to breed the finest thoroughbred horses.

"It's in memory of Nancy and Ann, that's what they had in mind to do, so it is my memorial to my lovely daughter and her best friend, Inspector" said Riley before he proposed a toast to the young women.

"It's a wonderful opportunity for Mr Kelly" said Hadley.

"It is, but my Nancy knew a good horse man when she saw one, and I think Kelly will do well" replied Riley.

"I'm sure he will, sir, but he'll be anxious to see his mother before he goes to America" said Hadley.

"I've already sent him to Ireland to see her and say goodbye, Inspector" said Riley with a smile and Hadley was impressed by the American's kindness and generosity.

"And I'm going to have my daughter and Ann taken back home and buried together at my ranch in Kentucky" said Riley.

"If I may say so, that is very fitting, sir" said Hadley.

The meeting in the Commissioner's office the next day was a very pleasurable affair where Mr Riley heaped praise and admiration over Hadley and Cooper. Hadley reciprocated with his profound appreciation for Lone Eagle's help as well as the Pinkerton Agents', who risked their lives in the hunt for the killers. The Commissioner sat behind his desk and beamed at everyone whilst the secretary to the American Ambassador just smiled and nodded through the whole exchange. Mr Riley informed the Commissioner that they would all stay in London until after the trial and obviously the Americans would be material witnesses to what had occurred at Holcot.

"A most satisfactory end to a tragic affair, Mr Riley" said the Commissioner.

"Indeed it is, sir, but as I said at the very beginning, I was here with my boys to see the murderers brought to justice and hanged, then when they are, I will regard it as closure and will return to New York with some kind of peace" replied Riley.

"I do hope so, sir" said the Commissioner sympathetically.

Several weeks later the trial was held at the Old Bailey and after the jury had heard all the arguments they found Winters and Mortlake guilty of the murders of Lady Nancy and Ann Wells. Mortlake and Winters were sentenced to hang and Riley was duly satisfied with the verdict. Hadley was sad at the senseless killing of the beautiful, young and talented women, by men who had everything and a good future in front of them. Monstrous greed coupled with decadence had led to the deaths and Hadley was pleased that Lord Mortlake and Winters had been found guilty of the dreadful crimes and would face the hangman.

As promised, Hadley and Cooper took the Agents for a couple of drinking sessions at the Kings Head where they met Agnes and

Florrie, who offered their services to the Americans but they refused, saying that their physical condition was too delicate after their shooting to do justice to the ladies, which amused Hadley no end!

A week later, after farewells, Riley and his entourage left London for New York and the detectives were genuinely sad to see them go as they had grown to like and respect the forceful, outspoken, but genuine Americans.

The next day, whilst the detectives were sitting in their office drinking tea and chatting to George about paperwork, Jenkins, Chief Inspector Bell's clerk came with a message for them to report to the Chief immediately.

"I wonder what this is about, Sergeant?"

"We'll soon find out, sir" replied Cooper as he put his cup down and followed Hadley out of the office.

Follow Hadley and Cooper when they investigate the complex and fast moving case of the South African DIAMOND MURDERS.

Printed in the United Kingdom
by Lightning Source UK Ltd.
132338UK00001B/1-30/P